cold legacy

avril dahl
book two

L.T. Ryan

with
Biba Pearce

LIQUID MIND MEDIA

Copyright © 2025 by LT Ryan, Biba Pearce, and Liquid Mind Media, LLC. All rights reserved. No part of this publication may be copied, reproduced in any format, by any means, electronic or otherwise, without prior consent from the copyright owner and publisher of this book. This is a work of fiction. All characters, names, places and events are the product of the author's imagination or used fictitiously.

For information contact:
Contact@ltryan.com
https://LTRyan.com
https://www.facebook.com/JackNobleBooks

avril dahl series

Cold Reckoning
Cold Legacy
Cold Mercy

chapter
one

THE PROTEST CHOKED THE STREET, A SEA OF BODIES PRESSED shoulder to shoulder, banners raised like battle standards.

NO MORE OIL was painted in bold strokes across a white bedsheet, sagging between two wooden poles. Chants echoed off the glass high-rises, the rhythm pulsing like a drumbeat.

Avril stood near the front, her hood pulled low over her face, her hands clenched into fists. She had rehearsed this moment in her head—just another activist in the crowd, waiting for the right crack in the tension.

A police line loomed ahead, riot helmets gleaming under the streetlights. The officers stood rigid, hands resting on their batons, eyes sweeping the crowd for the first sign of trouble. They were waiting for an excuse.

She had to give them one.

Next to her stood a real protester and the reason she was here. Runa Wiklund. According to Runa's profile, she was passionate, impulsive, an idealist dedicated to the cause. Runa was Avril's way in.

With Runa were several other members of the radical environmentalist group known as Terra Nova. Most noticeable was the activist's boyfriend, Jens Holst, suspected of being the group's enforcer. He was exactly the kind of person who would set off the chain reaction. Passionate. Angry. Easily provoked.

The crowd surged forward as one. Using the momentum, Avril allowed herself to be pushed into Holst. He stumbled, caught off balance, and knocked into one of the officers' shields.

She thought that might do it, but Holst held the line, even though the officer braced and gripped his baton. Avril didn't miss the anger behind Holst's eyes. She saw the frustration building, the urge to push back. It wouldn't take much.

Runa screamed anti-oil slogans beside him, her cheeks flushed, eyes bright and focused on the wall of police. With her fiery red hair in disarray and wild green eyes, she looked like a mythical warrior, a Valkyrie.

Avril shouted louder, causing Runa to glance over at her. Gaze fixed ahead, Avril raised her banner higher, mimicking Runa's adrenalized excitement.

A bottle flew overhead, smashing against the pavement near the officers.

Somebody shouted, and there was another surge through the crowd. The police bristled, their stance tightening, but they held their position.

Still not enough.

Avril gritted her teeth. She had to move now while the tension was high. This was her window. If she didn't do it now, the plan wouldn't work.

A long-haired, young man in front of her chanted into a megaphone, trying to rile up the crowd. When he lowered it, she knocked into his elbow, forcing his megaphone to slam against an officer's shield. It was a small, subtle action, a move that could be mistaken for an accident, but it gave her the spark she needed.

The officer reacted, shoving the youngster backward. The megaphone tumbled from his hands and the moment of restraint shattered.

Holst bent down to help the young man, but an officer grabbed him instead. Someone yelled out. More glass was hurled. The wall of riot shields surged forward, batons swinging, boots stomping.

And just like that, the crowd exploded.

Shouts turned to screams. A flare ignited somewhere behind her, washing the street in blood-red light. A woman tripped and went down, vanishing beneath the crush of bodies. Avril looked for her, but it was impossible to stay still. The air thickened with panic.

Giving up, Avril let herself be swept up in the chaos, moving with the tide of protesters. She needed to get arrested, but not too easily.

It had to look real.

She fought back—just enough—shoving an officer's arm away. "Get off me!"

A baton struck her ribs, pain bursting like fireworks beneath her skin. She staggered but didn't fall. Someone grabbed her hand. It was Runa, her eyes bright with adrenaline.

"Run!" she yelled.

It was too late.

A strong arm yanked her backward. The world tilted as she was slammed against the pavement and rough hands pinned her down. A knee pressed into her spine, crushing her into the asphalt as her arms were forced behind her back. Cuffs snapped around her wrists.

"Get off me!" she yelled, but it was no good. Nobody listened. Chaos had erupted all around her. Her cheek scraped against the ground. Boots pounded around her and she ducked her head, praying it wouldn't get stomped on.

On the periphery, she heard sirens, and a lot of shouting. Turning her head, she saw Runa lying face-down on the ground a few feet away, an officer straddling her back. As she watched, he yanked the activist to her feet. Her boyfriend, Holst, was nowhere to be seen.

An officer pulled Avril up. His eyes met hers.

Krister.

He gave a quick nod, then took a small plastic tube out of his jacket pocket and stuck it up her nose, squeezing. Dark red spray shot out, mimicking a bloody nose.

"Sorry," he muttered under his breath, as she winced. "You okay?"

"Yeah, let's go."

Krister handed her over to Karlsson, a young detective in the Swedish Police's Regional Investigation Unit. He was a nice guy—too nice to be a police officer. He'd toughen up, though, in this job. It was inevitable.

Krister's voice over the radio: "We got two. Moving them now."

As Karlsson and Krister hauled them—still struggling—out of the melee and into a waiting police van, Avril let out a relieved sigh, even as the fake blood dripped down her face.

The first part of the mission had been a success.

chapter
two

Two weeks earlier...

Avril stared at the email on her screen. It was from FBI Assistant Director Nolan Trent, her boss in D.C. While the tone was cold and formal, it had just enough diplomatic praise to keep up appearances. He'd never been her greatest fan.

Special Agent Dahl,

Following your recent involvement in the successful apprehension of Mikael Lustig, I have been directed to extend formal recognition of your work. While I understand your assignment to Stockholm was initially outside standard channels, your contribution to the case was both effective and commendable.

Given the high-profile nature of the Lustig investigation, and the Bureau's current operational tempo, your experience and capabilities would be of value to ongoing initiatives here in D.C. Your position within the Behavioral Analysis Unit remains available, should you wish to return. Please notify this office of your intentions at your earliest convenience so we can initiate the appropriate reassignment process.

On behalf of the executive team, I commend your results-driven approach. That said, I expect all returning agents to adhere to established protocol and contribute to the Bureau's collective priorities.

Respectfully,
Nolan Trent
Assistant Director
Federal Bureau of Investigation
Criminal Investigative Division
Washington, D.C.

Avril rolled her eyes. What a load of crap.

He'd obviously been told by his superiors not to let her go. The Bureau had taken credit for apprehending one of the most prolific and long-acting serial killers in history, even though they'd had absolutely nothing to do with it, while the Swedish Police Force, who'd had everything to do with it, had walked away with barely any acknowledgement.

Because of her. Because she was an FBI Special Agent.

Even thinking about it left a bitter taste in her mouth. Nolan had done nothing to support her. If anything, he'd gone out of his way to ostracize, ridicule and patronize her at every opportunity. When she'd taken a leave of absence and come here, to Stockholm, he'd pretty much told her not to hurry back.

Now he'd like to *reassign* her?

It had been over a month since the Frost Killer, as the media had called him, had been arrested. Justice had been swift. Faced with overwhelming evidence, as well as a confession, the jury at the closed trial had taken less than ten minutes to deliberate before they'd found him guilty on all counts. The judge had awarded the maximum sentence.

Fifty-four back-to-back life sentences, one for every murder victim, with no chance of parole. Already a sick man, he wouldn't even make one. He'd die in prison—and she hoped he rotted in hell.

Feeling jittery, she took off her glasses and pushed away from her desk. The email required a response. Problem was, she didn't know what that was yet.

Avril turned and gazed out of the window at the snow-covered driveway. Since it was March, the sun rose earlier now, but it was still weak and insipid and perpetually obscured by gray clouds.

Glancing next door, as had become a habit of late, she saw her neighbor and childhood friend, Krister, sweeping the driveway. His light brown hair was ruffled from the exertion, and he had a look of concentration on his rugged face. He always kept his parents' place—his place now—so neat and tidy. Unlike her.

Tugging on a thick coat and a pair of snow boots, she opened the front door and went outside. Her house was practically empty with all her late father's belongings either boxed up or donated to charity. There was nothing of his she wanted to keep.

Only a few of her mother's belongings remained, and she'd held on to those. A necklace, a pair of gold earrings, and a soft, petal-shaped brooch.

Even the photographs held too many painful memories now. She'd selected a few of her mother and herself, as well as a laughing one of the three of them at the lake one long-ago summer. They looked happy, before her father had discovered her mother's secret. It was in a silver frame now, on the mantelpiece.

It was strange how everything in her life had always been divided into "before" and "after." *Before* her mother's murder—the scene in the happy photograph, carefree summers with their friends, rambling through the woods with Krister.

And *after* it—the seemingly endless search, the bitter winters marred by images of frozen women, defeat at every turn. Then, returning to Sweden and finally, after an exhausting few weeks of mind games, the capture.

The nightmare was over.

Avril thought she'd be satisfied when she'd caught her mother's killer, or at the very least relieved, except what she felt was—

Nothing.

Hunting the Frost Killer had consumed her for over a decade, and now she felt lost. All that remained was a big, empty hole, and she had no idea how to fill it.

She could go back to D.C. and be reassigned—start work on another case. Have to tick a set of FBI checkboxes to get a favorable performance review? Work with a bunch of people who didn't like her, who thought she was an obsessed single-minded lunatic?

They weren't far wrong.

She stepped into the slushy snow, melting now. They'd probably seen the last snowfall of the season.

Krister looked up and waved. "Hey, you're up early."

Sunday. A day of rest, but all she felt was restless.

Shrugging, she called, "Case closed?"

He'd been so busy the last few weeks she'd barely seen him. Gone all day, back late. But then that's how it was in the Regional Investigation's Serious Crimes Unit.

She hadn't thought she would miss it, but she did. Catching a ride to the police station with Krister in the mornings, delving into the criminology of a case, exploring the psychology of the killer, the victimology of his victims, questioning suspects. It had been her life for the last ten years.

That monster had been her life for the last ten years.

Krister grinned. "Yeah, we raided several locations yesterday morning and the perpetrator was hiding at one of them. We got lucky."

"That's good."

He straightened up, holding the shovel. "You want to grab breakfast? I feel like we haven't talked in ages."

They hadn't.

"Sure, if you've got time."

He spread his arms. "I've got nothing but time today."

THEY WENT to a neighborhood café tucked down a cobbled side street, the kind with steaming mugs of dark coffee, warm cinnamon buns, and the comforting clatter of crockery and low conversation. Krister looked at her the way he always did when he knew she was holding something back.

"What?" she asked, tilting her gaze up at him.

"How have you been, Avril?"

She inhaled. "Oh, you know. Busy sorting through my father's stuff."

He pursed his lips. "Your house has been empty for weeks."

She didn't reply. It was annoying how well he knew her. He was the only person who did. Avril knew she wasn't exactly friendship material. Getting close to people had never been her strong suit. In fact, apart from Krister, she couldn't name a single friend. But then again, dedicating a decade of your life to hunting a serial killer wasn't exactly conducive to brunch dates and spa weekends.

"I got an email from my boss today."

"In D.C.?" He arched an eyebrow. "What did he say?"

"He wants to reassign me."

A flicker crossed his hazel eyes. "You're going back?"

"I haven't responded yet."

He gazed at her across the table. The waitress came back and set down two coffees, a pastry for Avril and a hot breakfast for Krister. He nodded his thanks, but his eyes never left hers. "Does that mean you're considering my suggestion and thinking about staying?"

She glanced away, down at her coffee. "I don't know. What would I do in Stockholm, Krister? I don't have a job, I don't even have a hobby."

He laughed. At her frown, he held up a hand. "Sorry, it's just hard to picture you doing something for fun."

"I can have fun," she said sulkily, even though she wasn't quite sure she believed that herself. Not anymore. Maybe once, when she was twelve.

Before.

"You could join the Serious Crime's Unit." He picked up his knife and fork. "They'd be happy to have you. You've got a great resume and a decade of experience—FBI experience—and Superintendent Sundström has already approved you as a consultant."

"Would he want me back, though?" She hadn't made life easy for him while she'd been there.

"Why wouldn't he?" He tilted his head as he chewed.

"You know. I'm not... I don't fit in easily."

He shrugged. "So what? You're not there to make friends. You're there to solve crimes, put away bad guys, and I happen to know that you are *very* good at that. He knows you're good at that too."

She stared down at her pastry, the raisins glistening in the fluorescent light.

"Besides, if you give the team a chance to get to know you, you might be surprised."

Avril thought back to the last case. "I took chances. I didn't listen to orders." She arched an eyebrow. "I deliberately put Ingrid at risk."

"You will have to promise never to do that again," he remarked dryly. Using Ingrid as bait to track the Frost Killer had been a necessary, calculated risk. Unfortunately, the rest of the department hadn't seen it that way.

She gave a noncommittal shrug. "I apologized. She got a medal out of it."

Krister nodded. "She did."

Krister had told her that now, after the trauma had subsided, Ingrid was quite proud of the fact she'd played an active role in bringing down the notorious killer. She'd lost her rookie status and was finally being taken seriously at work. She was even preparing for her Befälsutbildning, the command-level training exam that could lead to a promotion.

There was one thing that continued to plague her. She still hadn't told Krister her shameful secret. About Mikael being her biological father. Would she ever?

Maybe one day.

He winked at her as he ate his breakfast.

Her chest tightened. Probably not.

She couldn't afford to lose her only friend. The only person who actually meant something to her.

"So are you interested?" he asked, pointing his fork at her. "I'll have a word with Superintendent Sundström."

Still, she hesitated. It was like her brain was floating and couldn't settle on anything. "I don't know."

"Come on. What have you got to lose? Stay in Stockholm. Come and work with me. It'll be fun." He grinned again, before turning his attention back to his food.

It'll be fun.

She didn't know how much fun police work could be, but she needed a friendly face in her life. The truth was, she couldn't face going back to D.C. It felt like flying into hostile territory, and after everything that had happened, she wasn't ready for that.

Taking a deep breath, she glanced up at him. "Okay, I'll apply."

He gave a happy nod, his hazel eyes sparkling. "Good." He was about to say something else when his phone buzzed on the table between them.

Long and continuous. Urgent.

"It's work," he said, picking it up. "Hello. Krister Jansson."

Avril watched as his forehead furrowed, his eyes slanting into a frown. "When?"

Slowly, he set down his fork. "Shit. Seriously?"

His gaze flickered to her face, and she saw concern in his eyes. Something big had happened. "What?" she mouthed.

He shook his head.

"I'll be there as soon as I can. Ping me the address."

Avril reached around and grabbed her coat off the back of the chair. They were leaving, that much was clear.

Krister finished the call and fished in his pocket for some bills that he dropped on the table. "Sorry, Avril. I have to go. So much for having the day to myself."

"What's happened?" She tugged on her oversized coat and followed him to the door.

"I can't say." At her look, he sighed. "I guess you'll hear soon enough. Gustav Holmgren, CEO of Nordic Energy has just been assassinated."

Her eyes widened. "Really? I was just reading about the NordLinx Pipeline the other day. How'd he die?"

"Car bomb as he was leaving for work. Blew up in his own freaking driveway. Right in front of his wife."

Avril cringed. "You heading there now?"

"Yeah. Can I drop you somewhere on the way?"

"It's okay. I'll make my own way home."

His forehead creased, a cross between an apology and concern. "You sure?"

"Yeah, of course. I'll take the bus."

"Okay." He gave her a goodbye nod, but his eyes weren't sparkling now. They were serious, distracted. She knew his thoughts were already on the crime scene that awaited him. She knew the feeling.

Missed the feeling.

"See you later." She waved him away and went back to the table. Guess she was staying.

With a little sigh, she turned back to her coffee and what was left of her pastry. She wanted back in. As much as she thought she didn't, she did.

She was bored. Without something to occupy her, she was floundering.

Decision made. The first thing she was going to do when she got home was answer that email—and turn down her boss's offer.

It was time to get back to work.

chapter
three

KRISTER'S BOOTS CRUNCHED AGAINST SHATTERED GLASS AS he stepped out of the unmarked police car. The pungent smell of burnt rubber and chemicals sullied the fresh morning air.

Ahead was the smoldering wreckage of Gustav Holmgren's car, its frame twisted and blackened, smoke curling into the gray sky.

The explosion had torn through the vehicle's undercarriage, blasting out the windows and catapulting shrapnel across the Holmgren driveway and into the street beyond. The front gate hung askew, buckled from the force of the blast, and the brick façade of the CEO's pristine villa was peppered with deep, ugly scorch marks.

Krister let out a slow breath and turned his collar up against the lingering bite of winter. This was bad. Worse than he'd imagined.

A handful of uniformed officers had cordoned off the scene to keep back the growing crowd of reporters and curious onlookers who were, even now, pressing against the police tape. A white-clad forensics technician crouched near the wreck sifting through debris, while another snapped photographs of what remained of the driver's seat.

Krister didn't need to get any closer to know there wasn't much left of Holmgren. A car bomb of this scale was designed for one thing—absolute certainty. This wasn't a warning. It wasn't an attempt to scare him, to threaten or coerce. Whoever had planted it had made sure there'd be no walking away.

He spotted a man he didn't recognize near the house, talking to a pale, visibly shaken woman wrapped in a thick blanket. Alma Holmgren, Gustav's widow. She was talking, her lips moving, but he couldn't hear what she was saying.

A car bomb. In Stockholm.

While crime was on the increase, it was usually gang violence or drug-related offenses, not a blatant hit on one of their most prominent citizens. A car bomb was pretty non-negotiable—and telling. He glanced around at the blast zone, strewn with debris. There weren't many organizations who could pull this off.

Showing his ID to the officers at the cordon, he accepted a pair of protective shoe coverings, pulled them on, then cautiously approached the forensic photographer who had stopped snapping now and was checking the images on his digital screen.

He looked up as Krister approached.

"Are we sure it was Holmgren inside?"

The photographer nodded toward the shaking woman in the blanket. "His wife confirmed it. She'd just said goodbye to him and was in the living room when it happened. Saw the whole thing through the window. Terrible seeing your husband blown to pieces like that."

Right in front of you. It would have been a hell of a shock. No wonder she was quaking like a leaf.

The man in the suit approached Krister. "Carl Lindholm," he said, extending a hand. "Säpo."

Krister arched an eyebrow. What was the Security Service doing here? Sweden's intelligence and counter-terrorism agency usually only dealt with incidents of national security, terrorism, and other threats of that level. Did they suspect the car bomb was in that league?

They shook. "Krister Jansson, Serious Crime Unit."

"I know who you are." Lindholm gestured to the burned-out vehicle. "What do you know about the victim?"

"Only that he's a big shot oil magnate." Krister watched as the forensic tech took swabs from inside the car. He wished he hadn't eaten so much breakfast. It was churning around in his stomach, threatening to come up. "Nordic Energy, right? The NordLinx pipeline."

The agent nodded. "We've been watching Holmgren for months, ever since he became a target for radical eco-terrorist groups."

Krister's brows quirked. "Is this the part where you tell me this is your investigation and to back off?"

The serious, no-nonsense face cracked into a faint smile. "No, we like to encourage interdepartmental cooperation these days. We work with regional law enforcement, not against."

Krister nodded. "So what do you want from me?"

"Access to your files, complete transparency with regards to the investigation."

"Do we get the same in return?" he asked.

"Sure. As much as I'm authorized to give you."

Krister gave a knowing snort. That meant it would be them giving and Säpo taking, throwing them some breadcrumbs every now and then. Still, interdepartmental cooperation and all that.

"You got a specific group in mind for this?"

Lindholm lowered his voice. "You heard of Terra Nova?"

Krister shook his head.

"They're an extremist eco-terrorist group, fairly new on the scene. Only been around a couple of years, but they're serious contenders. Led by a murky figure known only as Odin, who nobody seems to have seen, they're extreme in their beliefs, particularly around oil production and the NordLinx Pipeline."

That was more than he'd been expecting from the Säpo man.

"Which is why you're liking them for this?"

He gave a tight nod. "They're growing fast. As far as we know, they have eighty to a hundred and fifty members throughout Europe, broken into cells. They're extremely well organized, run by a core leadership of only a handful of players, all intensely loyal to the cause."

"Got any names?" Krister asked.

Lindholm studied him, his dark eyes cagey. "Let's take this to the station. I need to get clearance before I share any more details."

Lindholm was right, this wasn't the appropriate place. "I'll meet you there. I need to brief my team."

The agent dipped his head, turned, and stalked back to his unlicensed SUV with tinted windows.

Krister watched him go, a mix of trepidation and adrenaline settling in his stomach.

There goes the rest of my Sunday, he thought—and probably his Sundays for the foreseeable future.

"WE KNOW the leader is called Odin," Lindholm said, back at the department. They were sitting around an oval table in the boardroom adjacent to Superintendent Leif Sundström's office. "We've picked him up on various online message boards instigating protests and spreading anti-corporate propaganda. The official threats received by various industry leaders were all signed by Odin."

"Code name." Krister rubbed his gristly chin. If he'd known he was coming into work today, he'd have had a shave.

"They all use aliases," Lindholm confirmed. "Mythological references. The other's we've managed to pick up are Runa, Gaia and Fang."

"Fang?" He slanted an eyebrow.

"Except that one. We think he's Odin's enforcer and a senior member of the organization."

"What about the others?" Fred Nyström, a dedicated detective and Krister's right hand man, asked, speaking for the first time.

"Gaia seems to have some sort of scientific background, although we're not sure what. Judging by her posts, she's clearly educated, possibly with a degree in something related to climate change, or that's what our experts think anyway."

"Based on her name?" Freddie asked.

He nodded.

"You're assuming she's a woman?" Krister interjected.

"For simplicity's sake, we're assuming Odin and Fang are men and Gaia and Runa women, however, that could be a ploy to confuse us. We're keeping an open mind."

Krister gave a nod of agreement. They couldn't assume anything, not until they knew for sure. "What do you know about Runa?"

"She's the youngest of the four. This is a cell based here in Stockholm, and we think they're part of the upper echelons of the organization. They seem to be calling the shots. Runa is clearly highly motivated and filled with passionate rhetoric. She's the only one who may have used her real name."

"Really? Isn't that risky?" David Karlsson, another young detective and recent member of Krister's team, asked.

Lindholm shrugged.

"How'd you figure that?" Krister asked.

"We traced a Twitter account to a Runa Wiklund. She lives here in Stockholm but was born and raised in Gothenburg, Sweden, to middle-class environmentalist parents."

"Fits the bill," Krister murmured.

"There's more. Her mother died of cancer linked to industrial pollution when Runa was just fourteen."

Krister whistled under his breath.

"Her father is a university professor at Uppsala University," Lindholm added.

Runa Wiklund was a textbook candidate. Odin, or whoever was in charge of recruitment, probably took one look at her and pinpointed her as an easy target for grooming.

"Well, we can start with her," Krister said. "Let's put her under surveillance, see where she leads."

Lindholm's lips quirked. "We've already done that. Had a team on her for a few weeks already."

Krister should have expected as much. "And? Any leads?"

"Yes and no. She's met with some lower-level activists in connection with a planned supposedly peaceful protest next week in the city center. It's been blasted all over social media. As for the other members of Terra Nova, we haven't spotted anything yet."

"What about a boyfriend or friend?" Krister asked.

Lindholm glanced down at the open file on the table in front of him. "She lives with an ex-soldier called Jens Holst. He's originally from Malmö but joined the military right out of school. He served in our peacekeeping forces in Afghanistan."

"What happened?" Krister asked, sensing a 'but.'

Lindholst's bushy eyebrows went up. "He was discharged for misconduct after punching a superior officer."

"A short fuse, then."

"Yeah. Something to do with a botched operation."

"This is the guy you think is the group's enforcer, Fang?"

"It's possible. Holst doesn't seem to care about politics, though. If he's involved with Terra Nova, it's because of his aggression and military expertise, not his dedication to the cause."

"Gotcha," Krister said with a nod. Some drifters just wanted a sense of belonging, and it didn't matter what the cause was. "He violent to his girlfriend?"

"Not that we've picked up, but it's early days. Like I said, our agents have only been on them for a couple of weeks. She hasn't filed any complaints, and there've been no domestic violence reports."

"So what now?" Krister leaned back in his chair. Säpo was already on the case, doing everything they would have done—monitoring social media and online activity, keeping the two key members under surveillance, and so on. What was left to do? "You want us to process the evidence? See what comes back from the bomb blast?"

They'd have people working on that too. Explosive specialists, counter-terror ops, bomb squad, you name it. They'd be much more adept at analyzing that sort of thing than the regional forensic techs. Give them a homicide, and they were the best in the country, but car bombs... That was not their area of expertise.

As expected, Lindholst shook his head. "No, we've got that covered. What we need is local knowledge. Can you do the door-to-door, see if anyone saw anything?"

Krister nodded. "We'll reach out to our informants, anyone who might know something."

"Good. We also need help with processing satellite scenes. Can you send forensics to Holmgren's office, interview his colleagues, the rest of the board, see if they were aware of the threat against him?"

Krister nodded, then looked at Freddie and Karlsson. "Freddie, can you organize the door-to-door? Karlsson, take Ingrid and head to Nordic Energy's company headquarters to speak to his colleagues."

They both nodded and left the room.

Lindholst waited for them to leave, then pursed his lips.

"Was there something else?" Krister prompted.

"Yeah, you could say that. This upcoming protest, we'd like your help with something."

"Okay. What is it?"

The Säpo man lowered his voice. "This must stay between our two departments. Nobody else can know."

Krister wasn't sure he liked the sound of that. "Yeah?"

Lindholst leaned forward and told them what he had in mind.

chapter four

I'm coming over. Got a proposition for you.

Avril pushed her glasses back up her nose and stared at Krister. They were sitting at the kitchen table, an open but as yet untouched bottle of wine between them. Krister had arrived half an hour ago after leaving the cryptic message on her voicemail.

"You can't be serious?"

"Of course I'm serious," he replied, leaning back in his chair.

She spread her arms. "Why me? Doesn't Säpo have specially trained operatives for that?"

"I recommended you. Thought you'd be perfect."

She frowned. "I've never done undercover work in my life. I don't know the first thing about it."

Krister rested his elbows on the table. "Listen, it's a way back onto the Force. I know you said you'd reapply, but this will circumvent that. You get cleared to do this and you're automatically back in. The Superintendent said so himself."

"I'm sorry, Krister. I just don't think I'm suitable."

"Listen, Säpo wants somebody who's not known in police or domestic criminal circles. Less chance of leaks that way. Nobody knows you here. If the organization is suspicious or well-connected enough to look up existing police officers or active undercover agents, they won't find you. You're an unknown, which makes you the perfect mole."

Avril raked a shaky hand through her hair. "I know you think this is a good idea, but I have a tough enough time fitting in—as myself. How am I going to do it as an undercover member of Terra Nova?"

He snorted. "That's why it'll work. Groups like Terra Nova are made up of socially awkward, damaged, passionate types. No offense, but that'll make it easier for you to fit in."

"Gee, thanks." She wasn't denying she was all of those things, although she wasn't sure she appreciated Krister pointing it out.

"Besides, you're not completely inexperienced," he continued with a grin. "You're an FBI Special Agent, for God's sake. You're well-trained, you understand the psyche of criminals better than anyone I've ever met, and you're a native Swede."

That was also all true.

She was beginning to see why he'd suggested she do it. "What does Säpo think?"

"They're eager to move ahead with this. There's a protest march next week. We were thinking of using it as an opportunity for you to make contact."

Her brain kicked in, thinking ahead, picturing the scenario. "How? You want me to go in as an activist?"

Krister sat back, smiling. "See? You're already thinking like an undercover operative."

She shot him a look.

Chuckling, he reached for the wine and poured both of them a glass. "To answer your question, yes. The riot police will be out in full force since this has the potential to turn nasty. There are already social media posts riling up the protesters. If you end up getting arrested with this particular person, it'll give you a chance to ingratiate yourself."

"Arrested? How am I supposed to do that?"

He set the bottle back on the table. "You're the behavioral sciences expert, you figure it out. Don't forget, I know you. You are skilled in the art of subtle manipulation." He masked a smile. "You out-manipulated me for years, back when we were kids. And judging by our last investigation, you've honed your craft. Poor Ingrid fell for it hook, line and sinker. So did the killer, for that matter."

Avril didn't want to think about how that had ended, so instead, she thought about Krister as a boy, with that wide smile, grazes on his knees, and a mop of unruly brown curls. "You were an easy target."

"Hey!"

She smiled. "You were always so eager to please."

"I wanted to impress you," he teased, picking up his glass. "Besides, most of the time I knew what you were up to—I was just humoring you."

She snorted at that.

He took a sip, watching her over his glass. "So you'll do it?"

"When is the protest?" she asked, deflecting.

"Next Saturday."

"That's not a lot of time to prepare."

He gave a deep chuckle. "I knew you were considering it."

She reached for her glass and took a gulp. This had to be the craziest idea she'd ever entertained. *Her*, undercover? It was laughable. The thought of having to insert herself into a criminal organization filled her with horror. People just didn't like her. She wasn't a team player. She was a painful introvert who preferred her own company to that of others and stayed out of the limelight. It was the main reason she hadn't objected when her role in taking down the Frost Killer had been kept out of the press.

"What if someone recognizes me?" She bit her lip.

"They won't. Your picture was never in the Swedish papers. The FBI took full credit. Even if they came across your name somewhere, they'd never connect it to you, not without a photograph. You're safe on that front."

A knot was forming in her stomach, making it hard to breathe. Why was she even considering this?

"I'll need an alias."

"Lindholm will set you up with an airtight legend. Fake identity, false social media profiles. If anyone Googles you, it'll stand up to scrutiny. You'll have a cover job, a plausible background, and a story that checks out."

She damn well hoped so. These guys had just planted a bomb in an oil CEO's car—they were dangerous. She didn't want to get made.

If she decided to do it.

"What about living arrangements? I can't stay here, obviously."

"You'd be put up in an apartment in the city. New job, new car. It has to be believable. You'll be provided with secure communication, a covert panic button, and a predetermined extraction plan if things go sideways."

She frowned. "There's not a lot of time. These kinds of operations usually take weeks of planning."

"We've got one week." His gaze turned serious. "Avril, they killed a man in front of his wife—a father of two teenagers. How many more people will they murder if we don't stop them?"

She pursed her lips, thinking.

"I'll have to read up on Terra Nova and their ideology, as well as this person I'm supposed to bond with."

"I'll get Lindholm to send you everything they've got on the group. The woman you're going to get arrested with is called Runa. She's younger than you, but we think she's in the top circle of the organization."

"How much younger?" Avril asked.

"A few years," he said with a wink. "She's twenty-four. Lindholm will tweak your legend to match. You'll be given a similar background, experiences, history of activism."

Avril was nodding slowly, processing everything.

She glanced up to find Krister smiling at her.

"What?" She tucked a hair behind her ear. Self-conscious.

"I knew you'd do it."

"I haven't said—"

"Yes, you have." He lifted his glass in a silent toast.

She sighed and reached for hers.

Yes, she had.

chapter
five

Present day...

Avril strained against the handcuffs, trying to flex her wrists. Her fingers were tingling from lack of circulation. Krister hadn't shown any leniency when he'd arrested her. The takedown had to look authentic.

The inside of the police van smelled like sweat, stale beer, and damp fabric. Runa sat beside her, her breath still ragged from the scuffle. Beside Runa were two more women, one sullen, one scared.

"What the hell?" Runa shouted at the two uniformed officers sitting opposite them, twisting her shoulders as if she could dislodge the cuffs. "We weren't doing anything wrong. You've got no right to hold us."

Technically true. It was meant to be a peaceful protest, and they hadn't done anything illegal. They'd just been caught up in the melee, as had the other two women, most likely.

The officers didn't engage, they'd been trained not to. They would only issue necessary instructions.

Runa glanced up at Avril's face and her eyes narrowed. "You're bleeding."

Avril shrugged, keeping her gaze low and her posture loose. She needed to project detachment—cool, disinterested, guarded. During her briefing, one of Säpo's behavioral advisors had drilled her on the psychological dynamics of undercover rapport-building. *Never push. Never appear too eager. A forced connection raises red flags. Let the target come to you. Let her think she's in control. That she's helping you.*

"You like beating up defenseless women, do you?" Runa snapped at the officers, taunting them. The scared woman's eyes grew rounder.

"You probably shouldn't antagonize them," she whispered.

Runa scowled at her. "Do you want to be here?"

The woman glanced away.

The two officers opposite them didn't react. They were only there to handle their transport and had nothing to do with their arrest or detainment. This was intentional and avoided personal biases or escalating tensions.

"I'm okay," Avril said, stonily. Runa couldn't think she was a wimp.

One of the officers, a stocky man with a buzz cut said, "Once we get to the station, you'll be booked and held until statements are taken. If you cooperate, you'll be out before morning."

Runa shot him a hostile glare but said nothing.

Avril knew the process. On arrival, they'd be offloaded one by one, patted down more thoroughly, then taken inside for intake. They'd be asked basic questions—name, date of birth, address. Their fingerprints and photographs would be taken, even for something as minor as unlawful assembly. Given the scale of the protest, there'd be dozens of arrests, meaning long waits in holding cells while paperwork churned through the system.

That was the idea, anyway. Give her a chance to get to know Runa.

The van rumbled to a stop. Outside, muffled voices carried through the metal walls. Orders being given, officers coordinating the arrival of the detainees.

The back doors swung open, and cold air rushed in.

"Out," one of the uniformed officers ordered.

One by one, they clambered out. The concrete yard behind the station was brightly lit and buzzed with activity. Protesters were lined up against a wall, their hands still bound as officers processed them in batches. Some shouted, others demanded lawyers, but most were resigned to the inevitable.

Avril and Runa were led inside through a set of double doors. The intake room was sterile and smelled strongly of detergent, with a bright fluorescent light that made everything appear starker and more jarring. White walls, metal benches bolted to the floor, a long counter where officers logged each detainee.

Avril was told to step forward. "Name?"

She didn't hesitate. "Astrid Dahlström."

Her alias. A simple, not-too-common Swedish name backed by an airtight cover story. Säpo had planted her digital footprint deep enough to withstand scrutiny.

The officer typed it into the system, barely glancing at her despite the fake blood that crusted on her face. "Date of birth?"

She rattled off the one she'd memorized. It would make her a year older than Runa.

Next came the mugshot. She stood in front of a screen and a camera flashed. Front, then profile. They didn't even bother to clean her up first. Avril could see Runa's curious gaze on her.

Good. The plan was working.

"Come," a voice ordered, and she went to have her fingerprints taken. The scanner beeped as she pressed her fingers against the glass. Luckily, this wasn't an ID check, or her real credentials would come up. Restricted, of course, for the duration of the operation.

Runa was next. She met Avril's gaze briefly as the officer ran through the same procedure. The fire in her expression hadn't dimmed. If anything, it burned even more brightly.

"Welcome to the system," the officer muttered as he finished processing her.

"Don't worry, I've been here before," Runa quipped.

From there, they were led down a corridor to the holding cells. Avril didn't know what had happened to the other two women, but the custody officers must have been instructed to place her and Runa together.

A thick, steel door swung open, revealing a cramped, windowless space lined with gray concrete. A metal bench ran along one wall, scratched with graffiti from past occupants.

The officer removed their handcuffs and gestured for them to enter the cell. "Sit tight. Someone will come for you."

The door clanged shut behind them.

They both massaged their wrists. It felt good to get the cuffs off.

"Bastards," Runa exclaimed. "I can't believe they wouldn't even clean you up."

Avril leaned back against the wall, wiping her nose on her sleeve. "It's nothing."

"I think it's stopped bleeding," the activist said, taking a closer look. It was then Avril noticed she had dark green eyes, like a forest after the rain.

"Thanks." The Säpo officer's words rang in her ears.

Be aloof, distant. Let the target come to you.

"I haven't seen you at any of the marches before?" Runa said, sitting down next to her. It was phrased more like a question than a statement.

Avril shrugged. "Just got back from the States."

"Yeah? What were you doing there, then?" Her gaze slanted across at Avril. She was obviously curious but still feeling her out. Avril didn't push it.

"Travelling," she said vaguely.

"I've never been to America." Runa's voice held a touch of wistfulness. "My boyfriend said he'll take me one day, but..." She shrugged as if there wasn't much chance of that happening.

Avril blinked. "Was he the one with you at the march?"

"Yeah, Fang." She gave a laugh. "He's called that because he has long eyeteeth, not because he bites."

Avril managed a weak smile.

"I know he looks tough," she continued, "but he's a big softie really."

That wasn't what Avril had heard. Jens Holst had been kicked out of the military for punching a superior officer. From what she could see, he had anger management issues and probably needed a whole lot of therapy.

She sniffed. Then again, who didn't?

"He get arrested too?"

Runa shrugged. "Don't know. I hope not. He won't take too kindly to that."

Avril didn't imagine a man like Fang would.

They lapsed into silence, and she wiped her nose again. The top of her gray hoodie was maroon with blood, and smears ran up both sleeves.

"What's your story, then?" Runa asked, turning to her again. "Why were you at the march?"

Avril clenched her fists. "I'm sick of the corporate bullshit. Greed, mismanagement, inactivity and widespread systematic failure. People are suffering because of it." Angry, and fearing she'd said too much, she lowered her head. "Sorry. I didn't mean to spark off. I just get so angry sometimes."

"No, it's fine," Runa said, pursing her lips. "I feel the same way."

"I lost someone," Avril said slowly, not looking up. "My mother. She died in the California wildfires back in '21."

"Shit, I'm sorry," Runa whispered. A long beat passed, then she said, "I lost my mother too, when I was younger. I know what it's like."

Avril lifted her head. "You did?"

"Yeah, cancer. Industrial waste in the water supply. She wasn't the only one."

"Oh, God. That's awful." Avril looked shocked. "Did you file a class lawsuit?"

"For all the good it did." Runa stood up and began pacing the small cell. "We were laughed out of court. They denied any wrongdoing. Nothing changed."

Avril shook her head. "That sucks, although it's not surprising. It's like they just don't care. Money means more to them than human lives."

Runa gave a slow nod.

There was another long pause, and then Runa said, "How do you feel about more... direct action?"

Avril shifted on the bench. "I don't understand. I thought that's what we were doing? The march—"

"I mean getting them to really sit up and take notice," Runa cut her off.

Avril stared at her. "If it'll make the bastards pay, I'm all for it. You know how many brutal police crackdowns I've witnessed in the US? They don't give a shit, and neither do I. Not about them."

Runa gave a thoughtful nod.

Avril waited, not wanting to push. She had to play it just right.

When Runa didn't say anything else, Avril swiped at an imaginary tear. "After my mother died, I realized there was nothing left for me there. I quit my job, packed my bags, and came back to Stockholm. It's where I was born."

"How long were you in America for?" Runa asked.

"Since I was eight. My mother and I moved there when my parents split up. She was all I had." She couldn't quite will her eyes to fill with tears. Crying wasn't something she did. Not ever.

Maybe Runa mistook her emptiness for grief, because she said, "Have you ever heard of an organization called Terra Nova?"

Avril shook her head.

"I joined a few years back. They're more... extreme than what you might be used to, but they genuinely care and want to make a difference." She hesitated. "They're willing to do whatever it takes."

Avril glanced up at her. "Really? You're not just saying that? Because most of the organizations I've belonged to in the past were—"

"I'm not just saying it." Runa stopped pacing and faced her. "They're for real. I think they're powerful, really powerful. They have money, too, and connections. They think big."

Avril gazed at her, openly curious, letting the silence stretch out.

Runa put her hands on her hips. "Why don't you come to a meeting and see for yourself?"

"A meeting?" She hesitated. "Okay, yeah. I would like that."

The sound of a bolt being shot back made them both look up. The door clicked open. "I'll let you know the details," Runa hissed, speaking fast. She just got it out before the door opened and an officer strode in.

"Runa Wiklund?"

Runa raised a hand.

"You come with me."

"What about me?" Avril got to her feet. A little more time would be good. Enough to make a definite arrangement.

"We're not ready for you yet."

Shit.

Avril sat back down again, thinking fast. How was Runa going to contact her?

"I work at an Indie book café called Grön Bok," she said hastily, trying not to sound too desperate. "You know, if you need to find me."

Runa nodded as strong hands grabbed her by the arm and led her out of the cell.

Avril could only hope that she would.

chapter six

"It's been a week, and nothing's happened," Avril muttered, straightening books on a display table. "The plan didn't work."

"You don't know that." Krister picked up a book, studied the cover, then put it back. "These things take time. It's a long game."

Avril sighed. "If only I'd had a little more time in the holding cell."

"That was unfortunate, but I think it was enough. You did a good job. Something is bound to happen soon."

She glanced at him. "What if she doesn't contact me?"

He shrugged. "There are other ways for you to bump into her."

"Won't that be too obvious?"

"We might have to."

Avril glanced at her watch. "The bookstore closes in an hour. She won't come today. It's Friday."

"Might be the ideal time," Krister countered, wandering over to the philosophy section. "Fewer customers, more chance of catching you alone. Besides, they've been watching the place all week."

Avril frowned. "You shouldn't have come here. What if they recognize you?"

"I'm a paying customer." He plucked a book off the shelf. "I'll have this one, please."

She raised an eyebrow at the title. "Didn't take you for a philosophizing romantic."

"There's a lot you don't know about me," he said with a grin.

Krister paid for the book and left, bag under his arm in full sight. Avril stayed behind the counter, but watched through the large window as he disappeared into the crowds. Outside, people hurried by, coats pulled tight against the biting wind. The sky, already a darker shade of gray, was deepening as the sun slipped behind the buildings.

Avril did a final walk-through of the store. The job had been part of her legend—arranged by Säpo, with the owner happily accepting a generous payout and signing an airtight non-disclosure agreement. Now, he and his wife were spending the rest of the month in Valencia, soaking up the sun, while she played bookseller and waited for something to happen.

At a quarter to five, the tiny bell on top of the wooden door chimed as someone stepped inside. Avril looked up—and her heart skipped a beat.

It was her.

Runa.

She'd come, after all.

Avril broke into an awkward smile—not too warm, not too eager. Trust was currency in situations like these, and she hadn't earned much yet. But she needed to seem open and approachable. "Hey. Good to see you."

Krister had been right. They'd picked their moment carefully. Close to closing time, after the last customer had left and when fewer eyes would be watching.

Runa's gaze swept the store, taking in every corner, checking it was empty. "Nice place you got here."

"Oh, it's not mine. I'm just holding down the fort while the manager's away." It was all true, but for some reason, she got the feeling Runa already knew that.

"You into books?" Runa paused near the display where Krister had been browsing less than twenty minutes ago.

They must have seen him leave. It was too risky for him to come here, she decided. They'd have to find another designated meeting point.

If these guys were as slick as Runa made out, they'd be watching. They'd notice patterns, people. It could bust her cover.

"I used to read a lot back in college. Not so much now."

"Where'd you go?"

"UC Santa Cruz," she supplied smoothly. "Political Science major. But I dropped out after my sophomore year. Couldn't afford it after my mother…" She let the words trail off, biting her lip. "Well, you know."

Strange how it was easier pretending to have emotions than actually showing them to anyone. She'd never been good with that, preferring to keep everything locked inside. Not healthy, as any shrink would tell you. Then again, it didn't seem to have affected her that much, and she had a shitload stored away.

Runa's expression flickered—something between recognition and understanding. "Yeah. I'm sorry."

Avril shrugged like it didn't matter. "How'd it go after they pulled you out of the holding cell?"

"Standard bullshit." Runa rolled her eyes. "Community service and a fine."

"Same," Avril huffed. "Some deterrent."

Runa snorted. "You learned your lesson?"

"Not even a little. In my opinion, the world's falling apart and no one's doing a damn thing to stop it."

Runa gave an approving grin. She'd appreciated that answer. "I told my people about you," she said quietly.

Avril raised an eyebrow. "You did?"

"Yeah. They're interested. I told them about your history and suggested we invite you to a meeting so you can see for yourself what we do."

And they could check her out in person.

Avril kept her stance loose, casual. She leaned slightly against the counter, folding her arms in a way that suggested mild curiosity. Interested, but not desperate. "Okay. Sure, why not?"

Runa gave a satisfied nod, then reached into her pocket and pulled out a folded slip of paper. She held it up for a moment, then set it on the counter. "If you're serious about doing more than just talking, be here. Tomorrow. 10 PM."

Avril glanced at the paper, but didn't touch it. "Okay."

Runa smiled. "See you tomorrow."

Avril watched her leave, listening to the door chime in her wake. A beat passed, then she reached for the note and unfolded it.

A single address.

She was in.

chapter **seven**

AVRIL ARRIVED AT THE DESTINATION ON FOOT AFTER walking through Södermalm's backstreets at a natural, unhurried pace. The neighborhood was a mishmash of old and new, where sleek cafés stood beside crumbling brick buildings tagged with graffiti and political slogans. If anyone was tailing her, they were very good. She hadn't seen the same face twice.

The address led her to a nondescript doorway, wedged between a closed thrift store and a bar that reeked of stale beer. The building was old and basic, a throwback to the neighborhood's industrial past. If she hadn't been looking for it, she might have walked past without a second glance.

Runa was waiting, leaning against the brickwork, scrolling on her phone. She broke into a smile when she saw Avril. "You came."

A small shrug. "I was curious."

Runa pushed a buzzer and the door clicked open. "Come on in."

They entered the dank interior. Avril scanned the narrow hallway. The walls lined with exposed pipes and raw concrete, and a bulb flickered dismally overhead. It wouldn't last long.

She followed Runa toward a single steel door at the end of the hall. There was no name plate, no markings, not even a handle with which to open it. Runa simply knocked and the door opened with a metallic click.

Interesting.

They stepped inside, and Avril found herself nose to chest with a muscular skinhead busting out of a too-tight leather jacket.

"Astrid, meet Fang." Runa touched the man on the arm.

So, this was Jens Holst, military outcast and alleged enforcer. She could see why. He looked like he could break necks with a quick twist of those massive hands.

"Hey." Avril forced a smile. She was so tense her jaw was hurting.

Relax, she mentally urged herself. *Or you're going to blow it.*

"Phone?" he asked, holding out a hand.

She reached into her pocket and handed it over before glancing over his shoulder at the room beyond. The space was not their base of operations like she'd expected, just a meeting place. It was bare and unassuming with rough cement walls, strip lighting, and plastic chairs set in a loose semicircle. A rickety camp table held a thermos, a few ceramic mugs, and an open box of biscuits. Overall, it was disappointing. There was nothing to justify the steel door, the secure access, or the out-of-the-way location.

It was just a gathering of people.

Apart from Fang, five others were already there. They were seated, relaxed but watchful, their eyes flicking to her the moment she entered. No one spoke.

Avril didn't react. She let them look. Let them draw their own conclusions.

Don't appear too eager.

Runa nudged her forward. "Come and meet the team."

She gave a shy nod and walked deeper into the room.

"This is Astrid," Runa said, looking around the group. "I'll let you all introduce yourselves."

"Welcome, Astrid," came a low, unhurried voice.

She glanced across the room as a willowy guy in round-framed glasses swiveled away from the coffee table. He glided, rather than walked, across the room, extending a hand. "I'm Echo. I'm in charge of this little cohort. I'm so glad you could join us."

She shook it. "Pleased to meet you."

He was tall, neatly dressed in jeans and a pressed shirt, with the lithe, sinewy build of a long-distance runner. His handshake was firm, and she sensed power beneath the relaxed grip.

Avril wasn't sure what she'd expected from the cell leader, but he wasn't it.

He studied her, the light reflecting off his glasses. "Runa speaks highly of you."

"Oh?" She glanced at Runa, who nodded.

"You've got fire, but you're smart too. I saw the way you acted when you were arrested. We need more people like you."

"Come and sit down." Echo waved his hand in the direction of the arch of chairs, two of which were vacant. Runa nodded, and they sat down.

"Did you search her?" A man with an angular face glanced up from his tablet.

"Rook—" Runa began.

Echo shook his head. "No, he's right." He shot an awkward glance at Avril. "I'm sorry, do you mind? We can't be too careful."

"Oh, er, no. I guess not." She got to her feet again and held out her arms. Out of the corner of her eye, she saw Fang hand her phone to Rook, who immediately glanced down at it. What was he up to?

Fang came over and patted her down. "She's clean," he confirmed, a moment later.

"Thank you, Astrid." Echo flashed her a grin. He was charming, she'd give him that much.

As soon as she'd sat down, the woman beside her uncrossed her legs and leaned over. She was in her fifties, slim and relaxed. Her wavy, dark hair was graying at the temples and hung loosely down her back. She was casually dressed in faded jeans and a knitted sweater that looked homemade, giving off aging hippy vibes.

"Welcome, Astrid. I'm Gaia." A large silver ring with a flecked green gemstone caught the light.

Avril smiled, and shook her hand, looking into a pair of sharp, intelligent eyes. Her first thought was that this was not a woman to be underestimated. "Thanks."

"Gaia is our resident scientist," Echo explained. "She works at the university, and we're lucky to have her."

Stockholm University. She stored it away for later.

"What kind of scientist?" Avril asked. It was a normal question that someone who was joining the group might ask.

"Environmental chemistry." She gave a soft snort. "I study how corporations poison the world and call it progress."

Avril just stopped herself from blinking in surprise. Instead, she tilted her head as if considering the weight of the words. She knew it was a statement designed to provoke a reaction, to see where the newcomer stood.

Avril tapped into her legend. She was someone who understood—someone who was here because she believed in the cause, not because she was looking for a way in.

A long beat passed, then she said, "Yeah, and they call people like us extremists for wanting them to stop."

Gaia's smile deepened, just a fraction.

Avril heaved an internal sigh of relief. Another hurdle down.

"The paranoid one is Rook," Runa said, earning herself a glare from the man with the tablet. "He's a tech genius, in charge of our social media strategy."

"Amongst other things," he mumbled, sliding her phone back to her across the table.

He'd be the one checking her out. A shiver shot down Avril's spine as she pocketed her device. She really hoped her backstory was strong enough to withstand his paranoid scrutiny.

She sent him a friendly nod, not that he bothered to return it.

Rook would be a tough nut to crack, and the one she would have to work on if she wanted to fit in here. Echo obviously relied on him, deferring to him about the body search, which meant he had standing in this cell of the organization. Maybe he was even part of Terra Nova's inner circle.

"Well, now you've met everyone, let's make a start," Echo said, taking up a position at the front. "Astrid, why don't you tell us a little about yourself. We know what Runa has told us, obviously, but we'd like to hear it from you."

Avril took a deep breath. This was it. She'd known this moment would happen, and she had prepared for it. Now, she had to deliver, without making it sound too rehearsed.

"I guess you already know the basics," she said, glancing at Runa. "I was born here, in Sweden, but moved to the U.S. when I was a kid. My parents split up, and my mom wanted a fresh start in California."

A pause—just long enough to make it feel unscripted.

"I was... like everyone else at first. Believing things could change. Believing if we shouted loud enough, if we did the research, exposed the corruption, that people would listen." She exhaled a short, humorless laugh. "Turns out, that's bullshit."

Echo's dark eyes were fixed on her, intense and unwavering. They burned with an inner glow behind the John Lennon glasses that she found quite unsettling.

Trying to ignore him, she kept going.

"I got involved in climate activism at UC Santa Cruz. Protests, petitions, direct action—nothing too radical. I was just trying to fight back against the same corporate parasites wrecking the planet." She shook her head. "During one particular march, the police arrested my friends, blacklisted them from jobs, and threatened their families."

Her fingers curled into her lap, a sign of barely restrained anger.

"I dropped out of college after my mom died in the wildfires." She let a flicker of pain surface, raw but not overwhelming—enough to make it real, but not a performance. "They called it a 'natural disaster.' But I saw what caused it. Drought, mismanagement, greed. The oil companies, the lobbyists, the politicians—they didn't care. They never do."

Silence settled for a moment. She saw Gaia nod slightly, as if recognizing something familiar in her words.

"I sold everything and came back here. Figured if the U.S. didn't give a shit, maybe Sweden still had a chance." She shrugged, keeping the bitterness light. "It appears I was wrong."

She stole a glance at Echo, whose expression was unreadable. At Fang, who was staring at the wall in front of him and not at her. At Gaia, who gave a nod of understanding. At Rook—who was watching her like he was waiting for her to slip up.

Echo, first to react, cleared his throat. "You'll be pleased to know that we do more than just talk. If you join our organization, you'll be able to take direct action against those very corporations you despise. The ones you blame for your mother's death. We seek to root out greed and corruption by any means possible."

Avril dropped her voice to a whisper. "Sounds good."

The meeting continued after that, with Echo giving an update on the protest march, nothing too important, since they were still feeling her out. She noticed he didn't mention Gustav Holmgren's murder, for which they were rumored to have taken responsibility. The police were still authenticating the claims. Maybe it was too soon. The trust wasn't there yet.

He did, however, mention her and Runa's arrest, and commended them for their resilience and dedication. She liked that she was included in that. It made her feel like Echo had accepted her, even though Rook clearly hadn't.

When it drew to a close, Echo called her over. "A word, Astrid."

She glanced at Runa, who smiled and gave her an encouraging nod.

Okay, this was good.

"What do you think of our little group so far?" Behind the glasses, his gaze was probing, like he was trying to see beyond her mask and through to the layers below.

She nodded, wanting to appear interested, but not too keen. "I like what I see so far. It's smaller than I expected, though. Just five of you?"

"Five in this particular cell, but the organization as a whole is growing every day. We have almost two hundred supporters in Sweden and more spread around Europe. They attend protests, donate money, and spread propaganda. We have thousands more online, as you can imagine."

Avril gave an intrigued nod. Echo had a way of talking that drew you in, a voice that was naturally loud, but when spoken softly, resonated with intensity. The contrast forced you to listen harder to catch every word. It was an effective technique.

"You must have questions," he said.

She pretended to think for a moment. "Are there other groups like this one?"

The fire in his eyes danced. She realized the dark irises were flecked with yellow, which was what gave them that enigmatic orange glow. "Of course. They all consist of five to ten committed members. We carry out specific tasks—sabotage, cyber-attacks, arson." He paused to gauge her reaction to the illegal activities.

"It must feel really good to be doing something that grabs attention, rather than just passive protesting," she replied, meeting his gaze with her own. "You don't know how long I've wanted to... act. Make people take notice."

"Well, you're in the right place," he reassured her. "The various cells work in isolation, to protect the organization."

"Makes sense." She paused. "Echo, are you in charge of the whole organization?"

He laughed. "No, Terra Nova's founder and president is a man known as Odin. Only a select few of the inner circle have seen him. I happen to be one of them, as are a few other cell leaders."

She nodded, transfixed.

"Tell me about your mother," he said, quietly.

For a strange moment, Avril thought he meant her real mother, not the wildfire victim belonging to her alias. As it happened, she could talk with some authority on grief, on loss, on having to live without ever understanding why.

"My whole world changed when my mother died," she said, honestly. "For a long time I couldn't understand what had happened. Why she'd been taken from me."

Echo gave a sympathetic nod, but his eyes were blazing.

"I looked into the disaster, discovered the budget restrictions and the ineptitude. The fire was avoidable, but they'd prioritized greed over the natural resources." She sniffed. "I was also probably in denial at that point."

He didn't say anything, just watched her closely.

"Anyway, it was then that I decided to dedicate the rest of my life to fighting the system that allowed this to happen."

Was she still talking about her legend?

"What did you do?" he asked.

"I dropped out of college and began protesting. I joined rallies and activist groups, I petitioned the state, but nothing changed. Nothing ever changes."

"Is that when you came home?"

She nodded. "I'd had enough of California, of the dysfunctional system of government, so I sold my mother's house, packed up, and came back to Sweden."

"I'm very sorry for your loss," he said, and she could tell he meant it.

"Thank you."

A long beat passed where he simply stared at her. Avril felt like he was absorbing her darkness, her grief.

"What would you say if I told you I could give you a chance to make a difference?"

She stared at him, remembering how she'd felt when she'd first joined the FBI. When her mother's killer had resurfaced in America, and she'd been given another opportunity to hunt him down. It had been a lifeline.

Her expression tightened. "I'd jump at it."

chapter
eight

It was a test.

Avril knew it, but she'd still go through with it.

This one, she couldn't tell Krister about. He wouldn't approve.

Her objective did not include engaging in criminal activity, but if she didn't pull this off, she wouldn't be accepted into the group. It was a no-brainer.

Avril scanned the street in Stockholm's city center. It was a misty, dull day, with bulbous clouds looming overhead, threatening to unleash at any moment. Being a Monday morning, there were a lot of commuters heading to work, collars up and heads down against the cold. Nobody was looking around them.

According to Echo, her target would be coming this way shortly. He supposedly took the same route to work every day—the train from Stockholm City Station, then a short, ten-minute walk to the office, a nondescript building that nobody ever looked at twice.

Gray against the gray.

She waited, pretending to read the headlines at a newspaper stand, gloved hands thrust deep in her pockets, beanie pulled low to obscure her blonde hair. The black scarf she wore hid her jaw and mouth, making her almost impossible to identify—in case of CCTV cameras. Echo had assured her that if she stuck to the predetermined spot, there would be no danger of that. A blind spot, he'd said.

How he knew, she had no idea. Rook had probably hacked into the city's CCTV network or something.

She shivered, but knew it had nothing to do with the icy wind.

"Come on," she muttered, eyes trained on the street.

Where the hell was he?

"You going to buy that?" the seller asked, glaring at her. She shook her head and moved on. Her teeth were beginning to chatter when she finally spotted him.

There.

Crossing the intersection from the station, just as she'd been told he would. Her pulse quickened as the reality of what she was about to do hit home. Avril had never in her life committed a blatantly violent act before. This was assault, pure and simple.

Steeling herself, she pushed away from the wall and followed the man. Unlike most of the other commuters, he wasn't dressed in a suit or a blazer. He wore jeans and a red checked shirt that stuck out from underneath his bomber jacket. A working man. He was carrying a worn briefcase, which told her he wasn't a manual laborer. This guy was heading to an office. She guessed a facilities or factory manager—or at a push, an engineer.

Not that it mattered.

Avril sucked in a shuddering breath. She could do this. It would be over quickly, a few seconds at the most, then she'd be on her way. Nobody would know who she was, or be able to identify her, if asked. She was safe on that front.

The man turned into a perpendicular street flanked by high-rises stabbing at the ominous sky. Adrenaline flooded her body, making her heart race. This was it.

She was actually going through with it.

Another ten yards or so and he'd be in the blind spot. Adjacent to the tobacco shop, that's what Echo had instructed.

Avril began counting down.

Nine... eight... seven...

The man was almost there.

Charging forward, she heaved him off the sidewalk into the street. It was pedestrianized, so there were no vehicles, thank God. The man gasped, slipped off the curb, and fell onto his side. Reaching down, Avril grabbed his briefcase, wrenching it out of his hand.

"Hey!" he yelled, as she took off down the street.

A couple of people turned around, but Avril darted around the corner. Out of sight, she pulled off her beanie letting her long hair cascade over her shoulders, unzipped her coat to show a bright blue power suit, and walked confidently away.

To the casual observer, she was a chic businesswoman on her way to the office. Nobody would think that a moment earlier, she'd mugged a man and stolen his briefcase.

It was 10:30 PM.

Avril waited outside the same address as the night before, clutching the briefcase in her hand. It was a cold night, made colder still by the icy wind that had been blowing all day. A dense shadow fell across the streetlamp and Avril swung around, pulse racing.

It was Fang.

"Shit, you scared me," she muttered, willing herself to calm down.

Her instructions had been not to open the briefcase. Under no circumstances was she to go through the contents. She simply had to hand it to a cell member tonight. Here.

Obviously, she'd tried to open it.

The briefcase was noticeably worn, the leather scuffed at the edges, with a flimsy four-digit combination code. Easy enough to pry open, but then Echo would know she'd sneaked a peek.

Instead, she'd taken it home, set it down on the kitchen table, and wearing a pair of latex gloves, systematically worked through every possible combination starting with 0001. When she got to 2723, it clicked open.

At first she'd simply stared at the open case, not quite believing she'd managed to hit on the right code. Luckily, the owner hadn't chosen a number starting with 9000, or it would have taken much longer.

The thought did cross her mind that it might be a trap, that the man might be a stooge, set up to see if she'd go through with it. The documents could be marked with chemicals or an invisible ink that would make her hands change color under an infrared lamp so they'd know she'd rifled through it and couldn't be trusted to follow instructions.

Was she overthinking it?

Avril had studied the pages through a magnifying glass, but they'd appeared normal. Next, she'd bent over and sniffed them. No chemicals. She didn't have an infrared lamp, but she was pretty sure the documents were clean.

So she'd looked through them.

At first glance, they'd been underwhelming. A print-out that appeared to be some sort of manual for an air conditioning system, a couple of invoices for scheduled maintenance, schematics for what could be a large arena or shopping mall, and an access card to an unidentified building. All that was written on the grubby plastic was: *Maintenance*.

She'd sat back in her chair, thinking. What did it all mean? Who was this guy? And why did Terra Nova want what was in his briefcase? Echo hadn't given her any clues.

Still, she had to assume there was a reason, and it wasn't just a random target for her sake. To prove her commitment to the cause.

Using the camera on the personal phone, she'd taken a photograph of every single document inside, in the correct order. It was too risky using the phone she'd been issued as part of her legend, complete with appropriate apps, a call list, and contact book of fake friends, especially after Rook had inspected it at the meeting. If he was their resident tech genius, he could have inserted a tracker or some sort of spyware onto the device. She couldn't afford to take any chances.

As an extra precaution, she'd wiped the photos off her personal phone once they'd been uploaded, making sure to clean out the deleted files too.

Once she was done, she'd repacked the briefcase, careful to stack the documents in the right order, close it again, and set the combination lock to what it had been before she'd opened it.

There.

No one would be the wiser.

She hoped.

"Can I have the briefcase?" Fang asked.

She hesitated. "What's in it?"

He gave an uninterested shrug. "Don't know."

So Echo hadn't told him either. Maybe it was just a test, and there was nothing more to it. Nah, she didn't think Echo was the sort to send her into a potentially risky situation for no reason. He must be getting something out of it.

She should have stuck around after the assault to see where the target went. Except she'd panicked and got the hell out of there, concerned with being spotted. He could have led her to his place of work, for which he had the access card.

Still, all was not lost. If he walked that route every day to work, as Echo claimed, she could just pick up his trail tomorrow, or even the next day.

Avril handed Fang the briefcase.

He grunted, then turned and hurried down the street until his hulking frame was swallowed up by the darkness.

chapter **nine**

Later that night, Avril used her laptop to scroll through the photographs she'd uploaded to the cloud, hoping to find something that would tell her where they were from.

"Not a single clue," she muttered, rubbing her eyes. No logos. No company names. No obvious links.

The two receipts weren't much help either. They were from a chain of building supply stores, which meant narrowing it down would be tricky. She could pass them on to Krister—maybe Säpo could trace which branch the purchases came from—but the guy had paid in cash both times. No name, no card, no way to link the items back to him.

Was that intentional?

The lack of useful information in the briefcase brought her back to her original thought. Had this been a setup? Was the victim in on it? Was that why there was nothing noteworthy in his briefcase? Had they known she would open it all along?

To be fair, it wasn't that hard a combination. Anyone with patience and time would have got there in the end—like she had.

Avril decided to take a hot shower to warm up before turning in for the night. As the steaming water washed away the tension of the day, she was left with one thought.

Should she tell Krister?

There was no doubt that she *should*, but would she?

Säpo might be able to make heads or tails of the documents, they might be able to access CCTV footage further down the street and trace the man she'd mugged to his place of work, or maybe they could identify him using facial recognition software. By not telling Krister, she was essentially withholding information.

Except, she'd broken the law. Mugging *and* theft. A clear violation of both Swedish criminal law and the operational parameters Säpo had laid out. How would they handle it? Would they pull her out and terminate the assignment?

In theory, they'd have to. Undercover agents were expected to observe strict boundaries. She hadn't gotten pre-approval for the mugging, therefore her actions could jeopardize the entire case in court. Evidence could be thrown out. Charges could collapse.

But this is what Säpo did. They knew ops like this weren't clean. If they thought the outcome was worth it, they might look the other way. Bury it in the post-op review. It all depended on what she got them in return.

One thing she did know, however, was that they wouldn't get this chance again.

Avril got ready for bed, moving around the unfamiliar flat. With a sigh, she decided to sleep on it—see if things were any clearer in the morning.

Avril opened her eyes, and for a confusing moment, forgot where she was. In the semi-dark room, she didn't recognize anything, and it was only the gap in the blinds and the unenthusiastic yellow of the morning light slicing through it that brought her to her senses.

Astrid Dahlström. Terra Nova.

The bookstore!

Throwing back the covers, she got out of bed. Half an hour later, she left the apartment to walk to the bookstore, grabbing a coffee on the way.

Should she go back to Stockholm's downtown area and wait for the man she'd mugged? Glancing ahead of her up the street, she shivered and pulled her coat tighter around her. If they were watching the bookstore, they'd notice her absence. They might even have someone following her. She doubted it, but you couldn't be too careful. It was probably best not to do anything to arouse suspicion.

Avril was halfway through the morning shift when a teenager walked in. It had been a slow day so far with only a handful of browsers and one sale. The kid nodded at her, placed a folded piece of paper on the countertop, and left again.

Another missive.

She unfolded the note and read the message. There was another meeting tonight, except this was at a different venue. They moved around to prevent detection.

Once she got home, she'd take a picture of it and send it to Krister. He never replied, he couldn't. She kept her personal phone switched off and hidden away, never on her person. But it was enough knowing he was out there, ready to move in should things go sideways.

THE MEETING WAS HELD above a bar in Södermalm, a hip and happening area of Stockholm. By day, the streets were filled with bohemian cafés, art galleries, and record shops, but at night, the neighborhood was very different. Bars overflowed onto the sidewalks, neon signs cast flickering reflections on the wet cobblestones, and the soft throb of music and conversation drifted through the narrow streets. Avril had always liked it here.

The bar itself, Gjutaren, looked unassuming enough. Tucked between a tattoo studio and a falafel joint, it catered to a kind of grungy, alternative crowd.

She pushed open the door and stepped inside, immediately assailed by the rank odor of cheap booze and stale cigarette smoke that seemed to cling to everything. The lighting was low, and the walls were lined with vintage band posters. She scanned them, raising an eyebrow at the better-known acts that had once performed here.

But she didn't linger. Following the instructions, she slipped through the side door and took a steep spiral staircase to the second floor. The space above was quieter, separated from the noise below by a thick wooden door, painted black and covered in scratches and faded markings.

Unlike the door at the last meeting, this one had a handle. She tried it, but it didn't open, so she knocked instead.

This must be the right place, but there was no one else around. It had just turned 10 P.M. so she wasn't late. Where was everybody?

Avril hesitated, unsure what to do. Despite her attempts to remain calm, her pulse raced like she was about to step into a warzone. Was this where they told her she'd failed the mission? That they knew she'd opened the briefcase?

Were they going to kick her out, or worse, force her to confess?

If they did confront her about it, she had her excuse lined up. She'd been curious, she meant no harm by it. Her problem wasn't disloyalty, it was curiosity. That's what made her so good at seeing through the corporate bullshit—she took the time to investigate.

Whether they'd believe her or not, she had no idea.

A moment later, the door cracked open. Fang stood there, his bulk filling the frame. He motioned for her to raise her arms before stepping aside.

Avril did as she was instructed. So, this was how it was going to be. A search for weapons or recording devices every time she attended a meeting. Was it the same for the others, all of whom were sitting around a wooden table in the center of the room? Or was the process reserved for newbies who had yet to prove their loyalty to the group?

Echo sat at the head, with Gaia beside him. Runa smiled as she walked in, while Rook glanced up from his tablet. She took an empty chair, as did Fang, but only after closing and bolting the door.

Echo looked up, smiled, and said, "Let's begin."

The meeting got underway.

"Firstly, I'd like to commend Astrid on passing the little test I set for her yesterday." There was a muted murmur of approval, and Runa gave her a thumbs up from across the table.

The dark gaze fixed on her. "I hope you didn't find it too upsetting?"

"Not at all." She kept her voice even.

"Fang mentioned you asked what was inside—" He left the statement hanging, waiting for her to confirm. She met his gaze, clear and direct.

"I was curious. I wondered what we needed it for."

He smiled. "All will be revealed in due course."

She had to be content with that.

At least she was in the clear. For the first time since she'd arrived, she began to relax.

"Now, since it's the first Thursday of the month, we have a scheduled call with Odin. For Astrid's benefit, Odin is the founder of the organization and chief decision maker. While we execute tasks and activities, he plans the agenda, along with his inner council, of which I am honored to be a member." There was no arrogance in his tone.

Avril straightened up. Great. She was about to find out more about the man behind Terra Nova. Up until now, he'd been this mysterious figure cloaked in intrigue. Not even Säpo knew who he was, other than his codename.

Odin—a Norse god associated with war, death, wisdom, and magic. Ruler of Valhalla.

Very appropriate.

Given the laptop Rook had positioned in the center of the table, she figured it would be an online video call. The tech genius leaned over and hit a few keys, and the screen flickered to life.

A video feed appeared, intentionally blurred so they couldn't make out the figure at the center. In addition, the lighting was dim, casting Odin's outline in shadow, but the transmission itself was seamless—no static, no lag, no distortion, just a smooth broadcast through whatever dark-web system Terra Nova had set up.

Avril was disappointed but kept her expression neutral. There was a sense of expectation in the room.

The voice that followed was electronically altered, but even so, it was low and controlled.

"Good evening, my friends."

The room fell silent. Even Rook, always half-distracted, leaned in slightly.

"Another month has passed, and once again, we move closer to

Cold Legacy

justice. The old-world order weakens with every strike we deliver. They're beginning to realize that their power is not absolute. Their reign is not eternal. We have proven that."

A pause.

"They called him untouchable. They thought his wealth, his bodyguards, his security detail made him immune. And yet, one man—one titan of industry who built his empire by choking the earth with oil—is gone."

Avril drew in a breath. She knew exactly who he was talking about.

Gustav Holmgren, CEO of Nordic Energy.

Europe was still reeling from the shock. Politicians condemned it. Corporations tightened security. Environmental groups distanced themselves, swearing they had no part in the violence.

Yet, in this room, there was no regret.

Odin's voice remained steady, unfazed. "He was just the beginning."

Avril tensed, bracing herself for what would come next.

"We have waited long enough," Odin continued. "We have fought in the shadows, but now, we must make them see us. We must shake them from their complacency."

There were murmurs of agreement around the table. Avril bobbed her head in accord with the others. Everyone was riveted by the blurry image on the screen.

"Something big is coming."

Avril glanced toward Echo, trying to gauge his reaction—but he was stone-faced, unreadable.

"Each of you will have a part to play," Odin went on. "My inner circle and I will determine the finer details. Echo will be briefed. He will ensure that everything proceeds as planned, and he will be in touch regarding your roles. Trust him. Follow his lead."

Echo inclined his head, just enough to acknowledge the statement. "Of course."

Another pause.

Then Odin's head turned slightly, as if looking at them one by one, though his blurred features gave no indication of where his gaze truly landed.

"Stay focused. Stay sharp. They thought we were scattered, leaderless, and divided, but they now know they were wrong. We are the storm on the horizon. And when we strike, they will never forget our name, Terra Nova."

A final beat of silence.

Then the screen cut to black.

chapter
ten

ODIN SAT IN HIS STUDY, CONTEMPLATING TONIGHT'S meeting. He'd just watched a replay, as he always did, scrutinizing the members, their reactions, his performance.

Now *that* had been interesting.

He studied the still image on the screen where he'd paused the video.

Astrid.

It had been a while since that particular cell had recruited a new member. All the others had been with them right from the start. Founding members, if you like. Rook, an essential part of the organization; Gaia with her sharp, scientific mind; Runa with her youthful passion; and then Fang, loyal to a fault. Of course, it had been Odin who'd dragged him out of his drunken haze of bar fights and misdemeanors, and given him a job, an income, and a purpose. Lastly, there was Echo, the glue who held it all together. He smiled to himself.

Rook had done a thorough background check on Astrid, as he did with everyone connected to the organization. Meticulous, relentless, borderline paranoid, the tech expert was exactly what Odin needed him to be. He'd even planted some sort of spyware on Astrid's phone so they could read her texts and see who she was calling.

Despite Rook's best efforts, however, they'd found nothing unusual in Astrid's story.

Perfectly ordinary, perfectly tragic.

A young woman with a fractured family history, a childhood spent between two worlds. An activist disillusioned by the slow grind of political change. A daughter who'd lost her mother to the wildfires that had ravaged California in 2021—a disaster that the media had called natural, even as the earth burned beneath the weight of human greed.

That grief, that fire, it had left a mark on her. He could sense it. A darkness, a hunger for something more than words, more than futile protests.

She was ripe for recruiting, her idealism battered but not yet broken. Someone who had learned that the system would not save her. Someone ready to take justice into her own hands.

He gazed thoughtfully at her image. Rook's report had confirmed everything she'd told them. UC Santa Cruz, political science major, climate activism, protests. In addition, there had been arrests, a blacklisting, her scholarship lost along with her mother to the flames. Astrid hadn't mentioned those, but then why should she?

And yet, it was the test that intrigued him most. The small task she had pulled off yesterday. Nothing too dangerous, nothing too revealing. Just enough to gauge her loyalty, her willingness to follow orders.

The briefcase she'd delivered had been intact. Even if she had looked inside, she wouldn't have found anything revealing, anything that made sense. But she hadn't looked. Her fingerprints had been on the case, as expected, but not the documents.

He was satisfied. She'd followed the instructions to the letter. A committed, trustworthy individual. Another Runa.

Odin pursed his lips. He prided himself in being a good judge of character. Astrid fascinated him. He could see the clouds in her eyes, the storminess she kept in check. There was a darkness there. Maybe even one that mirrored his own.

Grief had a way of shaping people, twisting them into something sharper, hungrier. He knew that intimately. He had wielded that focus like a blade more times than he could count. And he saw that same potential in Astrid.

She was still raw, still clinging to the edges of what was acceptable, still believing that what she was doing was just and righteous. But she could be worked on. She could become something more. A valuable tool in his arsenal.

Odin leaned back in his chair, steepling his fingers. Astrid was the perfect recruit. A woman who could exist in the real world but thrive in one full of secrets. If she proved herself, he would let her in deeper. Slowly. A piece at a time, until she was fully committed. Until she was bound as tightly to Terra Nova as any of them.

He stared at her image frozen on his screen.

"Welcome to the game, Astrid," he murmured.

chapter
eleven

Something big is coming.

Avril repeated the phrase over and over in her head. What was bigger than a public assassination of a prominent oil mogul? She dreaded to think.

Krister.

She had to talk to Krister.

He'd said not to come to him, that they'd be watching her flat, but glancing out, she couldn't see anyone around. That didn't mean they weren't there, of course, hiding in the shadows. She couldn't call him either, it wasn't worth the risk. She was under strict instructions not to use her personal phone unless it was an emergency, and obviously, the one Rook had handled was out of the question.

Besides, if she were honest, she wanted to see a friendly face.

Avril paced up and down her living room, surrounded by things that weren't hers, photographs of strangers smiling down at her. Fake relatives, fake memories. They all made up a life she hadn't lived.

Paranoia made her jittery. There could be cameras positioned outside on the street, or in the window of the building opposite, or even above her front door. She didn't know what surveillance tactics they had access to or were capable of, but she had to assume they were the best.

It was late, nearly midnight. The meeting had ended sharply at eleven, but it had taken her some time to get home. Outside, the night sky was like pitch, starless, any sliver of light blocked out by the thick cloud cover.

That could work to her advantage.

Decision made, she pulled on her black hoodie, a balaclava she kept for those frigid days where it felt like your face was freezing off—or when you needed to dissolve into the shadows—gloves, and tight, black leggings. Nothing that would attract attention or catch the light. She had to be invisible.

Her first-floor apartment faced the now silent street. Across the road was an empty sidewalk punctuated dully by a series of streetlamps. Overlooking it were other blocks of flats. This wasn't an affluent area. More like the type of neighborhood where a student or low-income citizen might live. Rents were cheap, but so were the buildings, amenities and budget stores.

She immediately discounted the balcony, which had a fire escape down to the street. Too many unseen eyes from the apartments opposite. Terra Nova hadn't gotten this far by being careless.

The front door was out too. That would be the obvious choice. The back door was a possibility. It led out onto a grubby side street, poorly lit, and filled with dumpsters and an empty parking lot. Except, if she were going to sneak out, they'd expect her to do it that way.

She had to think one step ahead like a game of chess in which she could quite easily become the pawn.

That left two options. Someone else's apartment balcony or the basement.

When she'd moved in, she'd scouted the building, and the laundry room was situated underneath the block, accessible by the stairwell just inside the entrance. It was unseen from the outside. If memory served, the basement had small, elongated windows just above street level to let in the light during the day. Was she small enough to fit through those? The basement windows faced the opposite side of the block. They couldn't have eyes everywhere.

Grabbing a flashlight, she slipped out of her apartment and along the drafty corridor to the stairwell at the end. Down one flight, then another, and she was at the basement door.

Opening it, Avril stepped into the blacker than black laundry room illuminated only by the unobtrusive beam of her flashlight. She couldn't put the lights on in case someone saw them from the outside.

Avril looked up at the windows. Yep, it was as she'd thought. About a foot and a half high and a yard wide. They opened outwards, held by a flimsy latch. Not very secure. Anyone could break in, but it would make breaking out easier too.

She climbed onto a washing machine and unlocked the latch, pushing it open as wide as she could. Frigid air seeped in and bit at her face. Avril hoped she wouldn't freeze. She was hardly dressed for a midnight stroll.

It couldn't be helped. Once out, she'd take a slow jog to the corner, then hop on a night bus to Täby, where Krister lived. He wouldn't be expecting her, but that was the point. She didn't want to risk any communication, not even by text message, just in case Rook was monitoring her phone.

She was about to slip out when she heard footsteps on the stairs. A burst of adrenaline made her freeze. The footsteps came closer.

Closing the window, she jumped down and scrambled behind a dryer. The light flicked on, and a young man carrying a bag of washing crossed the room.

Avril's heart sank. Really? Who did their laundry at this hour? Now she'd have to wait for him to finish before she could make her escape.

The man shivered, but thankfully didn't linger. He opened a washing machine door, stuffed his clothing in, added the detergent, the smell of which floated across to her, sterile and caustic, making her want to sneeze. She held her nose until the urge passed.

The washer went on, a phlegmy wheeze before churning into a low rumble. As it settled into a rhythm, the man straightened up, watched it a moment, then turned to leave.

Thank goodness.

Avril waited until the light was out and the door had shut, before she eased out from behind the machine. She couldn't afford any more delays. Hopping back onto the washer, she reopened the window, disconnected it from its hinges to maximize the gap, and crawled out onto the damp street.

. . .

Cold Legacy

KRISTER'S HOUSE lay in darkness. The bus had dropped her at the end of their street and she'd jogged the rest of the way, past her father's house, and around the back of Krister's. She knew it well, having spent many of her childhood summers in his garden.

Those had been happy times.

Before.

She stood on the back porch and looked up at his bedroom window. A low light glowed from within. He was still up, or he'd fallen asleep reading case files, as she knew was his habit.

Picking up a small pebble, she threw it at the window. It bounced off with a little tap, ricocheting back onto the frosty grass.

No movement.

Krister was a deep sleeper, far deeper than she was. He could sleep anywhere, even on the hard ground in a tent in the woods, in their den, or a treehouse.

Not like her.

She was plagued by the horrors that churned in her head. Icy tableaus from the Frost Killer's multiple victims. Unseeing eyes staring up at her, pleading for help that wouldn't come.

Even now that it was over, the faces were still there. Haunting her dreams.

Bending, she picked up another pebble, larger this time, and hurled it at the window. It hit with a loud pop. Avril cringed, hoping she hadn't cracked the glass.

This time, she sensed movement. The light flickered as a shadow moved across it and Krister appeared at the window. He scowled down into the garden, immediately suspicious.

She shone the flashlight onto herself and waved. The look of surprise on his face was almost comical, then she saw him curse under his breath.

He held up a hand and vanished from view. *Wait.*

Avril made her way onto the back porch. A moment later, the back-door opened and Krister stood there in track pants and a T-shirt. He was barefoot.

"Jesus, Avril. What the hell are you doing here?"

She couldn't stop shivering. "Can we take this inside, please? Before I freeze to death."

He ushered her in. "Why aren't you wearing a coat? You want a hot drink or something?"

She nodded and collapsed, trembling, at the kitchen table. It was the same one his parents had always had, the grooves and scuffs as familiar to her as her own. "P-Please."

"Hang on." He darted out of the kitchen, then came back a few seconds later holding a blanket. "Here, put this over your shoulders."

As he made her a hot mug of tea, she told him how she'd escaped without detection. "It was the only way. I had to see you."

"What is so important?" he asked, but she sensed the concern in his voice. "Is something wrong?"

"Krister, they're planning something big. I don't know what yet, but it's going to make the assassination look like a misdemeanor."

He paused, mug in hand. "Seriously?"

She nodded, teeth chattering. "I went to a meeting tonight, at that new venue. We had a live video talk with Odin."

Krister's eyes widened. "You saw Terra Nova's secret leader?"

"The one and only."

Krister placed the mug in front of her and eased onto the bench opposite.

"So he does exist."

"Very much so."

Krister tilted his head to the side. "What's he like?"

"Enigmatic, charismatic, engaging. All the things you'd expect. He spoke in a low voice, obviously disguised. I don't think it was prerecorded, or if it was, it was a damn good recording. He engaged with Echo, so I assume it was in real time."

"What did he look like? Can you sit with a sketch artist?"

She was already shaking her head. "He was blurred, I couldn't make out his features. White male, dark hair, slim build—that's about it."

"Fuck." He ran a hand through his hair.

Avril knew how he felt. They'd been desperate to ID the mysterious founder since the organization had first materialized, rocking the political and environmental landscape.

"Do you have any details about this event they're planning?" Krister asked.

"Not yet. He said he'd discuss the details with his inner circle. I know Echo is part of that, and maybe Rook, but I don't know if any of the others are."

Krister inhaled deeply. "We need to get eyes on them. Apart from Runa, we have no idea who the others are."

Avril took a sip of her hot chocolate. The feeling was coming back into her toes. "I'm working on it. Did you manage to follow Echo after the meeting?"

Krister shook his head. "Bastard gave the Säpo agents the slip. They followed Gaia, though. We now know her real name is Annika Ekström. Before she became a lecturer at Stockholm University, she studied environmental chemistry, later earning a PhD in toxicology and climate impact."

"She's well educated," Avril said, impressed. "How'd she become involved with Terra Nova?"

"We're not entirely sure, but she spent years lobbying for environmental policies, writing scientific papers on pollution, deforestation, and oil industry corruption, so she was ripe for the plucking, so to speak."

Avril nodded, savoring the warmth of her mug.

"We think the breaking point came in 2015 when her research exposed illegal dumping by a multinational corporation, which led to a government cover-up. The company was never prosecuted. After that, her funding was slashed, and she was pushed out of major academic circles."

"I can see how that might piss her off," Avril reasoned.

Krister gave a wry grin. "And Terra Nova was waiting to pounce."

"Echo is also very charismatic," Avril said after a brief pause. "He's got this intensity about him. I don't know—it's unnerving."

Krister's gaze narrowed. "Not getting to you, is he?"

"No, but he's not what I expected. He's not a fanatic. At least, he doesn't come across as one."

"What's he like, then?" Krister sat back, watching her.

Avril thought for a moment. "He's full of contradictions. Intense, but outwardly relaxed. He's got a loud voice but speaks softly. He's controlled, but there's this pent-up energy simmering beneath the surface." She didn't mention the penetrating gaze or the fire that burned in his eyes. Krister wouldn't get that. Wouldn't realize the impact it had. "I think he's dangerous."

Krister frowned. "I'll emphasize the importance of prioritizing him. We need to know who this guy is."

Avril finished her hot chocolate and stood up. Then, she hesitated.

"What?" he said, reading her immediately.

She took a steadying breath. "Krister, I did something illegal, a task for the cell. It was a test, and I had to go through with it."

He tilted back his head, his eyes slanted. "What did you do?"

"I assaulted a man—and stole his briefcase."

"You what? Was he hurt?"

She shook her head. "No, not that I could see. The task was to steal his briefcase. That's all. I left him on the street, but he was fine."

Krister gave her a long look. "What did you do with the briefcase?"

"I gave it to Fang, but not without taking a look inside first."

Krister gave a snort and shook his head. "I expected no less. What was in it?"

"Nothing telling. Like I said, it was a test. I loaded the files onto the cloud, so you can take a look, but I think they were designed not to give anything away. In fact, the whole thing was probably a set up."

"To see if you would go through with it?"

She nodded. "To gauge my commitment."

He exhaled. "If that's the case, then no reason to worry about it. Did you get a picture of the man?"

She gave him a look. "It's on the cloud too. I've wiped my phone, just in case."

He nodded. "I'll check it out. See if we can identify him."

"Okay. I'd better head back. I'm opening the bookstore tomorrow morning."

Krister slid out of the bench. "Let me drive you at least part of the way. It'll save you catching the bus. They're few and far between at this hour, and I don't want you dying of hypothermia."

She gave a relieved nod. "Thanks."

. . .

"I'll touch base with you in a couple of days," Krister said, when he dropped her off a few streets away from the apartment block. "If you need me, you can always call."

"I don't think the phone Säpo gave me is safe," she said.

At his confused look, she explained, "I had to give it to Fang the other night, and he passed it to Rook. I'm pretty sure he planted something inside, although I can't be sure. They might be tracking my calls and texts. Maybe even my location. That's why I left it at home."

Krister whistled. "I'll get you a burner. We can't risk you using your real phone, either—it could blow your cover, but you need a way to contact me."

She gave a quick nod and opened the car door. The cold wrapped her in its damp shroud.

"Home safe," Krister said.

Avril smiled, and then slipped into the night, merging with the darkness.

chapter
twelve

KRISTER CALLED A BRIEFING THE MOMENT HE STEPPED INTO the office. Freddie and Karlsson were already there, still bleary-eyed, clinging to their first coffees of the day. Ingrid was running late, but that wasn't unusual.

"Where are we on the door-to-door?" he asked Freddie, who'd assigned uniformed officers to canvas the neighborhood after the bombing.

"Nowhere," Freddie admitted. "Everybody heard the blast. They ran out of their houses to see Holmgren go up in flames, but nobody noticed anything odd the night before."

"Frustrating," Krister muttered. He'd been hoping for a lead.

"Yeah. I interviewed an old lady across the road. She's got insomnia. Said she heard a car engine around three in the morning."

"Did she see it?" Krister asked.

Freddie shook his head. "Unfortunately not. It wasn't in her line of sight."

"She heard it leave?"

"Nah. She went to bed after that."

He sighed.

"What about CCTV?" They could check that to see the make and model of the three AM prowler.

"Nothing in the street," Freddie replied, grimacing. "I checked with the neighborhood watch, and one family has a surveillance camera, but they're away at the moment."

"We need that footage," Krister said.

"I'm trying to contact them," Freddie said, "but they're hiking in Peru, and I have no idea where."

Krister clenched his jaw. "Keep at it."

He turned as Ingrid breezed in, looking like she'd just stepped out of a hair commercial. Her chin-length bob shone like it had been styled ten minutes ago. Coral lipstick, matching blouse. Eyes lined and shimmering.

She smiled around the table. "What did I miss?"

"Nothing," Krister said flatly. "You're just in time to brief us on your side of the investigation."

Ingrid sat, crossing her legs with a little too much flourish. He wasn't blind to her games. The trauma of being kidnapped and nearly frozen had kept her quiet for a while—but now she was back to her old flirtatious self. Determined, it seemed, to win him over.

"Karlsson handled the forensics," she said. "I spoke to the Nordic Energy board members."

Smart move. Ingrid knew how to work people—especially men. She played to her strengths, he'd give her that. Still, if the last investigation was anything to go by, she was no match for Avril. The thought almost made him smile, even though Ingrid had been through the ringer.

"How'd that go?"

Her smile deepened. "They were very cooperative. I spoke to each one individually. No real leads, but they all knew about the threat against Holmgren."

Krister frowned. "Any of them receive similar threats?"

"Yes," she said, eyes gleaming. "All of them."

"What?" He jumped out of his seat. "All of them?"

She nodded, clearly pleased by his reaction. "They get threats all the time, apparently. Until now, no one took them seriously."

"We'll have to let Säpo know. I'll call Lindholm now and fill him in. They'll want to see your case notes."

"No problem. I'm almost done writing them up."

"What security measures are in place?" Freddie asked.

"They've hired a private firm. Personal protection details for the board members only. General staff haven't been threatened—though the company gets a ton of hate mail. I've got a pile of it on my desk."

Private protection was smart. "They'll need to stay vigilant until Säpo catches whoever did this."

"Sucks we can't be the ones to bring them in," Karlsson muttered.

Krister shrugged. "It's called interagency cooperation, which basically means we do all the hard work and they take all the credit." He shouldn't be so cynical. Karlsson was young and hungry. Krister didn't want to kill his spirit. "Anway," he added. "It's not important who brings them in, as long as someone does."

Karlsson nodded.

"Forensics find anything at his office?"

The youngster shrugged. "Nothing relevant. No threatening letters or notes, no spyware on his laptop or phone, and his personal assistant says she vets everything before it goes to him."

"You get her statement?"

"Yeah, but she doesn't know anything. She's distraught by his murder. Couldn't stop crying when I was interviewing her."

Understandable. The blast had rattled everyone.

"Okay, thanks." He wrapped it up after that, and everyone went back to their desks.

LATER THAT MORNING, Krister called Lindholm with the update.

"The explosive was homemade," Lindholm said. "Crude, actually. Not what I would have expected from these guys."

"Maybe it's all they could get," Krister offered. "They might not be as well connected as everybody thinks."

"Could be. Makes it harder to trace. Anyone with basic chemistry knowledge and a garage could've built it."

"I'll reach out to Organized Crime. They might know someone who fits the profile."

"Do it," Lindholm said. "Let me know what you find."

"Will do."

Krister hung up and stared at the whiteboard across from him. Odin had said something big was coming. What was bigger than the assassination of an oil magnet?

Taking out the rest of the board? Destroying the company? Sabotaging the NordLinx pipeline? It could be any number of things.

He dragged a hand through his hair. Avril was in the best position to find out—but without a secure phone, she was cut off.

"I'm heading out," he told Freddie as he grabbed his coat.

He needed to get Avril a burner phone, something that couldn't be traced. She'd have to be careful not to let anyone see it, but he didn't like the thought of her out there with no way of contacting him.

Crude or not, these guys were dangerous, and he wasn't about to underestimate them. Not when Avril's life was at stake.

chapter
thirteen

AVRIL OPENED THE BOOKSTORE EARLY THE NEXT MORNING, then immediately perched behind the counter on the tall stool to drink her coffee while the rain pelted down outside. It had been almost three a.m. when she'd finally crawled back through the unlocked window, frozen solid, and made her way up to bed.

To say she was exhausted was an understatement. As the caffeine hit her system, she began to switch on, however, and the fog cleared.

It had been worthwhile sneaking out to talk to Krister. Not only had she warned him about the upcoming threat, but she'd also learned more about Gaia, the radicalized science professor at Stockholm University. Echo, on the other hand, was almost as much of a mystery as Terra Nova's elusive president, Odin.

The first customers wandered in around ten o'clock. When it was this cold and rainy outside, nobody wanted to get out of bed before that. Avril couldn't blame them.

Most of her customers were students of environmental sciences, political ecology, or sustainable development, their conversations peppered with discussions of climate models, carbon offsets, and policy failures. Others were academics, urban planners, and aging activists who had once marched against nuclear power in the '80s and now railed against the same corporate greed in a different era.

It was an interesting mix of people—passionate, well-read,

committed—but she had little in common with any of them. She hadn't gone to college, unless you counted the Swedish Police Academy or the FBI Training Center at Quantico.

Her education had come from chasing killers, learning on the job, and figuring it out as she went along. She'd taken a handful of courses with the Bureau's Behavioral Science Unit, the closest she'd come to formal academic training. Profiling violent offenders had fascinated her —not just the 'who' but the 'why' of human psychology.

If she ever did decide to go back to school, it wouldn't be for climate policy or environmental law. It would be for criminology or forensic psychology. Something that made sense of the minds—or mind—she'd spent her life hunting.

At lunchtime, she closed the shop and went to a nearby café for a sandwich and another coffee. No point in standing there, starving. If there was a meeting scheduled, a runner would come in mid-afternoon with a note, like before. She didn't expect one today—it was too soon— but she wanted to be ready, just in case.

As expected, nothing happened.

It was four o'clock, and she was contemplating closing early when the door opened and Echo walked in, coat billowing behind him like a villain in a superhero movie. He did enjoy a dramatic entry.

She smiled, even though she was unnerved by the unplanned visit. "Echo, this is a surprise."

"Not an unpleasant one, I hope?"

"Not at all. Welcome to Grön Bok." She waved an arm around to indicate the store.

But Echo didn't so much as glance at the shelves linked with reading material, his eyes were fixed solely on her.

Her stomach clenched. Was she in trouble? Had they found out about the briefcase? Was he about to tell her she was out?

Krister would kill her if she botched this operation. They were relying on her to get intel. They'd spent a fortune on setting her up in the apartment, the alias, the backstory. She couldn't blow it now.

Steeling herself, she asked, "Is something wrong?"

"No, not at all. I just wanted to see how you were getting on. We didn't get a chance to talk after Odin's address."

In other words, he was checking up on her.

"Oh, I see."

Thank goodness. For a moment, she'd thought her cover was blown.

"I'm fine. Had a boring day, actually. I was about to shut up when you arrived." All true.

"I'm glad I could alleviate your boredom. What did you think of our esteemed leader?"

She thought for a moment. "Intriguing. Is he always so... mysterious?"

Echo chuckled. "That comes with the territory, I'm afraid. Odin has to keep his identity secret for his own protection, and that of the organization."

Sounded like it was more for his own protection than the organization's, but anyway.

She nodded, not wanting to appear cynical. "It was exciting hearing from him. I'd be interested to know more about what he has planned."

"Would you?" Those dark eyes didn't waver as he watched her.

"Yes, this is what I've been waiting for. A chance to do something. To make a difference. I'm done talking. Done protesting. That achieves nothing."

She broke off and took a hurried breath. Was that too much? She didn't want to come on too strong.

"If you really want to be involved, I do have a job that needs doing."

Her eyebrows shot up. "Yes?"

"It involves breaking the law. Again."

"I'll do whatever it takes," she whispered.

"Not here. Meet me after closing at the café where you had lunch. It stays open until seven."

A shiver snuck down her spine. He'd been watching her since lunchtime.

"Okay."

She didn't move as he nodded to her, turned, and billowed out again.

. . .

AVRIL DIDN'T USUALLY GET nervous, but she definitely had the jitters now—and it wasn't just the copious amount of caffeine she'd ingested today. She did not have a good feeling about this.

If the mugging was a test, what would this entail? How far would she go for the job? Assault? Murder? Where did you draw the line?

Where did *she* draw the line?

In her last case, she'd knowingly put a fellow officer at risk. Sacrificed her like a pawn to win the game. Luckily, it had worked out the way she'd planned, and the killer had been caught.

But that had been personal.

This was not.

The bar wasn't as high.

As she pushed open the café door and spotted Echo sitting at a table at the back, she hoped she'd never have to find out.

"Hey." She walked over and slid into the chair opposite.

He smiled at her. "I took the liberty of ordering us both coffees."

Not more caffeine.

"Thank you." She stared at it like it was laced with arsenic.

Maybe it was. She had no way of knowing.

Now she was getting paranoid. Trying to relax, she wrapped her hands around the mug, savoring the warmth.

"Rook doesn't trust you."

Her eyes flew to his face, surprised by the statement. That wasn't what she'd been expecting. "Excuse me?"

He pinned her with his gaze. "You heard me."

Shit. This was an ambush.

Echo had lured her into a false sense of security, making her think he wanted to talk to her about the assignment, when in fact he wanted to quiz her about her alias. Had Rook found something?

"I'm sorry to hear that." She matched his gaze with her own clear blue one. It annoyed her that she'd walked straight into his trap. She ought to have known better, known not to trust him. Well, she wouldn't wither under his scrutiny. She was made of sterner stuff than that. "Did he say why?"

The corners of his mouth lifted. "Apparently your background is too perfect."

She frowned, pretending to be confused. "What does that mean?"

A nonchalant shrug. "Everything you said checks out. No mistakes, no white lies, no embellishments."

"And he's surprised by that?"

Echo tilted his head. "Most people exaggerate to some extent, it's human nature. Wouldn't you agree?"

She shrugged. "I guess so."

"Except you didn't."

"Well, not about the stuff I told you," she clarified. "I mean, you don't know me very well. If I talked about my relationships, my college life or my exam scores, you might get a different picture."

He gave a nod of acknowledgement. "Well argued. I'll remember to tell him that next time I see him."

Avril held her tongue. Had that convinced him?

"He also said there isn't much about you online other than what would be expected. No messy drunken night out photographs, no spring breaks, nothing other than college, the fire, some activist propaganda, and then radio silence."

Obviously not.

She was getting tired of this. "I wasn't in the mood to be social after my mother died."

"I get that. Rook, on the other hand, doesn't. He may need more convincing."

"What do you want from me?" She laid her forearms on the table, hands upward. An open gesture, a surrender. "How can I prove my loyalty?"

His sly grin made her pulse quicken. "Now that's what I was hoping you'd say."

chapter
fourteen

"You're going to break into a man's home."

Avril stared at him. Breaking and entering. She could do that.

"He's a security consultant named Henrik Ahlström. Specializes in counter-surveillance. I believe he worked for Säpo, before going into the private sector."

Avril nearly choked on her coffee.

A security expert. Was he out of his mind?

Echo slid a thin file toward her. Inside was a grainy surveillance photo of a middle-aged businessman stepping out of a Volvo. His posture was sharp. Military sharp. She'd trained with enough of them at Quantico to know.

"He founded Ahlström Security Solutions, the firm responsible for protecting Nordic Energy's corporate headquarters."

She was beginning to understand.

"He has access to everything," he went on. "Building schematics, security layouts, emergency protocols. Astrid, we need those files."

Her mind was racing. Did the "something big" have anything to do with Nordic Energy?

She glanced up. "How will I get in?"

There was that half-grin again.

"He lives alone in a townhouse in Östermalm."

She frowned. Östermalm was an expensive, well-patrolled district.

Not an easy place to move around unnoticed. Plus, a security expert's property would be well protected. He'd have state-of-the-art surveillance systems, burglar alarms, the works.

"Don't worry, the alarm won't be on," he said, as if reading her mind.

She gave an involuntary shiver. "How do you know that?"

"Because Ahlström is going to be home at the time."

"What?" Avril blinked at him. "You want me to break into a man's house *while he's there*?"

Was he crazy? It would be a suicide mission.

Echo leaned back, unfazed. "That's exactly what I want you to do. Ahlström will be distracted. He won't even know you're there."

"I don't understand."

He gave a knowing grin. "Runa will make sure of it. They've got a dinner date at seven o'clock on Saturday. At his place. Apparently, he likes to cook."

The pieces were finally falling into place. This was a double act. Runa would distract the mark while she broke into the house and robbed it.

"Won't he be furious when he discovers his place has been ransacked? He'll realize he's been set up. I don't want to put Runa in any danger."

Echo nodded, like he understood. "She won't be in any danger because he's not going to find out. You're going to take photographs of what we need and leave everything as you found it."

Seriously? This guy had obviously never done a house search before. It would be quicker stealing the files than photographing them. She didn't even know what she was looking for.

"How much time do I have?" she asked, trying to strategize.

"As much as you need. Runa will take care of that. The idea is to get the intel without him ever knowing you were there."

Avril let out a shaky breath. She didn't like the sound of this. It was risky and meant putting Runa in a potentially compromising position. "Wouldn't it just be simpler to break in while he's out?"

Echo shook his head. "The place has way too much security. We'd never get away with it."

She sighed, conflicted.

"This is the only way," Echo said, quietly. "We've considered every angle. The plan is feasible. It will work."

"Does this have something to do with what Odin has planned?" she asked, as if the thought had just occurred to her.

Echo's gaze narrowed behind his glasses. "That's need-to-know at this stage, but I can assure you it will become clear in the weeks to come. Right now, however, I need you to do this with Runa. Do you think you can do that?"

Don't ask too many questions.

Avril downed the rest of her coffee, then gave a stoic nod. "Yes, we can do it."

"Good." He nodded, pleased. "I'm going to send Runa around to your apartment tomorrow evening. The two of you can plan the job in more detail, iron out all the creases."

At least she wasn't in this alone.

"Can I count on you, Astrid?" A gaze that saw too much held her in place.

"Yes," she whispered. "I won't let you down."

She hoped she could live up to her side of the bargain—for him, and for the operation.

Echo left shortly after that.

Avril waited less than a minute before she pulled a black scarf out of her backpack and wound it around her neck, obscuring the lower half of her face. Next, she slipped on a grey beanie and followed him. Since Krister and his team kept losing him, maybe she'd have better luck.

Echo walked with purpose, his stride long and even. She kept her distance, adjusting her pace to blend with the flow of pedestrians along the narrow streets. Remembering her Quantico training, she kept him in her peripheral vision, rather than her direct line of sight. If he stopped, she stopped. If he sped up, she adjusted her pace, slipping into a throng of commuters or darting inside a shop so he wouldn't spot her.

So far he hadn't looked around. Not once.

Echo turned onto Hornsgatan, a busy stretch filled with late-night cafés, kebab shops, and vape stores. The street was well-lit, making it harder to stay hidden.

This wasn't ideal. Avril hung back, tracking him by the occasional flash of his dark coat as he weaved through the foot traffic.

Then, he stopped.

She side-stepped into a recessed doorway, flattening herself against the wood.

Echo glanced around once, then walked into a dimly lit café with floor-to-ceiling windows.

Avril counted to ten, then followed.

She hovered outside, just out of view. A menu board advertised baklava and Turkish coffee, but from her vantage point, she scanned the interior through the glass. Echo had taken a seat near the back, in a booth with two men already waiting for him. His back was to her. Avril strained her eyes to make out his companions' features.

Arabic-looking. Late thirties, maybe early forties. One wore a navy-blue coat, dark stubble shadowing his jaw. The other had close-cropped hair and a neatly trimmed beard, a long leather jacket draped over his chair. From their relaxed mannerisms, she could tell they were familiar with Echo. This was a pre-arranged meeting, and not the first one.

She wished she could hear what they were saying, but she could tell a lot just by watching.

The owner of the leather jacket leaned forward, gesticulating. This was a negotiation. The other sat back, listening and nodding occasionally.

Echo seemed completely at ease. He lifted his hand, summoning a waiter. After giving an order, he turned back to his acquaintances. The conversation continued.

Who were these guys?

Avril checked the time. She'd been standing here watching for two minutes. It was time to move on. Unfortunately, there was no way she could get any closer without being obvious, and going inside was out of the question. If only she had that burner phone Krister had promised her, or even her personal phone, but that was still hidden back at the apartment. Without a way to take photographs, she committed their faces to memory. Maybe she could pick them out of a slideshow.

She didn't go far. Ducking around a corner, she waited for Echo to leave. The sky was darkening rapidly now, and the streetlamps had flickered on. It was bitterly cold, and she hugged her coat around her.

Twenty minutes later, a black Mercedes S-Class pulled up in front of the café. Avril watched as Echo strode out, coat flapping behind him. He slid into the back seat and the car drove off.

Avril huffed in annoyance. After all that, he'd sped off in a vehicle and she couldn't follow because she was on foot.

A short time later, the two men emerged. Avril stepped out from behind the corner and walked slowly toward them. They had no idea who she was, so she felt safe being exposed. Her main priority was to get a closer look at their faces in the streetlights.

No such luck.

An even bigger black SUV rolled up and the back door opened. The two men ducked inside, and the SUV pulled away from the curb, its taillights glowing red against the wet asphalt.

By the time she got home, Avril was cold and wet, but she was still buzzing. She needed to share what she'd learned with Krister, and to tell him about the planned burglary. Maybe his contacts at Säpo could ID the men Echo had met.

She unlocked her apartment door and stepped inside, her thoughts on a hot shower and a night plotting on the couch. A voice cut through the silence, making her jump.

"Now we're going to talk about why you were following me."

She froze.

Echo.

The fiery glow in his eyes was downright demonic. He was waiting for an answer.

Shit.

chapter **fifteen**

Avril's heart thumped against her ribs, threatening to leap right out of her chest.

She didn't move. Not yet.

The air in her apartment felt charged, crackling with tension. Her training screamed at her to stay calm, control her breathing, and not react too fast, but her thoughts were racing. Had he searched her apartment? Had he found her personal phone, or the weapon she had hidden in the mattress? Could he have planted a bug?

Echo stood in front of the window, his silhouette half-shrouded in darkness, but his presence was like a blade pressed against her skin. He was waiting, watching, measuring every second of her silence.

She exhaled. Slow. Even. Buying herself time.

Then, she took a careful step forward, dropping her bag onto the couch like she wasn't rattled to her core. She needed to own this moment—turn it into something else before it turned on her.

"I was curious," she admitted, keeping her voice even. She slipped off her coat, as if this was a normal conversation, like he wasn't standing in her apartment judging her. Like she wasn't on the edge of being exposed.

"Curious about what?"

She turned to face him fully, letting the pause stretch just long enough. If she rushed this, she'd sound defensive. And if she sounded defensive, she was busted.

"You," she said finally. The words settled, weighted with meaning.

His head tilted, those dark, unreadable eyes burning into hers. She could feel his mind working, running probabilities, sorting through possibilities.

"Why?"

"Because—" She paused, then dropped her voice, just a little, as if sharing a secret. "I feel drawn to you. I can't explain it. It's not something that's ever happened to me before. I mean, you're like this brave, enigmatic leader, and I'm a nobody, but I—Well, I feel a connection." She took her beanie off and ran a hand through her hair, shaking it out. "Was I imagining it?"

He didn't react. But something shifted. She could sense it.

"No, you weren't wrong," he murmured, eventually. "I feel it too. We're similar, you and me." She nodded, praying his ego was such that he'd think she was confessing, not spinning out of control. "We've both felt pain. We're both drawn to the darkness."

She glanced up, surprised at his choice of words.

The corners of his mouth twitched. "Don't try to deny it, Astrid. I can see you're empty inside. Just like me."

She sucked in a breath. How had he known that? A long moment passed where they stared at each other.

Shakily, she said, "Sometimes I wake up in the morning and I can't think of a reason to get out of bed. It's like the day stretches ahead filled with nothingness. I think I lost the ability to feel when... when my mother died—and it hasn't come back."

She was whispering now. The truth. Except not as he knew it.

He was studying her, that deep, probing look that seemed to singe her soul. This man had an uncanny ability to read people.

Every instinct told her she needed to be wary of him.

Even with her Quantico training, her obsessive dedication to the job, and her stoic resilience, she was not immune. For an undercover operative, he could be her undoing.

Time to get back onto safer ground.

"This... The organization... You..." She waved a hand around. "All give me a sense of purpose. For the first time in ages, I feel like I have a reason to get up in the morning."

He pursed his lips, and she knew he understood.

A faint sigh. "That's why I followed you. I wanted to find out more about you, get to know you better. I thought if I did, you might let me get more... involved."

A longer pause this time. He was weighing her, feeling her out. Deciding.

She held her breath.

Eventually, "You could have just asked me."

She gave a small shrug. "You don't exactly make it easy. You said Rook doesn't trust me. None of you do, really. Not yet. But this means so much to me. I want you to know that."

That was what tipped the balance.

His shoulders loosened slightly, and she knew she had him.

He stepped forward, closing the space between them. Not enough to threaten, just enough to unnerve. "You want to get more involved?"

"Yes," she whispered.

"What if I took you to meet Odin?"

Her stomach tightened. The guy kept throwing curve balls at her, catching her off guard. She wasn't used to it. He was the most unsettling man she'd ever met.

"Really?" she whispered.

He gave a tight nod. "I think it's time you two talked."

Stockholm's Nationalmuseum was quiet at this hour. After their little talk, Echo had gone outside to make a phone call, then came back to collect her. An hour later, they were pulling up outside the museum. The grand entrance, framed by arched glass doors and classical columns, was flanked by two silent security guards.

Before they went inside, he confiscated her mobile phone, slipping it into his jacket pocket. "Just until we leave," he assured her. A precaution so she couldn't record or photograph the enigmatic leader of Terra Nova.

Butterflies in her stomach, Avril followed Echo down the soaring

Cold Legacy

corridors, past gilded portraits of long-dead aristocrats, their painted eyes tracking her movements as if sensing she was an imposter.

Echo moved quickly, his hands tucked into the pockets of his coat, his gaze flicking up toward the security cameras. Aimed at the artwork, they were there to protect the treasures, not to spy on the visitors. She doubted anyone watching would notice anything strange going on.

They stepped into a dimly lit gallery of Nordic masters, where the oil paintings loomed large, heavy with centuries of frozen landscapes, naval battles, and stark winter skies. The only other occupant was an elderly guard, half-asleep in his chair, head nodding to his chest.

It was the perfect place for a ghost to appear.

Echo stopped near a marble bench positioned in the center of the room, facing a large Rembrandt. He turned to her, voice low. "Take a seat. Wait here."

Avril hesitated but obeyed. The coldness from the bench seeped through her jeans.

"Don't turn around," Echo instructed. "No matter what."

She frowned, confused. "Why?"

"Odin doesn't allow anyone to see his face," he told her. "This is how it's done. It's for his security, as I'm sure you can appreciate."

Was Odin someone well known? A wealthy figure in the political or industrial landscape? Was the silent benefactor and controller of the eco-terrorist organization someone whose identity needed protecting?

Her stomach knotted, but she nodded. Echo walked away and positioned himself at the far end of the gallery. He stood feet apart, hands clasped behind his back, as if admiring the artwork. He wasn't looking at her, but he was close by if needed.

Then, she felt it.

A shift in the air. The unmistakable sensation of someone standing behind her.

Her fingers curled against her thighs, but she kept her gaze fixed on the painting in front of her. She didn't need to see him to know he was there.

A voice, low and deliberate, cut through the silence. "Hello, Astrid."

Avril swallowed. Her breath felt too loud in the stillness of the room. She didn't recognize the voice. The one from the Zoom meeting had been disguised, but this wasn't. It was masculine, evenly pitched. Nothing distinctive.

"Hello." She fought the urge to spin around and look him in the eye.

A pause. Then—"I believe you've been asking about me."

Avril kept her breathing steady, her hands resting loosely on her lap, but her muscles were coiled tight. "Yes, I want to find out more about Terra Nova. About how I can get involved."

"You've impressed Echo," Odin said, almost conversationally. "That is not an easy thing to do."

Avril gave an eager nod. "I want to prove myself."

"Why is that? Why are you so keen to ingratiate yourself in our little organization?" As if they were nothing more serious than a book club. As if they hadn't just assassinated an oil magnate and thrown the Swedish petroleum industry into turmoil.

She heard the suspicious edge to his voice. He wasn't convinced as to her allegiance—yet. She had to tread carefully.

"I need this," she said, knowing this was her chance to convince him. "I don't know how much Echo has told you about my past, but for the first time in a very long time, I feel like I've got something to live for. I've been dead inside ever since—" She struggled to get the words out. Even now, it hurt talking about it.

She sensed Odin move a fraction closer, his body heat warming the air around her. She caught a faint tinge of something minty. Gum, maybe? "I heard about your mother. Tragic circumstances."

Avril exhaled, just loud enough for him to hear. She had to tread carefully, give him enough truth to earn his trust, but not enough to expose herself. "This is the only thing that makes sense in my life right now."

He hummed, as if he understood.

Another beat of silence, then Odin spoke again, his voice softer now, contemplative. "You were right to come back. Sweden has lost its soul, just like everywhere else. People sit back, watching the world burn, waiting for someone else to act."

Avril kept her focus on the painting in front of her. It was a dark and brooding Rembrandt, the oil paint rich with age. She understood now why they had chosen this place. The weight of history, of power, of revolution. It was woven into every brushstroke, every gilded frame.

Odin continued, "We don't wait." His voice was measured, steady. "We take action. That's why we exist."

Avril nodded. "That's what I want. To act. I'm tired of nobody listening, of being ignored. There's no accountability. Ever."

"You've already proven yourself. You didn't hesitate when Echo gave you a task." A slight shift in his tone—approval. "That tells me you're serious. That you're ready for more."

She seized on that. "I am."

"Good. Well, as you are aware, we have something big planned. Something that will make the world sit up and take note."

Her throat tightened. "Yes."

"I'd like you to play a part."

"I'm ready." Avril unclenched her fingers, forcing herself to stay calm, though her pulse thrummed with anticipation. "What do you need me to do?"

A beat passed before Odin spoke again, this time with quiet finality. "Echo will be in touch with the details."

And just like that, she knew the conversation was over.

She stayed perfectly still as she heard movement behind her—clothing shifting, the soft scrape of a shoe against the marble floor. Then, silence.

She waited for a full breath. Then another.

Slowly, she turned her head, expecting—hoping—to catch a glimpse of his retreating form. But there was no one there.

Only the paintings, the dim glow of the gallery lights, and Echo, still standing at the far end of the hall.

Odin was gone.

chapter
sixteen

After Astrid left, Odin decided to take a stroll through the gallery. The beauty of the art, the cultural relevance of the old masters, and the coolness of the interior always had a profound effect on him.

Astrid.

His lips curled back in the hint of a smile. She was something of an enigma herself.

He didn't often meet with members, and never with new recruits, but she was different. He'd known that the moment he'd seen her.

Lost, filled with pain, searching for answers—and yet she wasn't an open book. She'd held back, he could sense it. She'd been holding back right from the start. He didn't know why, but he would find out.

Before him, a painting stretched across the canvas. The Sacrifice of Iphigenia. A woman, her body rigid with tension, lay draped across an altar, her face turned skyward in mute horror. The priest's knife hovered above her, poised for the kill. The gods had demanded blood, and she, a pawn in a war not of her making, would be the offering.

A necessary death.

A worthy sacrifice.

He studied the fine brushstrokes, the interplay of light and shadow. The artist had captured the moment exquisitely—the last breath before inevitability. A hush before the blade fell.

Cold Legacy

Astrid didn't know it yet, but she was standing at the edge of that altar.

He turned, glancing toward the empty bench where she had sat just minutes earlier. She had done as Echo had instructed. From his position, he could tell she'd been nervous but composed. Keen but not desperate.

Odin had read countless people in his lifetime, dissected their tells, peeled back their layers until there was nothing left to hide. Astrid was proving more difficult. That made her interesting. And a tad dangerous.

He moved through the gallery, his footsteps echoing on the marble floor. After a while, he stopped in front of another great masterpiece. This one was a personal favorite, not because of its subject matter, but because of what it represented.

A fiery, Dante-style inferno symbolizing hell. A flutter of nymphs frantically trying to escape, twisted screams on their once-angelic faces.

A reckoning.

It was coming.

After that, the world would wake up to a new reality. If Astrid played her part well, she would be a footnote in the history of that change.

Odin studied the looks of terror on the nymphs' faces.

Could he trust her?

He sighed. *No.*

But then, he trusted no one.

A pang of guilt flared somewhere in the vicinity of his chest, but he quickly extinguished it. The time for emotion was over.

Terra Nova, a group he'd built from the embers of his loss. From burned memories forever etched into his brain. It was time to put it to its full use.

His flock... They believed they were fighting for the earth like self-righteous warriors. He snorted. They were fools. They were but pieces on a chessboard.

Sacrificial pawns.

None of them would live through what was coming.

Except for Echo. Echo, who had been there from the beginning. Echo, who understood that ideology was a tool, not a solution. That it couldn't give you answers; you had to create those for yourself. That nobody listened to quiet protests, to ideologized views of utopia. It was all bullshit.

But Astrid...

He turned away from the grotesque tableau on the wall. She was different. Smart. Cautious. She asked the right questions at the right time, and more importantly, she knew when not to ask them.

Most recruits came in wild-eyed and reckless, too eager to prove themselves. They wanted violence for the sake of violence, anarchy with no purpose.

Astrid was controlled. She wanted something deeper, something real. For her it was a means to an end. Vengeance. Justice. Not just a sense of belonging, or a way to make a difference. Her darkness made her useful.

It also made her vulnerable.

And yet... There was something about her he couldn't place. That part she kept hidden.

He frowned, stuffing his hands into his pockets. Maybe he should take a lesson out of her book. Get to know her better, discover her secrets.

Odin couldn't. But Echo could.

Or even Runa.

He sighed. He shouldn't worry so much. It didn't even matter. Astrid was a means to an end, nothing more. He didn't need her to be loyal, only obedient. She would serve her function, just like the others. Then, when the moment came, she would be forgotten.

Why did the thought of that make his chest tighten?

Odin headed toward the exit. Suddenly, the weight of history, of what he was doing, felt suffocating. He needed to get out. Away from the thousand judgmental faces glaring down at him.

He stepped into the crisp afternoon air, inhaling through his nose. It gave him clarity, stilled the flutter of guilt that had been plaguing him.

The job he had in mind for Astrid was important. Integral. But not in the way that she thought. Let her assume she was climbing the ranks. Let her believe she was gaining their trust, stepping into the inner sanctum. It would keep her motivated, hungry. She would try harder, dig deeper, push herself further.

One thing he was confident of was that the outcome had already been decided. Astrid, and the others: Runa, Gaia, Fang, Rook. They were all walking dead. They just didn't know it yet.

Tomorrow, she'd get a chance to prove her worth. The house burglary—Ahlström's files, the schematics, the blueprints—they were secondary. The real test was Astrid herself. How she handled the break-in. How she worked under pressure. If she succeeded, she'd be promoted, given a bigger role to play.

The ultimate role.

If she failed... Well, then she wouldn't be around, so it didn't matter.

Tomorrow was the decider.

And he would be watching closely.

chapter
seventeen

Runa came round the following evening, just as Echo had said she would. Avril had just gotten home after a long day at the bookstore, but she was eager to find out what Runa had to say. In anticipation, she'd bought a frozen pizza and a bottle of wine. That's what you did with your friends, wasn't it?

She hadn't really had a chance to talk to the female activist in any depth since the jail cell. This would be good. It would enable them to bond—a word Krister would have used. Avril didn't think she'd ever 'bonded' with anyone in her life.

Still, she was good at pretending.

A short while later, the doorbell buzzed, a loud grating sound that resonated through the apartment.

Here we go.

She picked up the new burner phone Krister had had delivered to the bookstore earlier that day and initiated the voice memo app. It started recording. Hastily, she stood it in a dry vase filled with fake flowers on the coffee table, mic turned upwards to catch the sound. After making sure it was invisible to anyone standing in the room, she answered the door.

"Hello," she said brightly, gesturing for Runa to come in. She hoped the apartment would stand up to scrutiny.

Runa entered, took off her coat, and glanced around. "This is cozy."

Avril held her hand out for the coat. "It's temporary, just until I can afford something better." The excuse would explain the sparseness and the lack of personal touches.

"I forgot you haven't been back long, have you?"

"A couple of months. I'm still finding my feet. Up until recently I wasn't even sure I was going to stay in Stockholm." She hung Runa's coat on a hook behind the door, alongside her own. That much was true.

Runa sat down and glanced up at her. "What about now?"

Avril forced a grin. "Now I'm more inclined to stay."

"That's good. I'd hate for you to leave so soon. Things are just getting interesting around here."

"Oh?" Avril prodded.

"Yeah, until that CEO blew up in his car, we hadn't seen any direct action, despite what Echo kept telling us."

"Were you responsible for the car bomb?" Avril asked, getting the wine out of the fridge.

Runa shook her bright red hair, currently curling over her shoulders. "That wasn't us. Echo said it was another Stockholm cell, and he'd know. He's part of Odin's inner circle."

Interesting. She'd have to remember to relay that to Krister later.

She held up the bottle of wine. "Shall we have a glass?"

Runa smiled. "Great."

Avril unscrewed the bottle and poured them each a glass. "Have you met any members of the other cells?" Casual, just making conversation.

"Not yet. They keep the different cells separate, for our own protection. Why'd you ask?"

A shrug. "Curious, that's all." She handed Runa a glass and held up her own. "Here's to our upcoming mission."

They clinked, and Avril sank down next to Runa on the couch. Physical closeness wasn't something she gravitated toward. It never had been. She wasn't wired for casual intimacy, or unnecessary proximity. She had to be extremely comfortable with someone for that to happen. Like Krister. But in this moment, it served a purpose. Runa needed to feel at ease, and Avril needed her to let her guard down.

It had occurred to her—in her more reflective moments—that this assignment was breaking down a lot of personal barriers. Challenging her in ways she'd never imagined—or wanted. But she was in it now. There was no turning back. The only way was through.

"That's what I'm here to discuss," Runa said.

Avril took a sip, then set her glass down on the coffee table. "I believe you're providing the distraction, while I break in and search the study."

Runa's gaze flickered. "I met Henrik Ahlström in a bar last week. Perfect honey trap. Middle aged, divorced, lonely. His wife left him two years ago and his three kids all live with her. She got sole custody. According to the divorce settlement, he was never home, but he sees them every second weekend."

Avril took it all in. Rook must have dug up that information. Classified, of course, but that wouldn't stop him. The guy was obviously a skilled hacker. "You picked him up?"

"Technically, *he* picked me up. I just made myself available, if you know what I mean." She smirked. "Men are so predictable."

Avril thought about Echo and wasn't so sure. She'd never met a man harder to read.

Runa took another sip of wine, stretching out her legs as she settled deeper into the couch. "He thinks I'm some kind of disillusioned artist. Told him I used to paint but gave it up when the world started burning. Too much to fight for. Too much to be angry about."

Avril studied her, watching the way her fingers traced the rim of the glass. "And he believed you?"

Runa smirked. "Of course he did. They always do. Give a man a sad story and make him feel like he's the one who can fix you—he'll lap it up every time."

She wasn't wrong. Something else was obvious too. Runa knew how to play people, how to manipulate. That was useful to know.

"So, tomorrow night, I go over for dinner," Runa continued. "He's making steak. Some expensive cut, too. I made a fuss about how long it's been since I had real food, and he insisted."

Avril raised a brow. "You've got him wrapped around your finger."

Runa shrugged, swirling the wine in her glass. "Men like Henrik, they're used to control. Used to power. But the moment a pretty girl

Cold Legacy

looks at them like they're interesting, like they have something to offer, they crumble."

It was unsettling how easily she said it, how practiced she was in the game. But Avril wasn't judging. How often had she pushed the boundaries when on a case?

"You'll have a couple of hours," Runa said. "He'll want to talk, drink, maybe play some music. I'll keep him distracted. But you'll need to be quick. He's not an idiot. If something feels off, he'll pick up on it."

Avril leaned forward, elbows on her knees. "You're sure the office is where he keeps everything?"

Runa nodded. "Rook found some chatter in his emails. He gets sent reports, schematics, security layouts. He needs them on hand for consultations. But he's paranoid—he doesn't trust digital storage, at least not for everything. He keeps hard copies."

"So, I find those, photograph them, and get out," Avril summed up.

"Exactly."

Avril traced a finger over the condensation on her wine glass, considering. "How thorough was Rook's check on him? What are the chances he's got hidden cameras inside his house?"

Runa hesitated, but only for a second. "He doesn't. Rook's tapped into his security system. His paranoia is about external threats—intruders, cyber-attacks. Not people he lets in."

Very skilled.

That was something, at least. But it didn't mean they weren't at risk.

"What about you?" Avril studied her. "Are you okay with this?"

Runa smirked, but there was something guarded behind it. "I've done worse."

Avril wasn't convinced. Runa was putting herself out there, flirting with a stranger, opening herself up to abuse, all for the sake of the cause. "Fang knows about this?"

The smirk vanished.

"No. And he never will." She took a slow sip of wine. "He wouldn't understand."

Avril watched the subtle change in her posture, the way she suddenly seemed more closed off. "This could be dangerous. How far are you willing to go?"

Runa set her glass down with deliberate ease. "For the cause? All the way."

The words sat between them, heavy and absolute.

Avril gave a slow nod. "Me too," she said quietly.

The silence stretched between them.

She thought about Krister, about the burner phone recording everything. About Runa, who, for all her bravado, was still just a girl clinging to a cause that gave her a sense of belonging.

And she thought about Echo, and Odin, and the game they were all playing.

She had no illusions. Runa, herself, the others… they were expendable. Puppets on a string. Not for a moment did she believe any of them were getting away clean.

She swallowed the last of her wine and set the glass down on the table. "How about some pizza?"

chapter eighteen

"It was a massive explosion," Alma Holmgren, Gustav's widow, said. "I looked out the window and all I saw was this fireball in the drive."

She clutched her hands together, knuckles whitening.

Krister sat opposite her, a cup of tea on the side table next to him. On Lindholm's instructions, he'd given her time to come to terms with her husband's murder. Now that the rawness of her loss had eased, he thought it only prudent to interview her.

"She isn't involved in his work," Lindholm had said the last time they spoke. "She didn't even know about the threats. He kept all that from her."

"Still, I'd like to get her take on it," Krister had insisted.

Lindholm had shrugged. "Sure, go ahead."

Krister knew the Säpo agent had already written the wife off as a useful source of intel. In Krister's experience, partners and spouses often knew more than they admitted—sometimes even more than they realized. He wasn't ready to discount her just yet.

"That must have been such a shock," Krister said. "What was your initial reaction?"

"I called an ambulance, obviously. Not that it did any good. Poor Gustav died instantly—or so I'm told."

"I'm very sorry for your loss," Krister murmured.

"Thank you. He was a good man. No, he was a great man. Nordic Energy was his life, and it was because of him that the company was so successful."

"What kind of husband was he?" Krister asked. "What kind of father?"

Her eyes widened. "He was wonderful. I mean, he worked a lot, but he provided for us. We never wanted for anything."

What about attention? Compassion? Love?

But he didn't say these things. Lindholm would say they weren't important, but Krister had the impression Gustav Holmgren hadn't been the best husband or father. He made a mental note to talk to the two grown-up children about it. Kids were less forgiving than doting wives—or spouses concerned with public opinion.

He rubbed his chin. "Mrs. Holmgren, did your husband mention the threats he'd been receiving?"

Her voice wavered. "No. The other policeman asked me that. I wish I had known. We might have been able to take precautions. He might still be alive if—" Her voice caught. She flicked a hand in the air. "But there's no point in ifs, is there?"

He gave her a weak smile. "Not really."

She nodded to the burly security guard standing outside the front entrance. "The company sent him. They think I might still be at risk. God forbid, or the children."

"Where are your children?" he asked. The couple had a son and a grown-up daughter.

"My son, Morten, works for the company. He's also on the Board. My daughter was here. Of course she was. But she had to go back to work. She'll come back for the funeral, when the police release Gustav's body." She gulped and took a shaky sip of tea.

"Could you give me their contact details? I'd like to speak to them—just to make sure they're okay." They'd also need protection, especially Morten, if they didn't have it already.

"That's very nice of you, but unnecessary. You know youngsters, they're more resilient than people my age."

"If you could give me their details anyway, I'd appreciate it."

She gave a slight nod.

"Mrs. Holmgren, did your husband ever mention an organization called Terra Nova?"

She frowned, then shook her head. "No, I don't recall that name. Is it a company he worked with?"

"No, nothing like that. What about the name Odin?"

"Odin who?"

"Just Odin."

Another shake of her head. "No, we don't know anyone by that name." She wiped a hand over her brow. He could see she was tiring.

"I won't be long, Mrs. Holmgren. Just a few more questions."

She nodded.

"Was your husband acting strangely at all before his death?"

"Acting strangely? No."

"He wasn't behaving differently? Stressed? Nervous? Agitated?"

She arched a thin eyebrow. "He ran a multi-billion-euro enterprise—he was all of those things."

"But anything out of the ordinary?" Krister pushed.

"Nothing out of the ordinary," she said with a little sigh. "But then, he didn't talk much about the business. Not with me, anyway."

There was something in the way she said it that gave him pause. "Who did he speak to, Mrs. Holmgren?"

Her gaze flickered as she turned away. "Morten. His colleagues. The board of directors. Not me."

So he'd been right about Gustav. Not the best husband.

"Okay, thank you for your time." He got up, and she followed, still fragile from her trauma.

"Are you any closer to finding out who did this?" she squeaked as she opened the door.

"We're exploring several avenues of inquiry, ma'am," he replied. "We'll be in touch if we need anything else."

She gave a weary nod. "I understand."

He walked away, leaving her standing there, staring vacantly into the past.

. . .

KRISTER DIDN'T GO to the office—he veered toward Södermalm and the bookstore. Avril's message had concerned him.

Need to talk. Met Odin.

That last part had made him sit up and take note.

Progress, at last!

He was proud of her. She'd done well. He'd always known she could do it, that she'd blend in with the activist crowd. With her quirky ways and social awkwardness—which he found endearing, because he understood her—she could easily pass for a misfit. Plus, she had that obsessive nature some found tiresome, but which was vital in police work. He got it, but even he knew when to draw the line.

She didn't. Never had. Even as a child, she'd always pushed harder, gone farther than he had. He'd been the one to reel her in, to caution her, and sometimes to pick up the pieces. Not that she ever listened.

He gave a soft snort. Nothing much had changed.

It was a risk going back to the bookstore. They could be watching. The same man showing up twice in as many weeks would raise suspicion. He still had the book he'd bought last time in the back of his SUV. Maybe he was returning it. Looking for something else.

It was feasible, at a push.

Krister parked and took a moment, surveying the exterior. There didn't appear to be anyone lurking around. No surveillance cameras outside the store to hack into, nothing across the street either. The only CCTV camera was at the far end of the road.

Still, he wasn't assuming anything.

Keeping his head down, book in its brown paper bag tucked under his arm, he strode across the road. Avril looked up, and her blue eyes widened.

"Krister, what are you doing here?"

"I had to see you. We need to talk."

"I know, but it's not safe coming here. You could blow my cover."

"I won't come again. Just wanted to return this." He held the book up. "It's the wrong one."

She sighed, then scoffed. "Knew you weren't the philosophical type."

He grinned. "Tell me all about Odin."

"There's not much to tell. I didn't see his face. He came up behind me and I was told to sit still and face forward. He had a normal masculine voice, no inflection, no accent. Nothing notable."

He frowned. "You never saw him?"

She shook her head.

"Damn it. I thought you might have something."

"I do."

He stared at her, noting the gleam in her eyes.

"But I need permission to go ahead. It's not strictly legal."

He slanted his gaze. "What do they want you to do?"

"Echo asked me to break into some hotshot security expert's home and search his study. I'm looking for schematics on Nordic Energy's corporate headquarters."

He sucked in a breath. "Nordic Energy? As in Gustav Holmgren's company?"

"The very same. I think it could be the 'big something' they were talking about."

"The next target," he murmured. "Okay, well if that's the case, you'd better do it."

"What will Säpo say?"

"Let me deal with Säpo. This is necessary to gain intel on a possible terror attack. As long as nobody gets hurt—" He shot her a stern glance.

"Nobody is going to get hurt," she assured him. "It's not like last time. This is a straight B and E."

"Shouldn't be a problem then."

Avril put her hands on her hips. He could tell by her stance that she had more news.

"What?" he asked, pre-empting her.

She took a deep breath. "They pretty much admitted Terra Nova was responsible for the car bomb."

His pulse kicked up a notch. "They did? When?"

"Runa came round last night and told me. She said it wasn't us, but one of the other cells."

"Us?"

A shrug. "You know what I mean."

He massaged his forehead. "There's something that doesn't add up about that attack. I mean, I know they are said to have taken responsibility, but that was rumors in the mainstream media, and you know how reporters love to hype stuff up. My team looked into it. Terra Nova have not issued an official statement. Also, the bomb was a rudimentary IED. Homemade, if you like. According to Lindholm, anyone with basic bomb-making knowledge could have thrown it together."

Avril blinked at him. "What are you saying? That they didn't do it?"

He spread his hands. "I don't know. They probably did. I'm just saying it's strange, that's all. From what we know about this organization, they are more sophisticated than that. They have access to money, to military-grade explosives, advanced tech. Why would they use a crude, rudimentary device?"

"There are several reasons," Avril said, adjusting her glasses. "Price, for one. I'm sure they don't want to waste money on an expensive device if a cheap one will do. Also, perhaps it was just easier and quicker to go with someone local. The device itself would be harder to trace, as well. If anyone can make it, it detracts attention from them."

"But then they claim responsibility anyway?" He clenched his jaw. "I don't know."

He had to admit Avril was right about the other reasons. It could just have been easier and more cost effective. Maybe he was reading too much into this.

He sighed. "It's just a feeling I can't shift."

"Well, you are right about the tech. Rook has expert computer skills. I suspect he hacked into the marriage register, along with other encrypted databases. I hope my legend is airtight, because it's going to need to be."

Krister nodded. "I'll let Säpo know, although they would have made sure. This isn't the first time they've done this."

"I know, but he's good, Krister, and he's digging into my background. I'm worried about him."

"You won't be there much longer," Krister said, trying to reassure her. He could tell she really was concerned, and that wasn't like Avril. She was tough. This guy must be good if he'd rattled her. "As soon as we know the date of the attack, we get you out. I'm not putting your life at even more risk."

She gave him a brave smile. "Deal."

Krister wanted to stay, but he had to get back to the office. He selected a new book, paid for it, then turned to leave the store.

Just in the nick of time, too.

As he walked out, he brushed shoulders with the fiery redhead who'd been arrested with Avril at the protest. Runa.

His first thought was that they'd been busted. That she was coming in to check up on him. Then he saw the smile on her face, and how she waved at Avril, and relaxed.

Nope. This was a social call.

They were in the clear.

chapter
nineteen

AVRIL TURNED TO RUNA. "GIVE ME A MINUTE TO CLOSE UP, and then we can talk."

She drew the blinds, locked the front door, and flipped over the CLOSED sign. The faint drone of traffic outside dulled as the store settled into silence.

"Better," she said, dusting off her hands. "Now, how are you feeling about tonight?"

Runa shrugged, leaning against the counter. "I've got a game plan. Dinner, some light flirting, maybe a little after-dinner entertainment... After that, I'll make an excuse and call it a night."

Avril appreciated how cool Runa played it, but she knew this was all about the mission.

"How about you?" Runa asked, green eyes turning on her.

"I'm ready."

Officially, no police surveillance would be watching the house, but Krister had said he'd be nearby. Just in case.

At seven o'clock, Runa would arrive at Henrik Ahlström's townhouse, all charm and sexy confidence. He'd welcome her in, pour them drinks, and start cooking. At some point, Runa would excuse herself and go to the bathroom where she'd unlatch the window, giving Avril a way in.

According to Echo, the bathroom window was wide enough for her to squeeze through. It wasn't barred, but made of thick, reinforced, dappled glass, almost impossible to break.

Once inside, Avril would locate the study. Thanks to Rook's hacking into the architect's database, they knew it was down the hall and to the left of the staircase. Runa's job was to keep Ahlström occupied while she searched through his files.

Schematics of the Nordic Energy headquarters. Floor plans, ventilation shafts, structural weaknesses. Anything that would help Terra Nova bypass security and navigate the office block once inside.

That had to be the target.

"I've got to go home and get changed," Runa said, taking a steeling breath. "See you later."

"I'll be there." Avril gave a firm nod. Runa would be reporting back to Echo, who was sure to ask how Astrid was feeling about the mission. Was she uneasy? Was she nervous? Was she confident?

Echo, in turn, would report back to Odin. A man whose heat she'd felt in the confines of the gallery, but whose face she'd never seen.

CLAD IN BLACK LEGGINGS, a black hoodie and gloves, Avril lurked in the shadows outside Henrik Ahlström's townhouse. The small, but powerful flashlight on her headband was off, but she knew she'd need it later.

Farther down the street, under some gangly, leafless trees, was a parked Volvo. It was a perfectly normal suburban housewife's car, except Avril knew Krister was inside, hunkering down, waiting for her to commit a crime.

She shook her head. This was crazy. She was a law enforcement officer, and all she seemed to be doing since she'd started working for the Swedish police was break the law.

All she needed was a date for the attack, and then she was out. Säpo would arrest them, and she could get back to normal crime-fighting.

She gave a soft snort. Who would have thought hunting down killers would be normal?

What she didn't admit to Krister was that Odin scared her, and

Echo unnerved her. They both had the same intense presence that messed with her emotional defenses.

The others were more straightforward. Fang was a bully, but she knew how to deal with those. Gaia was genuinely a nice person, albeit passionate and misguided. Rook was clever and suspicious, but she could handle him, and Runa was naive and impressionable, despite being tough and passionate about the cause.

She watched as a cab pulled up in front of the house and Runa climbed out. The redhead looked fantastic in a body-hugging green dress that clung to her pale curves. Her flaming hair shone in what little moonlight there was, and her three-inch heels clacked on the asphalt as she walked up to the house.

It was then Avril noticed the streetlamps outside Henrik Ahlström's townhouse were out. She sniffed, impressed. Echo had thought of everything.

The door opened. A male voice said something, his tone warm, welcoming. A few seconds later, Runa disappeared inside the house and the door shut.

That was her cue.

Ducking down, she snuck around the side of the house and hunched down underneath the bathroom window. No security light came on, no dog barked. There was nothing to give away her presence.

It was cold, and she wasn't wearing much padding, so she gritted her teeth to stop them from chattering. Any moment now—

"Come on," she muttered, when ten minutes later Runa still hadn't appeared. It was freezing out here.

Finally, a light flicked on. Avril exhaled. Thank goodness.

A figure moved to the window and fumbled with the latch. There was a soft *click* and the window creaked open.

Avril straightened up, stiff with cold.

"Sorry," Runa hissed, rolling her eyes. "The man can talk. I couldn't get away without making it obvious."

"It's okay." Avril didn't waste any time shimmying through the gap. Runa helped her up.

"I'd better get back." She gestured in the direction of the living room.

Cold Legacy

"Good luck." Avril hid behind the door as Runa went back to her date.

It took a moment to thaw out, but then she sprang into action. Opening the door a crack, she peeked out into the dimly lit hallway. The lighting was turned down low. Meant to be romantic, no doubt.

She tiptoed down the hallway towards the study. Pulling down the handle, she exhaled when it opened. No reason to lock it when you lived alone, she supposed.

A quick glance down the hallway, and she ducked inside, closing it softly behind her.

Switching on the headlamp, she took a look around. Henrik Ahlström was not a neat man. Paperwork littered the desk, piles of folders were stacked up in the in-tray, and several files lay on top of the cabinet against the wall.

Great.

She decided to start with the desk and systematically work her way through every single piece of paper she could find, checking to see if it related to Nordic Energy.

Ten minutes later, and she was still empty-handed.

She was almost done with the desk when she spotted a gray binder with Nordic Energy written down the side.

"Bingo," she whispered, lifting her phone.

Click, click, click.

She captured the documents without using the flash. They would still be legible in the light of her headlamp. Rook would be able to enhance them even more—as would Säpo.

After the desk, she moved on to the filing cabinet, but didn't find anything of interest there.

A noise in the hallway made her look up. Footsteps headed her way.

Shit.

"I'll be right back," Henrik Ahlström called, as the doorhandle turned.

Heart pounding, Avril scanned the room, desperately searching for a place to hide.

The door opened.

chapter
twenty

"Can I have some more wine?" Runa's voice, calling from the kitchen.

Henrik Ahlström paused, his frame silhouetted by the hall light. "Sure, help yourself."

Avril stayed completely still beneath the desk, pressing herself deeper into the shadows.

Please don't come in.

A second passed. Then another.

The light flicked on.

Avril didn't dare move a muscle as Henrik Ahlström strode across the hardwood floor to the desk. He cursed, rifling through some papers. A soft rustle. A grunt of satisfaction.

Avril shrank into herself, her back pressed to the wood. She could see his legs from her hiding spot, shifting as he adjusted his stance.

"Found it," he said, voice carrying back toward the kitchen. "This is what I wanted to show you."

Avril stayed put until his footsteps receded, then she let out a shaky breath. That was close! The study door was still open, pale light tumbling in from the hallway.

She waited five seconds. Ten.

Only then did she move.

Cautiously, she crawled out from underneath the desk. Every nerve was on edge as she crawled across the floor to the window.

She could hear Runa's laughter from the kitchen, and the slightly nauseating aroma of sauteed onions.

Stuffing her phone back into her leggings, she opened the window. It creaked, and she tensed, hoping he wouldn't hear it from the kitchen.

Avril heard more laughter, and the clashing of cutlery. Runa was playing her part to perfection.

With the stealth of a cat burglar, Avril crept out of the window, then lowered herself down onto the ground. Once out, she reached up and pushed the window shut. The latch snapped into place.

Adrenaline still pumping, Avril slunk away from the townhouse, keeping to the shadows. She'd done it. Henrik Ahlström would never know she'd been there.

It was 10 P.M. Avril stared up at the run-down, no-name hotel on the fringes of Stockholm and shuddered. The buzzing neon sign outside flickered like it was on life support.

Avril had never been to this part of town before, and just walking here had been an experience. The streets reeked of spilled beer and the sidewalks were littered with cigarettes, chewing gum and the occasional syringe. She'd half expected to get mugged before she even made it to the hotel.

It was perhaps the only time she'd been relieved to see Fang who was leaning against the graffitied wall outside. "First floor," he muttered, jerking his head upwards. "Room 8."

She stepped past him, through the peeling entrance, and bypassed a reception desk where a half-asleep old man was sitting. He didn't glance up.

The lobby smelled of stale coffee and disinfectant that didn't quite mask the deeper, more permanent odor of mildew and unwashed bodies.

Avril went up the creaking staircase, too afraid to touch the railing in case she caught something. Number 8 was on the right, and she heard voices emanating from inside.

A quick knock and the door opened. Gaia beckoned her inside. Everyone was there, apart from Fang, who she assumed would come up soon. Runa perched on the bed, while Rook leaned against the window overlooking the street. Echo stood in the middle of the room, legs slightly apart, arms folded.

He broke into a grin when he saw her. "Excellent job last night. Both of you."

Avril gave a quick smile, while Runa flushed. It wasn't often Echo dished out praise. The others clapped lightly, but she didn't miss the scowl Rook threw in her direction.

After she'd gotten home, she'd texted the photographs to Echo. Unfortunately, she couldn't send them to Krister too, in case her phone was being monitored. She couldn't even upload them to the cloud. Not from this device.

She had written down the phone number Echo had given her, however, even though she knew they wouldn't be able to glean anything from it. Rook would have taken care of that.

Ignoring the glowering tech geek, she gazed around the uninspiring hotel room. Peeling wallpaper, a threadbare carpet, and a double bed that sagged in the middle.

"It's not much but it serves our purpose," Echo said, watching her.

How did he do that?

"Now we have this information," Gaia said, turning to Echo. "What are we going to do with it?"

He gave a secretive grin. "As you've guessed, Nordic Energy's corporate headquarters is our new target. Now that we have the blueprints, we can determine the best way inside."

"Then what?" Fang came into the room. He closed the door behind him, which locked automatically from the inside.

"Then we cause havoc."

Echo's voice was calm, deliberate, and unmistakably menacing. A shiver ran down Avril's spine.

He didn't elaborate, just sat back, fingers interlocked as he surveyed the group. "We're still ironing out the details. Once Odin has reviewed the information you secured, he'll determine how to proceed. Then, I will let you know."

"Are we carrying out the attack?" Runa asked, her eyes gleaming with anticipation.

"I believe so, yes."

There were murmurs of excitement. Even Rook straightened up, his interest piqued.

Avril noted the shift in the room. They were eager. Hungry. She got the impression they didn't often get a chance to take direct action, despite their manifesto. This was huge for them.

This was why they'd joined.

She tried to mirror their enthusiasm, tried to look just as eager, just as engaged, but she couldn't quash the trepidation that held her in its grip.

They were plotting mass murder.

Echo's gaze settled on her. "Problem, Astrid?"

She swallowed. Up until now, she hadn't thought she was that easy to read.

"Not at all. I just can't get excited until I know all the facts."

"Very wise," he mused. "You won't have to wait long."

She let out a silent breath when he turned away, forcing herself to relax.

Don't blow it.

The meeting continued, with Rook explaining how he had done a deep dive into Nordic Energy's workforce, identifying key employees they might be able to extort. People with financial troubles, gambling addictions, or vulnerable family members. The kind of people who could be coerced.

Avril tried to commit the names to memory, although exhaustion tugged at the edges of her concentration. Her gaze drifted back to Echo. He moved fluidly, a predator pacing the confines of his space. His glasses caught the dim light as he frowned, adjusting them with an absent flick of his fingers. The sharp intelligence behind his eyes was always at work, calculating, dissecting.

There was something both magnetic and dangerous about him, she decided.

Avril knew that intelligence like his often came with a price. Genius had a way of tipping into obsession. Into madness. He was always thinking, always analyzing, always playing a longer game than anyone else in the room.

Not a man to cross.

Yet, that was exactly what she was doing.

What would he do if he found out she was a spy? That she was working for the very institutions he despised?

She blinked, eyes gritty. Her quest for answers, for order, ran contrary to his, which were geared towards chaos, disruption, and anarchy.

Would he be furious? Fly into a rage? She couldn't imagine Echo angry.

What would Odin do? Would he have her killed? Make her disappear? Another nameless body dumped in the snow.

Shaking her head, she tried to dispel her exhausted paranoia.

That wouldn't happen. She wouldn't let it.

Nobody was going to find out. Not Rook. Not Echo. Not Odin. Not until this was all over, and they were apprehended. And by then, it wouldn't matter.

For some reason, the thought didn't make her feel any better.

chapter
twenty-one

BEFORE SHE LEFT FOR WORK THE FOLLOWING MORNING, Avril called Krister on the burner.

"How'd it go last night?" he asked.

As usual, she'd had given him the location of the meeting, but he hadn't been there. They'd decided it was too dangerous. Runa had seen him at the bookstore, and if he got spotted outside the meeting place, red flags would be raised.

"I think Runa's keeping tabs on me."

"You think they're suspicious?" Krister asked sharply.

"Not suspicious, just wary. Also, I need a scanner, just in case my apartment is being bugged."

"You think Runa—?"

Or Echo.

"I don't know. I might be paranoid, but... maybe. It would be good to sweep it."

He paused. "Avril, if you think it's too dangerous... that we should pull you out..."

"I'm good," she said hurriedly. "At least for a while longer. Can you get someone to drop a scanner off at the bookstore?"

"I'll see to it."

"Thanks. Once we know the date of the attack, we can set up a sting." The entire cell would be arrested and thrown in jail where they couldn't harm anyone again.

"Okay, but just be careful."

"I will."

She heard a dull clunk and knew he was setting his coffee cup down on the kitchen table. She could picture it now—the worn wood, the deep striations made from years of use. A pang of longing hit her in the gut.

How weird? She'd never been homesick before. Then again, she'd never really had a home before. She'd always been too focused on the hunt.

Right now, however, she wanted nothing more than to sit at Krister's kitchen table and drink coffee with him, laughing—or at least smiling—at his bad jokes.

She let out a slow breath. This case was getting to her. There was no time for sentimentality. She had work to do.

"You have any more details about the attack?" Krister was asking.

She shook off the funk. "They confirmed the target is the corporate HQ. Nothing else yet."

"Okay, I'll update Säpo tomorrow."

"What are you going to tell them about the break-in?"

"Nothing. They don't need to know how you came across this information, only that you've seen the plans, and we think that's the most likely target. Holmgren's eldest son has taken over the running of the company. He was voted in by the board this week."

"They were going through a staff list," Avril recalled. "I think they're going to blackmail someone into helping them. I'm not sure who, though."

"Call me as soon as you find anything," Krister said. "No matter how insignificant."

"Will do."

"Look after yourself Avril. Any hint of trouble and you get out, okay? Call me and I'll come get you."

He was always looking out for her. "I will."

. . .

AN HOUR BEFORE CLOSING, Runa and Fang arrived at the bookshop. Her last customer took one look at the brawny skinhead and exited in a hurry, leaving the book she'd been browsing open on a table.

"Hey." Avril broke into a fake smile. They were definitely keeping tabs. She hoped they hadn't noticed the female operative who'd bustled in earlier that day and left the bug detector in a shopping bag in a dark corner of the store. "Good to see you both."

Fang's expression didn't change. It was like he had a permanent scowl etched into his face. She couldn't understand what Runa saw in him. Then again, she was the last person to judge. She'd never even dated anyone, apart from Krister, and they were just friends.

Deep down, she knew he'd like them to be more, but she didn't know if she had more to give. Not yet. Not until she began to heal.

What she'd told Echo hadn't been a lie. There were times when she felt so empty inside, she didn't know what to do with herself. Especially now that the *Frost Killer* was behind bars.

She was in limbo. Trapped in a weird, alternate universe where her "friends" were her enemies, and her oath to serve and protect meant breaking the law.

"What are you guys doing here?"

Runa came over, but Fang took up his default position inside the door. Habit, she guessed.

"We came to invite you to a party," Runa said, smiling.

"A party?"

"Yeah, tonight. It's at a hostel in Västberga."

Avril knew that area. It was popular with travelers and transient workers in the city. It was also near to where Mikael Lustig, the Frost Killer, had lived when he'd gone on his first killing spree, except that house was no longer there. It had burned down in a fire over a decade ago.

Runa was saying something. "I'm sorry, what was that?"

The young activist frowned. "Are you okay, Astrid? You seem miles away."

"I'm fine. Just a long day. Tell me about this party."

Runa gave her the details. A rare chance to meet other Terra Nova members, as well as supporters and those sympathetic to the cause. "There will be other cells there," she added, eyes gleaming.

"I thought the point of having decentralized cells was so we aren't seen together?" It seemed contrary to the purpose of the model.

"It is, that's why this is so exciting. We're not to tell anyone which cell we belong to, though, but Echo says it's good to mingle and make friends. That way you know who you can trust should you need to."

She supposed that made sense.

But why now?

"Have you ever been to one of these parties before?"

Runa shook her head. "No, never. Have you, Fang?"

Fang gave a gruff shake of his head.

Avril frowned. There must be a reason. Odin wouldn't have agreed to it otherwise.

"We think it might be because we're going to collaborate with them on this upcoming mission," Runa said, dropping her voice.

"We are?"

"That's what Echo said, but don't tell anyone I told you. He hasn't announced it yet."

She smiled. "I won't."

Now that was much more likely.

"There are rumors that Odin will be there." Her eyes shone with excitement.

"Really?" Avril doubted that. Odin didn't get seen in public, let alone at a party. She recalled the rustle of clothing and the heat she'd felt on her back at the museum. The way the hairs on her neck had stood up when he'd gotten close—and she gave an involuntary shiver.

"Where is it being held?" she asked.

Krister would have to station someone outside with a camera. With multiple cells and members from all over the country, it was too good an opportunity to miss.

"I don't know yet. Secret location. We'll receive a text message at nine o'clock tonight."

Avril gritted her teeth. Too late to mobilize a surveillance effort. She'd have to tell Krister to get someone on standby.

Runa grasped Avril's hand. "You will come, won't you?"
"Of course." She smiled at Runa. "I wouldn't miss it for the world."

chapter
twenty-two

AVRIL PUSHED OPEN THE FRONT DOOR AND STEPPED INSIDE. The heavy bass of the music resounded through the house, and the air was thick with the scent of sweat, smoke, and weed. She was running a few minutes late, after thoroughly sweeping her apartment for bugs. She hadn't found anything. It seemed neither Echo nor Runa had gone that far. It was a relief, for it meant she was in the clear.

The hostel in Västberga was the kind of place where travelers and drifters came and went, and the landlord didn't ask questions. Nobody stayed long enough for him to care.

The common area was packed. Several groups of people deep in conversation occupied the mismatched sofas, some with stuffing spilling out of the seams, drinking cheap beer and passing around hand-rolled cigarettes. Others stood around drinking, smoking and chatting, but Avril didn't recognize anyone.

She scanned the room, searching for Runa, Gaia or even Echo. Parties like this made her uncomfortable. She had no time for small talk, and didn't care to socialize with people she'd never see again. Plus, the number of people made her want to escape back outside into the fresh air.

The party was a cover, or at least that's what Runa had implied. Members of the two Stockholm-based Terra Nova cells were both here tonight, but no one knew who they were.

Layers upon layers of secrecy, she mused as she wandered around.

Finally, she found Runa leaning against a rickety table in the kitchen, a bottle of cheap wine in her hand. Her red hair tumbled over one shoulder in loose waves, she had multiple strands of beads around her neck and wore a white top with bell-bottomed denim jeans.

Avril crossed the room. "There you are! I've been looking for you."

Runa swayed and gave her a watery smile. "Hey, glad you could make it."

Avril frowned. "Are you drunk?"

"A little." She raised the bottle. "Cheers."

It was then Avril saw the bruise blooming along her cheekbone. Judging by the underlying deep blue color, it was recent too.

"What happened?" Avril asked.

Runa touched it self-consciously. "It's nothing."

Avril frowned. "That's not nothing."

Runa blinked at her. "I walked into a door."

Bullshit.

Avril studied her, waiting. She knew the power of letting a silence linger.

"It was a misunderstanding," Runa said eventually. "Honestly, I'm fine."

Avril sighed. "Fang?"

A flicker of something behind her eyes. Regret? Sadness? Embarrassment? A micro expression. Most people wouldn't have noticed.

"Like I said, it was a misunderstanding. He didn't mean it. Fang can be... overly possessive sometimes."

Avril pursed her lips. That was no excuse for violence. If she had to guess, she'd say Fang had found out about the fake date at Henrik Ahlström's house. What Runa had done for the cause didn't sit well with him. "He must know it was all a pretense?"

Runa glanced down at the floor. "He knows, but he still doesn't like it."

Avril shook her head. Runa should leave him, but of course, she wouldn't. She didn't have anyone else.

"Come on," Avril said, as more people filtered into the kitchen. "Let's find the others."

Runa hesitated, put down the bottle, and followed her out of the room.

Upstairs was less crowded than below, but they still had to squeeze past a group on the landing. They found the others in one of the bedrooms, talking amongst themselves.

Avril was about to join them when she got cornered by Rook. He was all bristling indignation and sly suspicion.

"I'm on to you," he hissed, under his breath.

"Excuse me?" She was startled by the naked animosity.

"You heard me. They might trust you, but I know you're not who you say you are."

She went cold.

What did he know? Had he discovered a crack in her legend?

There was no choice but to brazen it out. "What do you mean?"

A smirk. "There is no record of Astrid Dahlström on the DMV database. Everything else is too perfect, like it was manufactured. I know it's lies."

"Honestly, Rook, I have no idea what you're talking about. I don't drive. Never have."

He scowled. "Who doesn't drive in America? Everyone has a car."

"Not everyone." She spread her arms as if to say, *I didn't*.

He studied her with dark, suspicious eyes. "You think you're so smart, but you can't fool me. Echo believes you, but be warned, once I find evidence that you're a phony, he'll change his tune. He doesn't take kindly to liars."

She met his gaze, her own heated. "I'm not lying. Search all you want, you won't find anything on me, because there is nothing to find. Not everyone is out to get you, Rook."

He blinked, but his gaze hardened. "You don't want me as an enemy, Astrid."

"Why? Because you'll hit me over the head with your laptop?" She scoffed. "I'm just trying to make a difference, like everybody else here."

He took a step toward her, invading her space.

"Everything okay here?" Echo asked, coming over. His timing was impeccable. He glanced at Avril, then over to Rook.

"Everything's fine," she said, breaking into a smile.

Rook gave a sulky nod. That told her a lot.

Despite his suspicions, he hadn't mentioned anything to Echo yet, otherwise she'd be getting a much frostier reception from the cell leader.

He didn't have anything concrete.

It was a problem though. If Rook kept digging, it wouldn't be long until he found some inconsistency, some tie-in with her real identity. A photograph, a news article, a police report.

Right now he was obsessing about what he couldn't find, but there was information out there that he could, once he knew where to look.

"Good. I'm glad you could make it." He was addressing Avril, and Rook, knowing when he wasn't wanted, turned and stalked off—but not before shooting her one last withering look.

"There are a lot of people here." That was as close as she got to small talk.

"It's an open party. Since we're using it as an opportunity to mix with another activist cell, we thought it would provide more of a—" He paused, searching for the right word.

"Smokescreen?" she suggested.

He quirked an eyebrow. "Exactly."

"Are they here? This other cell?"

"Indeed they are. Most of them are in this room as we speak. We're just waiting for a few more and then we'll get started."

"Started?" She frowned.

"Yes, didn't Runa tell you? We're having a meeting."

"No," Avril said slowly. "She forgot to mention that part."

He shrugged. "It doesn't matter. You're here, that's the important thing."

She got the feeling Echo knew full well that Runa hadn't told her about the meeting ahead of time. Was that so she couldn't tell anyone else? To ensure she came alone?

Was it natural caution, or did he suspect something? Maybe Rook's paranoia was rubbing off.

A shiver sliced through her, violent enough that she couldn't hide it.

"Are you cold?" he asked, gaze slanting.

A self-conscious laugh. "No, just excited. This is a big deal, right?"

He grinned. "It will be. Tonight, Thor and I will introduce our respective groups. That reminds me, what do you think of Freyja?"

"Who's Freyja?"

He laughed. "You. We all have code names in the organization. I thought it was fitting."

Freyja.

A memory tickled the back of her mind. "Wasn't she the Norse goddess of love?" Her knowledge of mythology was a little rusty, but she thought she remembered reading about it with her mother once, a long time ago.

He gave a pleased nod. "Correct, but she was also the goddess of war and death."

Avril caught her breath. She'd forgotten that part, or maybe her mother hadn't mentioned it.

He leaned closer, his dark gaze flecked with orange, like embers in a fire. They drew her in. "Freyja's soldiers who were slain in battle went to Valhalla."

"Odin's Valhalla?"

"Ah, so you know Norse mythology?"

"Only a little."

"Well, Freyja was fearsome in battle, but also cunning. She made deals with giants and outwitted gods."

What did that mean? Was he implying something?

She stared at him, partially mesmerized by his fiery gaze, quite godlike in its intensity.

To her surprise, he raised his hand and twirled a finger around a loose strand of her hair. She froze. What was he playing at? She was about to pull away, when he whispered, "She also had blonde hair."

Avril let out a shaky breath. "Then I think it's perfect."

chapter
twenty-three

"What were you two talking about so intently?" Runa asked, as Avril went over to join her. The meeting was about to start, and she felt flushed and agitated after the cryptic conversation with Echo.

She mustn't overreact. Echo was probably just feeling her out. Rook's suspicions must be rubbing off on him, and as a result, he was subtly questioning her, seeing if there were any cracks in her armor.

So why did it feel like he was playing mind games with her?

"Oh, he's decided my new name will be Freyja."

"Nice," Runa said with a nod of agreement. "It suits you."

"Thanks."

She leaned forward, a smile tugging at her lips. "He likes you, you know."

A chill shimmied down her spine. "Who? Echo?"

"Yes, Echo." She broke into a cheeky grin and in that moment looked much younger than her twenty-four years. "He didn't pay this much attention to me when I first joined, and I see the way he looks at you. It's like he can't tear his gaze away."

"He's just very intense."

It probably hadn't helped that she'd admitted she wanted to get to know him better. But she'd been caught on the spot and had to think fast. Being attracted to him was the first thing that had popped into her head. It had worked, but had she cultivated an unhealthy interest?

"Mm-hm," Runa murmured, her gaze lingering on Echo. "He is kind of sexy, though. Isn't he?"

Avril didn't reply.

Unnerving. Disconcerting. But sexy? She wasn't sure about that.

Echo and a man who she guessed was Thor stood in front of everyone. Using a pen, Echo tapped dully on the neck of his beer bottle, garnering everyone's attention. Avril noticed the bottle was still full.

"Can we have everyone's attention please?" All eyes turned his way. Looking around the stuffy room, Avril counted fifteen members, across both cells. A joint task force, so to speak.

Echo introduced himself and then Thor, who—like his namesake—was a hulking giant of a man with jet-black hair and deep-set eyes that never stopped moving. He looked like he could crush skulls with his bare hands, in addition to summoning bolts of lightning from the sky.

You'd think Echo would look geeky beside a man of that size, but when he spoke, he commanded the room with ease. Immediately the murmuring stopped. It was his stillness, Avril decided, that was most captivating. Along with the fiery gaze behind those unusual spectacles.

In a standoff, she'd rather face Thor than Echo.

Echo let the silence stretch before he spoke again. It was deliberate. He knew how to control a room, how to make people lean in, waiting for his words.

"Welcome to tonight's meeting. I hope you've had a chance to get to know each other. If not, you will afterwards."

Nobody moved.

"I'll get straight to the point. As you've all been made aware, our target is Nordic Energy."

Avril could sense the hunger in the room. All eyes were fixed on Echo.

"We're going to bring them to their knees." Echo's gaze flicked around the room, assessing his audience, judging their reactions. When his eyes met hers, he held them for a fraction longer than necessary before looking away.

"Nordic Energy is more than just a company," he continued.

"They're a symbol. A monolith built on destruction, fueling the slow, inevitable collapse of the planet. They profit from the suffering of others, from ecosystems burned to the ground, from the slow death of our seas, the poisoning of our rivers, the corruption of governments. And worst of all?" He let the question hang. "They do it with impunity."

A few murmurs of agreement. Runa, standing beside Avril, nodded along, her eyes bright. She believed every word. They all did.

"They lobby, they manipulate, they bury their crimes under the cloak of bureaucracy," Echo went on. "And for years, the world has let them because they're too big to fight. Too powerful to stop. They have politicians in their pockets, police forces on their payroll, and judges willing to turn a blind eye."

His voice didn't rise, but it pulsed with conviction and a cold certainty she found terrifying.

"But we are not politicians," he said. "We are not judges—and we are not afraid."

Avril watched the way the room responded. The way his listeners bristled with indignation. Rook folded his arms, nodding slowly. Gaia seemed hypnotized. Thor's fingers flexed at his sides like he was itching to punch something.

Echo held them all in the palm of his hand.

"We will show them they are not untouchable," he continued. "That their walls, their guards, their cameras, their high-rise fortresses will not protect them from our justice."

A beat of silence. Then, a slow ripple of agreement.

"Nordic Energy is the head of the proverbial snake," Echo continued. "It's where the executives sit in their glass offices and make their dirty deals. It's where they plot their next environmental crime, where they hide their secrets—so that is where they will finally understand the consequences of their actions."

He stepped back, letting that thought settle before continuing.

"This is not a protest," he said. "This is not a symbolic act of resistance. This is an operation designed to disrupt, to send a deafening message that they, and the politicians in their pockets, cannot ignore."

Avril felt the energy in the room shift again. Rook was nodding, eyes gleaming with a dark fanaticism. Runa looked at Echo like he was the Messiah sent to save them. Even Gaia had the spark of idealism in her eyes.

Only Fang sat unmoved, a scowl etched on his rugged face. Did he resent Echo for what he'd made Runa do? Was there discord in the ranks? She filed that thought for later and turned back to the front.

Echo nodded to Thor, who stepped forward.

"The building is secured." His voice was deep and booming, a roll of thunder unfurling over them. "Private security on every floor. Keycard access only. Cameras at every entrance. Panic buttons in the executive offices." He exhaled through his nose. "It's not a place you just walk into."

A small smirk played on Echo's lips. "That's why we're going to be smart about it. The schematics we obtained—" His eyes flicked to Avril and Runa. "—will provide us with a way in."

Thor straightened. "It's going to require both our cells working together, which is why we called you here tonight."

Another murmur rippled around the room and heads turned, checking each other out.

"We're going to go round the room and introduce ourselves, using code names only. After that, you'll have a chance to talk amongst yourselves before rejoining the party downstairs. Remember, you're sworn to secrecy. Anyone caught divulging the details of our mission will face the consequences."

Nobody spoke, but a few heads nodded. Avril swallowed over the lump in her throat. Out of everyone here, she was the most at risk. Glancing around, she caught Rook's dark gaze on her and held it defiantly, refusing to show weakness.

I'm on to you, he seemed to say.

If she was going to see this assignment through till the end, she'd have to do something about Rook. She wasn't sure what, but he had to go.

chapter
twenty-four

IT WAS PAST MIDNIGHT WHEN AVRIL FINALLY GOT HOME. Pulling off her clothes and dumping them on the bathroom floor, she had a hot shower to wash off the sweat, smoke and tension of the night. As she stood there watching the water swirl down the plughole, she thought about Runa's bruised cheek, Fang's jealousy, and Rook's suspicion.

I know you're not who you say you are.

Rook was a problem. A serious one.

She could handle the others. Fang was predictable, Runa was too emotionally invested, and Echo, despite his unnerving ability to read her, wanted to believe in her.

But Rook? He was digging. Prodding. Waiting for her to slip up.

If she didn't do something soon, he would expose her.

The tank emptied, the water turning cold, shocking her back to the present. She shut it off and stepped out, watching the droplets slide down the drain, washing away the last remnants of the night.

She had a plan.

But to execute it, she needed help. And it couldn't be Krister.

IT WAS Sunday and the bookshop was closed. Avril slept late and then ate breakfast in her flat, sitting at the small table in front of the window.

It was a bright but chilly morning, and yet the sunshine had brought everyone out onto the streets.

She needed to go to the grocery store to get some supplies, so she messaged David Karlsson to meet her there. When she'd called him yesterday, she'd stressed that he had to wear casual clothes and couldn't tell anyone where he was going. She couldn't risk her cover being blown.

Avril waited until a few minutes after ten, then left the apartment with her shopping bags. Nothing strange in that.

There was a small shopping plaza at the end of her street. Along the way, she stopped for coffee, keeping her eyes on the window as she ordered. Once, she bent to tie her shoelace, and on more than one occasion, checked behind her in store front reflections.

It didn't look like anyone was tailing her.

The square was bustling with weekend shoppers. Avril walked into the grocery store and picked up a basket, before heading to the back where there was a frozen food section. She hovered over the freezer, as if trying to decide what to buy.

"You'd better make it quick," a voice said. "I'm not supposed to be here."

She knew it was Karlsson, she could see him in her peripheral vision. He was standing behind her, looking at something on a shelf. To anyone watching, they were just two shoppers standing in close proximity, each minding their own business.

"I need your help," she whispered.

"I feel bad about not telling the boss."

"I will tell him," she explained. "But this can't come from him. It has to be anonymous. I know you have a friend in the IT department."

He shuffled, obviously uncomfortable. Karlsson had just started dating a young IT specialist, but they hadn't told anyone. Inter-departmental relationships were frowned upon.

"How'd you know that?"

"Woman's intuition," she lied. Krister had told her. "Don't worry. I won't say anything."

"Thanks."

There was a pause.

"What do you need?" She saw Karlsson reach for something on one of the shelves.

Avril bent down and rummaged through the freezer. While she did, she told him what she wanted him to do.

AVRIL GOT BACK to her apartment to find a disheveled Runa huddled in the doorway. Her face was blotchy, and it looked like she'd been crying. Dirty hair hung limply around her shoulders, while the bruise along her cheek bone had turned purple. She was also hugging herself, holding a hand over her ribs.

"Runa, what are you doing here?" Avril asked, her hands full of shopping bags, but she already knew.

Fang.

Runa sniffed, blinking back tears. She was trembling violently from the cold. Avril gestured for her to come inside. "Let's get you warmed up."

Runa followed Avril into the apartment block. They walked up the one flight of stairs and along the drafty corridor to Avril's flat.

Runa didn't say a word. Avril sensed she was fighting not to burst into tears.

Once inside, she set down the shopping bags and directed Runa to an armchair. "Sit down, and I'll make us some tea."

Leaving her there, she went to the kitchen and brewed them both a mug of chamomile with honey.

"Drink this," she told her friend when she got back. "It'll calm you down."

Runa wrapped her hands around the mug, and Avril was pleased to see she'd stopped shaking.

"It will be okay," she whispered, sitting beside her on the couch. "He can't hurt you now."

Runa turned her liquid green eyes to Avril. "I don't know what's gotten into him lately. He's never normally like this."

"Violent?"

"Yeah. He's been agitated, aggressive, jealous. It's like he's using any excuse to have a go at me."

Avril noted Runa was slouching a little on one side.

"Are you injured?" she asked.

"It's only a bruise. Nothing serious," Runa replied. Avril didn't question her, but by the way she was holding herself, she could tell it was more than a bruise.

"What can I do to help?" Her cop brain was urging Runa to file a restraining order and leave her abusive boyfriend, but she wasn't a cop now. She was a friend, and she had to act like one.

"Do you mind if I stay here for a few nights?" Runa asked, sniffing. "Just until things calm down."

Avril stared at her, aghast. Every fiber of her being wanted to refuse, but she knew she couldn't. "Er..." She hesitated, unable to bring herself to say yes.

How would she cope having someone else in her space? She'd lived alone since she was seventeen years old. Besides, she had a job to do. How would she communicate with Krister if Runa was here? How would she know if Karlsson had held up his end of the deal?

"It would only be for a few days," Runa insisted, pleading now. "I can't go back. He'll be waiting for me."

She couldn't put Runa in harm's way either. The woman needed a safe place to stay.

Forcing a smile, she said, "Sure. You can sleep on the couch."

To her surprise, Runa leaned over and hugged her. Avril froze, momentarily stunned.

Move! her brain told her.

Tentatively, she patted Runa on the back. Her friend didn't appear to notice her awkwardness. "Thank you, Astrid. You're the best."

"You're welcome. I hope Fang comes to his senses soon. He's lucky to have you."

Runa did burst into tears then.

Avril stared at her, intrigued by the tears that rolled freely down her bruised face. What was that like? she wondered. It had been so long since she'd cried that she couldn't remember the last time.

Her theory was that she'd cried for so long and so hard after her mother's murder that she didn't have any more tears left. Her ducts had dried up and were now defunct.

"I'm sorry," she murmured stiffly. "I didn't mean to make you cry."

"That's okay." Sniff. "It's my fault. I'm the one who was stupid enough to get involved with him in the first place. I should have listened to Echo."

"Echo?"

"Yeah, he told me it was a bad idea, but I went ahead anyway." She gulped in some air. "He was just so big and protective, and I've never had anyone looking after me like that." Her eyes begged Avril to understand.

She got it, she really did. It was nice knowing someone had your back after years of isolation. Krister's face sprung to mind, but she blinked it away.

This was about Runa, not her.

"It's so good having a friend like you." Runa smiled through her tears. "I'm so glad we were arrested together."

Avril chuckled at that. It lightened the mood.

What would Runa say if she knew it was all an elaborate set-up so that she could infiltrate Terra Nova?

"Me too."

A pang of regret sliced through her, but it didn't last. She was fond of Runa. Her first grown-up female friend. What with all the traveling she'd done while at the FBI, she'd missed out on a lot of "normal" stuff.

Friendships, relationships, community associations were all foreign to her. Avril wondered briefly what her life would have been like if her mother had lived. If she'd been normal.

Would she have had friends and sleepovers? Would she have frequented parties at college? Would she have dated, had a boyfriend, got married?

Sighing, she pushed those thoughts aside. That wasn't her reality. It never would be.

And this wasn't real. None of it.

It was an undercover assignment—and she mustn't forget that.

chapter
twenty-five

THAT NIGHT, AVRIL PLANTED THE SEED.

She and Runa sat in the living room, sharing fragments of their past over a bottle of cheap red wine.

Runa was open, unguarded. She had nothing to hide. A mother who died when she was fourteen. A father who buried himself in academia, treating his only daughter like an afterthought. Avril couldn't deny the parallels.

Runa had gone to university to read political science, full of fire and ambition, but disillusionment quickly set in. She dropped out in her second year. That was when *Terra Nova* found her. Or, more accurately, recruited her.

Avril listened as her friend told her the story. Echo had "bumped" into her at a café, and they'd gotten talking. He was all fire and passion and told her about this group he belonged to. He outlined their philosophy and she'd felt an affinity right from the start.

Runa thought it had been serendipity, but Avril didn't believe in coincidences like that. Echo—or maybe Odin—had been watching, waiting for the right moment to reel her in. A casual meeting at a café, a conversation that felt organic. It was anything but. Avril knew how it worked.

Runa, young and idealistic, had never stood a chance.

"I had a run-in with Rook the night of the party," Avril said, lowering her voice. "I don't think he likes me."

Runa frowned. "Why? What did he say?"

"That I'm not who I say I am." She swirled her wine. "He thinks I'm lying about my mother, about my time in America. Everything."

Runa's brows pulled together. "Why on earth would he think that?"

She shrugged. "I don't know. I just want to help. This..." She spread her arms. "Terra Nova is the first thing that's felt real to me in a long time. Before I met you, I had nothing. I don't feel like that anymore."

A simple confession, but as she said it, Avril realized it was kind of true. The organization, misguided though it was, did give her a sense of belonging in a way the FBI never had. With law enforcement, she'd always felt like an outsider—different, obsessive.

Here she felt accepted.

They made her feel valued.

It's not real.

That was the danger of extremist groups. That's why they targeted the misfits and neglected members of society, because they offered something those people didn't otherwise have. A family.

"Do you want me to have a word with him?" Runa asked, eyes flashing.

"No," Avril said quickly, shaking her head. "I don't want to cause friction. Hopefully, he'll realize he's got nothing to worry about and it'll pass."

Runa nodded. "Don't take it personally. He's just paranoid. He digs into everyone's background. He did it with me, too."

"What's his story, anyway?" Avril asked, casually.

"I don't know much about him," Runa confessed. "He joined a couple of months after me, but Echo was pretty keen to get him onboard. He needed a cyber-security expert."

Avril nodded, letting her talk.

"I heard that he got kicked out of university for hacking into a government database." Runa snorted. "He did some time but was out in under a year. His family has money and contacts."

"They know he's involved with Terra Nova?"

"Don't know. From what I can gather, he doesn't see much of them.

Doesn't see much of anyone. I tried to befriend him when I first joined, but he wasn't interested."

Typical hacker type. Avril had worked with men like Rook before—paranoid, socially stunted, more comfortable behind a screen than in a room full of people.

Still, she couldn't talk. Her obsession had been tracking serial killers, not code. People at the Bureau thought she was weird—and to anyone looking in from the outside, she guessed she was.

But not here. Here, she could be as weird as she liked. As long as she had the cause at heart, she was accepted. In this upside-down world, Rook was a valued member of the team. He was respected, and he had a vital function, which meant Echo, or indeed Odin, couldn't do without him.

That had to change.

"Really?" Avril feigned surprise. "Because I saw him getting into a black SUV the other night, near Odenplan."

Runa's brows drew together. "A black SUV?"

"You know, the big gas-guzzlers with tinted windows." Avril took a sip of wine. "It was weird. He looked over his shoulder before getting in. I waved, but he didn't see me."

Runa's expression hardened.

Avril pushed a little further. "I guess it was a family member. I mean, why else would he be meeting someone in a car like that?"

"Where exactly?" Runa asked sharply.

"Odenplan, just off Karlbergsvägen."

Runa's fingers tightened around her glass. "His family doesn't live anywhere near Odenplan. They've got a house in Djursholm."

Avril widened her eyes. "Oh... well, maybe I was mistaken." She forced a laugh. "I thought it was him, but you know, it was dark—"

Runa didn't look convinced.

"You didn't get a license plate?"

Avril laughed. "What? Of course not. Rook is the one who vets people, not me. I didn't even think to look."

Runa was chewing on her lower lip, clearly turning what she'd heard over in her head. Avril let the silence settle, knowing that doubt—once planted—would grow all on its own.

"Funny, isn't it?" she said lightly. "Rook knows everything about us, but we know nothing about him. I guess Odin must trust him, else he wouldn't have brought him onboard."

"He's not just on board," Runa admitted. "He's part of Odin's inner circle. That's why Echo respects him so much. He's connected all the way to the top."

Now that was interesting.

"Do you want something to eat?" Avril asked, getting up. "I bought a ton of groceries today, so we can make a vegetable stew or something?"

Runa hesitated, then nodded. "Yeah. Sounds good."

Avril noted the moment Runa's shoulders relaxed—when she mentally shelved the thought, at least for now.

But the damage was done.

The power of suggestion was subtle but deadly. Avril had watched experts manipulate murderers and terrorists in interrogation rooms, planting ideas that slowly unraveled their defenses. She had learned from the best.

Now she was using it against Terra Nova.

And with Karlsson's help, she was going to bury Rook.

Without losing a moment's sleep over it.

chapter
twenty-six

AVRIL WOKE UP TO THE BURNER PHONE VIBRATING UNDER her pillow. Half asleep, she pulled it out and glanced at the screen.

Krister.

Although she wanted to talk to him, she couldn't. Already she could hear Runa moving about in the next room. Cutting the call, she glanced at the time. Eight o'clock.

She'd overslept.

The wine last night had knocked her out.

She was due to open the bookstore at nine, and she wanted to shower, dress and grab a coffee on the way.

When she walked into the living room, Runa was already dressed and applying make-up in the mirror.

"You're up early."

"Yeah, Echo messaged. He wants to meet up. Says he's got a job for me."

"Oh, really? Did he say what?" Hopefully Runa would mention what she'd said about Rook's clandestine meeting with the mysterious people in the black SUV.

"No, but—" She shifted, not meeting Avril's gaze.

"What is it?" Avril asked.

"I just hope it's not something that involves flirting with another man. I'm not sure what I'd say to Fang."

Avril stared at the bruise still visible under the make-up. "Runa, I know it's none of my business, but given the type of work you do—that we do—I'm not sure if dating Fang is such a good idea."

Runa grimaced. "I know, you're right. I was awake most of the night, thinking about it. I hardly slept a wink. Anyway, I've come to a decision. I'm going to break it off with him today. I'll move my stuff out this afternoon."

"You can stay here," Avril offered, now she was used to the idea. It wasn't so bad having Runa here if it was just for a short time. "At least until you find alternative digs."

"Thank you, Astrid." Runa gave a watery smile, and Avril could see the genuine relief on her damaged face.

"Don't mention it. You'd do the same for me."

"Course I would," Runa confirmed. "That's what friends are for."

Avril swallowed over the strange knot in her throat. Runa actually meant it.

She watched as Runa applied more foundation over the bruise on her cheek, carefully blending the edges until it was nearly invisible. Nearly.

"Where are you meeting Echo?" Avril forced her mind back on track.

"Stockholm City Station—and if I don't go now, I'll be late."

Before she could ask any more questions, Runa grabbed her bag and headed for the door. "Maybe we can grab a drink later?"

"That would be great," Avril said, watching her go. "Good luck with Fang this afternoon. Let me know if you want a hand moving."

Runa flashed her a sad smile. "Thanks. Will do."

Then, she disappeared out the door.

ONLY WHEN SHE was sure Runa had left did she call Krister back.

"Jesus, I was getting worried," he said, tersely.

"I know, I'm sorry. I've got a houseguest."

There was a stunned pause. "Who? Not Echo?"

Avril frowned. "No, why would you think it was Echo?"

"I don't know." He sounded flustered. "Just the way you were talking about him the other day. Anyway, it doesn't matter. Who is it?"

She told him about Runa's surprise visit and that she'd invited her to move in for a while.

"You should see her face," she told him. "Fang's a brute."

"Can't say I'm surprised," Krister grunted. "Given his background."

Avril hadn't been either. "Krister, Echo is meeting Runa at Stockholm City Station at nine o'clock. He's got a job for her. I think Säpo should send someone to follow them."

"Nine? Crap. Do you know what's happening?"

"No, but it might involve Nordic Energy. Runa's worried about how Fang will react, but I don't think it's another honey trap. I reckon it's more important than that. Don't ask me why, it's just a feeling."

"Okay, fine. Thanks for the heads up."

Avril hung up and got ready for work. She would be late, but who really cared? She'd spoken to Krister and put a tail on Runa, that was the main thing.

THE BOOKSTORE WAS quiet and decidedly chilly when she walked in forty-five minutes later, coffee in hand. A small pile of mail lay on the mat, having been pushed through the slot before she'd arrived.

Picking it up, she noticed there was a small note lying on top. It had one line of text on it.

Be careful. He's on to you.

Avril froze. It was unsigned, but the message had been handwritten.

Holding her breath, she turned it over. The back was blank.

Who on earth could it be from? The obvious conclusion was someone in the organization?

Fang? Gaia? Echo?

And what did they mean? *Who* was onto her?

Rook? Or was it someone else?

She walked over to the counter and set her coffee cup and the mail down, still clutching the note in her other hand.

Rook was the most likely candidate, but if someone was warning her, that meant they knew who she was too—and that was not good.

Taking a shaky breath, she stared at the handwriting, committing it to memory. The orderly letters, even print, no twirls or curls. Could be a man or a woman's hand, she wasn't sure, but if she ever saw it again, she'd know.

Opening a drawer, she took out a box of matches, then she took the note to the small basin in the musty kitchenette at the back of the store and lit it. She watched as it shriveled up and disintegrated in a swirl of glowing embers.

Of course, this could be a fiendish play by Rook, testing her, seeing if she'd panic. If she thought someone was onto her, what might she do to cover her tracks? She couldn't assume anyone else knew who she was.

Even if they did, they had opted to warn her instead of telling Odin, which meant she was still safe. For now.

AVRIL'S DAY got progressively worse. The heating in the bookstore wouldn't work, so she had to call a gas specialist to fix it. That meant contacting the owner, who wasn't particularly keen at forking out for the repairs.

It would look odd if she paid for it, however, and if the police settled the account, there would be a paper trail. She had to act as if she was a real employee of the bookstore, which meant bothering the owner on his vacation.

Still wearing her oversized coat, Avril waited for the repairman to arrive while trying to help a customer. A soft vibration in her pocket drew her attention.

Her burner phone!

She was slipping. She must have slipped it into her pocket without thinking. That was the last time she was drinking on the job. It messed with her brain.

It was Krister's number. What the hell was he doing calling her in the middle of the day? He knew how dangerous that was.

Ignoring it, she tried to explain to a teeth-chattering customer that the heating would be back on soon. Not that it mattered, the woman left anyway.

Her phone rang again.

Krister.

It must be important, or else he wouldn't risk exposing her. Twice.

The store was empty, so she hung the "Closed" sign on the door and disappeared into the back office.

"What is it?" she hissed, answering in a whisper. "You know I'm at work."

"Avril, I've got some bad news."

Her heart did a flipflop. "What is it?"

"There's been an accident—or something. I don't know what." She could hear by the tone of his voice he was rattled.

Her heart skipped a beat. Säpo officers were trailing Runa.

"What's happened, Krister? Is Runa okay?"

"No, Avril. She's not." His voice broke. "She's dead."

chapter
twenty-seven

THE GROUND SEEMED TO TILT AND AVRIL GRASPED THE DESK in the office, shakily lowering herself into the chair. "What do you mean she's dead?"

"Dead. She fell, or was pushed, under a train at Älvsjö Station."

"Oh, my God." Her head spun. "Are you saying she was murdered?"

"Yes. No. Fuck, I don't know. It's chaos down here. I've closed the station and called forensics. It only happened twenty minutes ago. A high-speed train, it wasn't stopping at the station. Somehow she stumbled, or was pushed, onto the track. There was no time for the train driver to stop."

Avril closed her eyes, an unwanted mental image flashing behind her lids. Runa's bright green eyes wide with fear, her mouth open mid-scream. Then a screech and the flash of sparks as the brakes activated, all too late.

"That's terrible," she murmured, feeling moist heat behind her eyelids. Was she crying? Opening her eyes, she stared unseeing at the dirty wall in front of her. No tears fell. Just a burning sensation, and a horrible dark hole where her heart had been.

Runa. So young, so idealistic.

Gullible.

Expendable.

He's got a job for me.

She blinked, her brain kicked into action. "Did they follow her? Did they see who she met? What was the job she was doing for Echo?"

"Whoa, Avril. Slow down," Krister said. "I haven't managed to talk to the undercover officers who were following her yet. As soon as I got the call about the accident, I raced down here. Once I get this under control, I'll talk to them and fill you in."

"Do you think it was Echo?" she whispered.

"I don't know." Krister sounded weary. "I'd better go, Avril. Watch yourself. We'll talk tonight."

"Okay. Bye, Krister."

Avril dropped her head down onto the desk. How could this be happening? What had Runa done that had gotten her killed?

No way it was an accident. She knew Krister didn't believe that any more than she did. Echo had used Runa and then brutally discarded her.

She gasped—

Or was it Fang?

Had Runa told him she was leaving him, and it had pushed him over the edge? They knew he was capable of violence. Had he lost it and pushed her in front of that train? Had he killed her rather than accept she was breaking up with him?

Avril frowned against the pounding in her brain.

That's what friends are for.

Avril let out a ragged breath. She'd felt a connection to Runa. A bond, if you like. Not an easy thing for her to achieve. They had similar backstories, they both knew how it felt to be ostracized, to be neglected. Alone.

She scowled at the wall, feeling the rage rise up like bile. How dare Echo think he could dispose of her friend in this way? She was a human being, a woman fighting for a cause. She had hopes, dreams.

Had.

Avril paused, as a thought struck her. There was one other possibility.

Rook.

Had Runa told him what Avril had said? Had she confronted him about the SUV? Did Rook really have something to hide, or was he just scared the rumor would propagate, casting suspicion on him?

Could he have been waiting for Runa at Älvsjö Station?

She shook her head. That was the least likely scenario. Runa wouldn't have had time to contact Rook this morning. If anything, she'd have spoken to Echo about it first.

Too many questions. No answers.

Feeling like she was in a daze, Avril got up and walked back into the bookstore. Unable to focus on anything, she stared out of the blurry glass panels in the front door.

He's onto you.

A shiver shot through her.

Was she next?

"You need to view any and all CCTV footage from the station," Avril told Krister later that evening, when he'd finally gotten a chance to call. It was late, but she was still wide awake. It wasn't grief that had settled in her heart, it was anger. Anger at a wasted life.

Anger at what they were doing.

At everything.

"I've already asked for it," he replied, his voice raspy from overuse. Avril lay on the couch, phone to her ear. The apartment felt empty now that Runa wasn't there. Her open suitcase still lay in the corner, clothes tumbling out onto the floor. Her make-up was still on the mantelpiece, left underneath the mirror. If Avril closed her eyes, she could picture Runa standing there.

"I want to come in. I can help you analyze it."

"You can't break cover, Avril. If you do, this will all be for nothing."

She clenched her jaw. As much as she hated it, Krister was right. She owed it to Runa to see this through, if for no other reason than to bring down the bastard who'd murdered her.

"They're saying it was suicide," Krister told her.

Avril gave a hard scoff. "You don't believe that."

"Obviously not, but the world will. Her father will."

Avril thought about the absent figure who'd been more interested in his research than his own daughter. "A troubled university dropout mixed up with an extremist organization. I can see the headlines now."

Krister grunted. "Anyone on your end said anything?"

"Not yet," she told him. "They're assuming I don't know. I suspect someone will tell me in due course. Maybe tomorrow."

"Do they know she was staying with you?"

"Fang does."

"Be careful, Avril. If this is how they handle loose ends, you're walking a tightrope."

"I know." She hesitated. "Did you talk to the Säpo guys yet?"

"Yeah. And it's not good news." His tone darkened. "They followed Runa from Stockholm City to Älvsjö but lost her in the crowd. Last time they saw her, she was heading toward the Stockholm International Fairs and Congress Center. They didn't pick her up again until she was back at the station."

Avril let out a sharp breath. "You're kidding?"

"I wish I was. When the... accident happened, they weren't on the platform. They didn't even realize it was their target who'd gone under the train until later. Thought they just lost her in the chaos."

"What's the point of having them if they can't follow one woman? It's not like she blends in either, not with that flaming red hair."

"I know, Avril. It was sloppy police work and there will be an internal investigation. That doesn't help us right now, though. Runa's dead, and we have no clue what she was doing there."

Avril groaned in frustration.

"Look, I have to go. I'll call you when I know something."

And she had to be content with that. It was only after she'd hung up that she remembered about the note.

chapter
twenty-eight

AVRIL HAD SCARCELY HUNG UP WHEN THE DOORBELL WENT. She jumped, spinning to face it.

"Who is it?" she called, hoping someone had got the wrong apartment.

"Echo," came the gruff response.

What was he doing here? But she knew. He'd come to tell her the bad news. And she had to act appropriately.

"Coming!"

Avril darted into the bedroom to hide the burner phone and grab the gun. Krister had insisted she keep one in the apartment, a fact she was very grateful for now. The Säpo team had even inserted a secret compartment in her stringy mattress where nobody, other than a pro, would know where to look.

Stashing the burner with her real phone, she retrieved the gun and took it into the living room. Heart pounding, she looked around, then thrust it under a cushion on the sofa. Echo could have been the one to kill Runa. There was no way in hell she was going to face him unprotected.

Exhaling, she went to open the door.

"Hi." She hoped she didn't sound too flustered or out of breath.

"Hey, mind if I come in?"

"Sure." She held open the door and he strode past her into the apartment. His forehead was furrowed, and those amber eyes were downcast. He looked sad.

"Astrid, I've got something to tell you, and it might come as a shock."

She stood facing him, her arms hanging loosely by her sides, her feet bare. She still wore her jeans and a cream jumper that she'd had on earlier that day, her hair hanging loosely around her face.

"What is it?"

"You might want to sit down." His gaze drifted to the suitcase in the corner, and his jaw tightened.

Avril sat on the couch, leaning back against the cushion with the gun. Echo remained standing, as she knew he would. Even when delivering bad news, he needed to have the upper hand.

"It's about Runa."

"Runa?" Avril's gaze drifted to the make-up on the mantelpiece. She couldn't help it. If she stared hard enough, maybe she'd see her friend's reflection in the mirror.

"She's dead, Astrid. They think she committed suicide."

So that was the line he was going to go with?

Not an accident. Not murder. If he'd been with her this morning, he'd have known she wasn't suicidal. Her eyes hardened, and she fought to maintain her composure.

She wanted to scream at him. Demand answers.

Yet she said nothing.

Echo mistook her anger for grief, or shock, because he shifted awkwardly and said, "I'm sorry. I know you two were close."

Yes, they were. And if he had anything to do with this—anything at all—she was going to make him pay.

"I saw Runa this morning," she said quietly, as if she was stunned by the news. Eyes downcast, in case he saw through her masquerade. Echo had a way of doing that. "She seemed fine. I can't believe she'd kill herself."

Echo nodded, sympathizing.

"How did she die?" Avril whispered, too afraid to look up.

"She jumped under a train."

Avril shook her head. "No, I refuse to believe that. She wouldn't. Not Runa." The indignation allowed her to vent some of her anger.

"It's true, Astrid. There were witnesses. They say she jumped."

Bullshit.

Avril did look up then, locking her gaze on him. "Who? Who were these witnesses?"

"I don't know. I only know what the police said."

"You spoke with the police?" Now she was surprised.

"Not exactly."

"Then how?"

"We have our ways. You know that."

Rook.

A cold chill swept over her. Did he have access to police databases? She had to warn Krister. If he did, nothing was safe. Not her. Not the operation. Not anything.

They could already know who she was. Maybe this was all an elaborate game, and they were playing her. Using her to feed misinformation back to Säpo.

Avril ran a hand through her hair. She had to get a grip.

"Are you okay?" Echo took a step toward her. "You don't look well."

"I'm fine. It's the shock, that's all. She was staying here for a couple of days, did you know that?"

Echo shook his head, but she could tell he was lying.

He knew. He knew everything.

She turned her head to the corner. "That's her suitcase over there. She and Fang had a fight. He didn't like the way... He didn't like what she had to do on our last assignment."

"Fang came to me," Echo said softly. "I reassured him it was necessary. Runa was good at her job. She didn't have a problem with it, but he couldn't handle it. I advised him to end it with her, and he said he would."

That was not what Runa had said.

"She had a terrible bruise on her face." Avril gasped. "You don't think—?"

It was a logical thought process given the man's violent nature, and

Echo would expect her to go there. She may as well get it out in the open, see how he reacted.

"No." He shook his head, his glasses catching the light. "Fang had nothing to do with this, Astrid. Runa was upset that their relationship had broken down and decided to end it."

Avril bit her lip. Hopefully he'd think she was trying not to cry.

"I'm sorry for your loss," he said. "We'll be holding a memorial for Runa tomorrow night. I'll send you the address."

She nodded bleakly. "I'll be there."

He turned and left the apartment, but not before he cast one last look in her direction.

Had she fooled him? She damn well hoped so, otherwise she was in a lot more trouble than she thought.

chapter
twenty-nine

KRISTER STARED AT THE GRAINY IMAGE ON THE SCREEN. It was of the platform at Älvsjö Station. Being a Monday morning, it had been packed with commuters.

The crowd swelled, a train stopped, they squeezed on, and it left, taking them with it. Then the cycle repeated itself.

Officers had been trawling the CCTV footage all night, and they'd isolated the frames in which Runa had been spotted. Slender, in a grey coat and head downcast, she was only noticeable by her hair, which gleamed in the weak morning sunshine.

She moved along the platform, trying to find a free spot in which to stand. Krister frowned and leaned forward. "Is that a strap over her shoulder?"

Freddie spun around in his chair. "Yeah, it looks like it."

"Did the responding officers find a laptop bag on the platform? Or on the tracks?"

Freddie frowned. "I don't think so. I'll find out." He turned back to his desk and picked up the phone.

Krister carried on watching. Runa shuffled along the platform until she disappeared off the edge of the screen.

"Dammit," he muttered. "Is that it?"

"That's all we've got," Karlsson said.

Krister leaned back in his chair. "So she supposedly jumps in front of the train in the only blind spot on the entire platform?"

Karlsson nodded. "That's right."

He stared at the screen. "No way. I'm not buying it."

"No bag," Freddie said, turning around. "Not on the platform or the tracks."

"So somebody took it?" Karlsson asked, shocked. "Who steals from a dead woman?"

"Someone who doesn't want anyone to know what was in that bag," Krister said. He glanced up. "Is there any other footage of her going into the station? What about before she went in? Was she with anyone?"

"They haven't got that far yet," Karlsson said with a grimace. "They started at the time of death and worked backwards. We'll have to wait for any more sightings of her."

Krister sucked in a frustrated breath. "Okay, but keep me posted. As soon as she's spotted, I want to know. We need to track her movements leading up to her death."

Freddie turned around. "Witness accounts differ. Several people we spoke to said it looked like she stumbled. One guy said she appeared drunk or drugged up. That's where the suicide theory came from. Another woman said she thought she could have been pushed, but she didn't see who pushed her, so they discounted that."

Typical. A platform full of people and nobody saw anything.

"I'm going to Säpo," he said, grabbing his jacket. "I want to talk to those goons myself."

SÄPO HEADQUARTERS WAS LOCATED in a modern, angular complex just outside central Stockholm, housed in the Swedish Security Service's secure compound. The lobby was sterile and silent, manned by armed officers in dark suits who wore the same sharp-eyed expression Krister had come to associate with federal-level security.

He signed in at the front desk and was escorted through a series of doors requiring keycard access. Metal detectors, reinforced glass, retina scanners—it was more secure than any police facility he'd ever worked in.

A plainclothes officer led him into a small, glass-walled briefing room where Lindholm was already waiting, his tie loose and his jacket draped over the back of a chair. A steaming coffee sat untouched on the table.

"Jansson," he greeted, standing up briefly before sitting again. "I'm sorry we don't have more for you. Like I told you on the phone, my men didn't have eyes on her when the incident happened."

Krister sat across from him. "Yeah, why is that?"

Lindholm hesitated. He wasn't going to admit they'd screwed up. "It was a Monday morning, and they lost her in the crowd. I wish to God they hadn't, but it happens."

"It shouldn't happen," he growled, feeling the heat rise to his face. "Your men had one job, to keep her in sight. She was meeting with the head of a terror cell that we suspect is planning an imminent attack. How much more urgent can it be?"

"She's not a key player," Lindholm said. "My men were looking for Echo, the cell leader. That's who we wanted. We still don't know who the hell he is."

"You wanted him to lead you to Odin," Krister surmised.

Lindholm nodded. "He's the big fish. We get him, we cut the head off the snake. The attack never happens."

"You've got nothing on Odin," Krister snapped. "Or Echo. You don't even know who they are. My agent is the only way we're going to stop this. We need evidence, intent, specifics. We need to know what they're planning."

"And your agent is still in play, is she not?" he asked.

Krister nodded.

"Then we have nothing to worry about. She'll give you the intel, and then we can arrest Odin and Echo and bring down their entire organization. Our goal here is to avoid another terrorist attack, not wait for it to happen."

Krister gritted his teeth, frustrated. "I understand, but I have a homicide to investigate—actually, two now, counting the car bomb—and I need to know if your men saw anything at Stockholm City or Älvsjö that might help."

Lindholm studied him for a moment. "I can tell you we didn't spot

Echo at Stockholm City Station. My team spent the last twenty-four hours going through CCTV footage. We studied it from every angle. He wasn't there."

Krister rubbed his jawline, agitated. "Yet we know she met with him."

Lindholm shook his head. "If she did, it wasn't there. In every frame, she is alone."

Krister sighed. "What about the laptop bag. Did she have that with her?"

Lindholm frowned. "A laptop bag? No, I don't think so. Why?"

"Because she had one on the platform at Älvsjö."

Lindholm's gaze darkened. "One second."

He took out his phone and stepped out of the office. Five minutes later, he was back, his brow creased. "That's a negative. She did not have a laptop bag with her at Stockholm City Station, nor when she was walking toward the Convention Center at Älvsjö."

"Then where the hell did she get it?"

Lindholm perched on the edge of the chair. "She must have made contact with someone. They gave her the bag."

"Exactly." Krister frowned. "But if it wasn't at Stockholm City Station, and it wasn't at Älvsjö, then where?"

Lindholm gave a weary shrug. This wasn't his priority. He was concerned about the bag, but not enough to become invested. Säpo were only concerned with Echo—and Odin.

"What time did your men lose sight of her?" Krister asked.

"I'll have to check and get back to you."

"If you wouldn't mind. I need to work out how much time passed before she appeared on that platform. It might help us figure out where she went, or what she did in that time."

Lindholm nodded. "I'll message you as soon as I know."

Krister got up. They didn't shake hands, nor did Lindholm show him out. Another officer did that.

Krister sighed. Well, he wasn't going to give up on Runa. Her life mattered, and he was going to find out who pushed her in front of that train.

chapter
thirty

Avril spotted him before she even reached the shop.

Fang.

He stood rigidly outside the bookstore, fists clenched at his sides, his bulk taut with barely restrained fury. His eyes locked onto her like a predator sighting prey.

She halted a few feet away. "Fang," she said, voice raw. "I'm so sorry."

He didn't answer. Didn't flinch. Just stared at her, something dark and volatile simmering behind his eyes.

She moved toward the door, fumbling with her keys, desperate to get out of the cold. But before she could reach the lock, a heavy hand gripped her shoulder and yanked her back.

"This is all your fault."

She wrenched free and turned on him. "What are you talking about?"

"I know you told her to end it." His voice rose with each syllable, the acrid sting of alcohol clinging to every word. "It's your fault she's dead."

"Fang, I know you're upset, but—"

"She's dead because of you."

The pain was clear now, etched in every tense line of his bruiser's face. His eyes—red-rimmed and ringed with exhaustion—betrayed a grief so raw it caught her off guard.

It told Avril three things.

One, he'd truly cared about Runa.

Two, he hadn't been the one to push her under the train.

And three, Echo had lied when he claimed he'd advised Fang to break things off.

"I didn't have anything to do with it," she hissed, glancing at the curious passersby starting to gather. "Keep your voice down."

"She told me it was over. Said she couldn't see me anymore. That was you."

"No, Fang. It was because you hit her. Everyone saw the bruises."

But he wasn't hearing her. "I loved her," he snapped. "She was everything to me, and you ruined that. You filled her head with poison. If it wasn't for you, she wouldn't have stepped in front of a goddamn train."

He was shouting now. People had stopped, openly gawking at the confrontation between the towering man and the slim blond woman.

"Let's go inside," Avril decided, turning her back on him.

He hesitated.

"Don't," she warned sharply. "Not out here."

The door clicked open and she slipped inside. The air was stale and cool—the heat hadn't kicked in yet—but it was better than the street. Fang followed her, slamming the door with a bang that made her flinch.

Avril returned the keys to her pocket and turned to face him. "I know you're hurting, but Runa being at that train station had nothing to do with me. She was on a job. For Echo."

His face fell. "What?"

He ran a hand over his bald head, struggling to process what she'd just told him.

"She told me Echo gave her a task," Avril pressed. "She didn't say what it was, but she was headed south. That's all I know. Then last night, I heard she'd died."

He stared at her, his eyes blank and hollow.

"I swear, Fang. She was fine when she left yesterday morning. I don't believe for a second that she jumped."

Cold Legacy

He shook his head. "But I thought...?"

"You thought what? That she was so devastated over you that she threw herself in front of a train? Fang, *she* broke up with *you*. That doesn't make sense."

He rubbed at his temple, as though trying to scrub the confusion out of his skull. "Then what the hell happened?"

"I don't know," Avril said. "But I intend to find out."

"How?" he asked, quieter now.

She hesitated, hating herself for using Fang to further her goal, but unfortunately it was necessary. "The night before she died, we were talking about Rook. Runa said she saw him getting into a black SUV. She thought it was suspicious and said she was going to ask him about it. Next thing, she's dead."

The big hands rolled into fists. "You're telling me Rook did this? He... what? He pushed her in front of that train?"

"I don't know," Avril repeated. "I'm just telling you what she told me." She didn't care about bending the truth if it helped catch Runa's killer.

"But why?" he asked. "Why would Rook do something like that?"

"If he was feeding information to the police—or the press—maybe Runa found out. Maybe he couldn't risk her talking."

Fang's fists curled. "You're saying Rook's a snitch?"

"I'm not saying that. I'm saying that's what Runa suspected."

He stared at her, a long and loaded moment, then dropped his gaze to the floor.

"If Rook did this..." He trailed off, shaking his head. "I'll kill him."

"We don't know that he did," Avril said, trying to contain him.

Fang began to pace, his boots thudding heavily against the hardwood floor. The door creaked open and a little old lady stepped inside, caught sight of him, then backed out like she'd walked into a crime scene.

"You're scaring the customers," Avril said.

"Fuck the customers. My girl is dead, and someone killed her. When I find out who that someone is..." He punched a fist into his hand, the message clear.

Not if I get to them first, Avril thought.

Turns out Runa did have someone else looking out for her. It was just a pity Fang's show of support had come too late.

THE MEMORIAL SERVICE was held that night in the courtyard of an old townhouse that had once been grand, but had long since faded and crumbled with age. Inside, the hall still held traces of its former glory. High ceilings etched with celestial motifs and a massive chandelier that had long ago lost its sparkle.

The black-and-white marble floors were scuffed and stained, but still charming. They filed across them in silence, through a pair of open doors, and out into the courtyard.

Terracotta urns filled with brittle, leafless trees lined the perimeter. In the center stood a dried-up fountain, its stone basin cracked and dusty. A weather-worn statue of a nymph clutching an urn stared eternally skyward.

Avril studied the soft curls of the sculpture's hair, the proud line of the jaw—and thought of Runa.

She wondered how the police investigation was going. Krister hadn't called her back yet, and she was dying to know if they'd found anything on the CCTV at the station. Maybe the killer had been caught on camera.

Maybe it was one of them?

Echo stood with his back to the wall. The pallid gray light brushed his angular face, giving him a spectral look. Dressed entirely in black, he appeared even paler than usual. The only thing that burned with life was the steady flame in his eyes, glowing faintly behind his glasses.

Fang stood a few yards away, glaring at Rook. The tech specialist noticed and frowned but quickly turned his back. Those two hadn't had a chance to talk yet. Avril suspected it would kick off after the memorial service.

She drifted over to Gaia, who stood alone, her eyes fixed on Echo. Shadows underlined her gaze. "Such a tragic waste," Gaia whispered.

Avril nodded. No argument there.

Gaia seemed composed, but there was a stiffness to her posture. A stillness that seemed unnatural. The whole group had taken Runa's death hard.

Avril studied her carefully, searching for any flicker of recognition—some telltale sign that Gaia knew who she really was, or that she'd sent the note. But there was nothing. Gaia didn't glance her way, didn't look smug or guilty. She just seemed upset, like the rest of them.

Then Echo stepped forward to speak. He told them how he'd met Runa when she was still young and idealistic, desperate to make a difference. He spoke of her passion, her potential, how she'd already changed the world in small ways.

Avril wondered what the job was he'd had her do the morning of her death.

Was that why she'd been murdered?

As soon as Echo had finished, Fang stalked across the courtyard toward Rook. Avril decided it was time to take her leave.

"I'll see you at the next meeting," she said to Gaia.

Gaia nodded absently, her attention locked on the confrontation now unfolding.

Fang was nose to nose with Rook—well, nose to forehead, given the size difference. Avril watched, heart pounding.

"What did she say to you?" Fang snarled.

Rook straightened, trying to hold his ground. "Nothing. I don't know what you're talking about."

"I know about the black SUV. Are you a snitch, Rook?"

"What?" Rook blinked, baffled. "You're out of your mind."

"You talking to the cops? Is that what Runa found out? Is that why you killed her?"

"You're insane!" Rook barked. "Echo, get this oaf away from me—he's lost it."

Avril knew she should leave, but she couldn't tear her gaze away.

"What's he talking about, Rook?" Echo asked, stepping in.

"I have no idea," Rook said, eyes wide. "He's making it up."

"What black SUV?" Echo pressed, voice low but sharp.

Avril allowed herself the faintest smile. With the cracks showing, and Karlsson's help, Rook's days in Terra Nova were numbered.

She slipped away through the open gates, unseen.

And disappeared into the night.

chapter
thirty-one

"WHAT DO YOU MEAN THERE WAS NO CCTV?" AVRIL ASKED. She stood next to Krister at a crowded bar, a few blocks from her apartment. It was late, but she'd asked him to meet her here for an urgent update.

"Runa was pushed in the only blind spot in the entire station," Krister said in a low voice, loud enough so she could hear. "Now, how is that possible?"

Avril thought for a moment. Turning sideways, she said, "Because the person who killed her knew exactly where to do it."

"Exactly. There's only one problem. How did the killer know she'd be standing there?"

Murmuring over her shoulder. "Maybe he was with her. He could've picked the spot, walked her there. Then, when the train approached, shoved her onto the tracks."

"He wasn't. She was alone."

Avril bit her lip. "What about Echo? She was meeting him."

"We didn't spot him on any CCTV at Älvsjö Station," Krister said. "Or Stockholm City, for that matter."

"He must have been there."

Krister shook his head.

"I need to see that surveillance footage," she hissed, under her breath. "I might recognize someone."

"That's what I thought too, but we don't have the time."

She sighed. He was right. Trawling through CCTV footage took hours. Hours they didn't have.

Krister frowned. "Maybe you should get out, Avril? After what happened to Runa—"

"I can't." She turned her gaze to his, only briefly. "You said yourself, if I don't go back, the whole case is blown. We're close, Krister. I can sense it. As soon as they give us the specifics of the attack, you can pull me out."

He hesitated. "Please be careful."

"I will."

He's onto you.

If that note referred to Rook, she was handling that. She just wished she knew what had transpired after the memorial service. Without Runa, she had no inside track on what was happening in the cell.

"I'd better go" Krister mumbled.

The bartender was looking at Avril. "Want something else?"

She'd been nursing the same beer since she'd gotten there. "No, thanks."

He shrugged and went to serve someone else. When Avril turned back, Krister was gone.

STILL IN HER black dress and coat from the memorial service, Avril walked the last few blocks home. The temperature was still hovering around freezing. If spring was coming, it was taking it's time about it.

She climbed the drafty stairs and walked along the corridor to her apartment door—slowing down as she approached.

It was open.

Instantly, her hand went to her hip—but of course she wasn't wearing a holster. Her gun and phones were hidden under her mattress. All she had was her purse and the compromised phone.

"Hello?" She nudged the door open with her foot.

"Where have you been?" Echo's voice sounded from inside.

Her heart skipped a beat. Was he here for her?

Did he know?

Cold Legacy

She calculated how fast she could get to the bedroom and grab her weapon before he got to her. Not fast enough. If he was armed, she wouldn't make it.

"Echo?" She peeked around the corner.

"Yeah, it's me. Come in, Astrid. Close the door. We need to talk."

She exhaled, heart leaping into her throat. This was not good.

Avril entered the apartment. Echo was slumped on the sofa, where she'd hidden her gun days ago. His glasses were pushed up into his hair. He looked tired, and for the first time since she'd met him, he seemed rattled.

"What's wrong?" She perched on the edge of the worn armchair across from him.

His eyes burned through her. "Where have you been?"

"I went for a drink on the way home." Leaning forward, she placed her purse on the coffee table. "I was upset. I needed it."

He stared at her. She stayed still, resisting the urge to fidget, but she avoided his gaze. Echo read people too well. If he saw her eyes, he'd know she was lying.

Finally, he glanced away, massaging his forehead. "Something happened tonight. After you left."

"Oh?"

"Fang accused Rook of being an informant."

She frowned. "An informant? As in, talking to the police?"

Echo looked haggard. A flicker of anger—or regret—dimmed the fire in his eyes. "Yes. Fang said Runa saw him getting into a black SUV. Do you know anything about that?"

Avril bit her lip. "Runa did mention she'd seen him get into one a couple of days ago, but I didn't think anything of it. Apparently he comes from a wealthy family. I just assumed he was talking to one of them."

"How do you know about his family?" Echo snapped.

Avril leveled her gaze at him. "Runa told me. She said they didn't get on. I didn't ask why. It's none of my business."

Echo drummed his fingers on the armrest, then nodded slowly. "We checked. He'd been corresponding with the police."

Avril gasped. "What?"

159

Inside, she was elated. Karlsson had come through for her. He'd got his girlfriend to send those encrypted emails.

"Or rather, they'd been emailing him. Instructions. Times, Meet locations."

Avril stared at him. "That's awful."

Echo dragged a hand through his hair. "Of all people to betray me, I never thought it'd be Rook."

"I'm sorry," she said softly. He was really upset by his friend's betrayal.

He gave a dismal shake of his head. "Not your fault. I'm just tired."

He looked it.

"Can I get you a drink?" she asked. "You look like you could use one."

He gazed at her, and something flickered behind his eyes. Longing? Maybe, but it was gone in an instant.

"First Runa. Now Rook. My team's almost halved. It's lucky we found you." He rose slowly. "I'll pull replacements from Thor's cell."

"Rook left?" she asked carefully.

He gave a tight nod. "Yeah. He won't be coming back."

The way he said it turned her blood to ice.

She gulped over a lump in her throat. "I'm sorry to hear that."

"So am I, Astrid. Trust me—so am I."

chapter
thirty-two

As Avril watched Echo command the room, she almost questioned whether his visit the night before had even happened. Gone was the disheveled, rattled man who'd collapsed onto her sofa. In his place stood the messianic orator—the magnetic leader they all believed would change the world.

He spoke with such conviction it was hard to believe he wasn't the top of the Terra Nova hierarchy. But she knew there was someone above him. The true leader. The one nobody saw.

Odin.

If she hadn't met him herself, she'd wonder if he was real.

A sudden thought prickled her skin. Had Odin been the one who pushed Runa under the train? Had he been at the station that morning? It would explain why Echo hadn't appeared on CCTV. Maybe he hadn't been there at all.

Odin could have been anyone. A man in the crowd. A rushed commuter glancing at his watch. A security guard in a hired uniform. A businessman scrolling on his phone.

They'd never know.

Avril exhaled slowly, glancing around the venue. The meeting was being held in the upstairs room of a grimy old bar near the city's business district. The once-glossy wood was dulled by age, the carpet was threadbare and tacky underfoot. The smell of stale beer clung to the walls.

Through the steamed-up windows, she could just make out the skeletal glow of the financial district's skyline.

"Regretfully, one of our own has left us," Echo was saying. Avril turned back to the front.

"You may notice Rook is absent today. His life has taken a different path, and his cause no longer aligns with ours. We wish him well."

Like hell you do.

She didn't know what had become of Rook. All that mattered was he wasn't here to expose her.

"You're all going to have specific tasks in this operation," Echo said, quickly moving on to the imminent attack on the energy corporation headquarters. "I'm going to outline them now."

The atmosphere shifted. No more philosophy. No more rhetoric. This was the moment they'd been waiting for. Avril straightened up, her full attention on Echo.

"Freyja, you'll be the one to access the building and let the team in."

For a moment, she thought he was talking to someone else, except he was looking right at her. Of course, the code name. He hadn't used it last night in her apartment, but he'd been upset then. In public, in the cell, she was Freyja.

Avril had no idea how she was supposed to access the building, but she gave a firm nod. No doubt all would be revealed soon.

"Once you're inside, Thor, Tyr, and Loki will plant the charges. Gaia will oversee wiring and ensure everything's ready for detonation."

Thor and the others gave brief nods of acknowledgment.

Avril inhaled sharply. They were going to use planted explosive devices to blow the building.

"As soon as your part is done, you leave," Echo told them, his voice smooth, almost hypnotic.

Avril glanced at Gaia and felt her skin prickle. The university lecturer nodded, her sharp blue eyes were focused on Echo with a dangerous intensity.

"I'll be in position with the remote trigger, ready to detonate the devices the moment everyone is clear of the building."

By everyone, he meant them.

Not Nordic Energy's employees. Not the security guards working a late shift. Not the maintenance staff cleaning the offices. They would still be inside when the bombs went off, incinerated in the blast.

A silence stretched through the room. No one flinched.

"We will wipe Nordic Energy off the map," Echo declared, his voice heavy with fervor, as if he were announcing something sacred. There were several nods and murmurs of agreement.

Avril watched him carefully from the back of the room. *He's completely mad,* she thought to herself. But at the same time, she couldn't help but be moved by his intensity.

Echo continued, but didn't give them any more operational information. The meeting broke up, and the two cells filtered out, talking quietly amongst themselves.

"Freyja, a word," Echo called, as she flung her bag over her shoulder.

She turned as he approached. "How do you like the plan so far?"

Was that a leading question? She wasn't sure.

"In theory, it works," she said. "But how am I supposed to get into the building?"

"Simple," he said. "You're going undercover. You're good at that."

She froze. "Excuse me?"

"You're going to go in as a temp. I've arranged for you to get a job on the cleaning staff."

"Oh, I see." She studied him, almost too afraid to ask. "How do you know I'll be any good at it?"

"I just mean you've got nerves of steel. You've managed to successfully complete all the other tasks asked of you. I know I can count on you for this too."

She straightened. "Yes, you can. When is it happening?"

He held up a hand. "We haven't confirmed the date yet."

We, being him and Odin.

"But when we do, you'll be one of the first to know. I'll sign you up with the agency a day or two before the attack, but you'll need to be ready. Can you close the bookstore for a few days?"

"That shouldn't be a problem," she said.

"Good." His gaze lingered. "How are you holding up?"

She shrugged. "Okay. I didn't know Runa that well, but I liked her, and we'd gotten close in the last few weeks since our arrest."

A sympathetic nod. "I understand. It's always unsettling when people are not who we think they are."

Was he talking about Runa now, or Rook?

Or her?

The problem with Echo, Avril decided as she left the bar, was that he always spoke in riddles. You were never quite sure what he meant.

BACK AT HER FLAT, Avril wasted no time in calling Krister.

"I've just come from a meeting," she said. "I know how they're going to attack Nordic Energy."

"How?"

She explained everything—Echo's plan, the cleaning job, the explosives, Gaia's role. "I don't know which agency yet," she added, "but it'll be one they already use."

"I'll check," Krister said.

"You're not seriously going to let them go ahead with this?" Avril asked.

"We don't have enough to arrest them yet," he said, frustration tightening his voice. "We need something solid. A conversation isn't enough—prosecutors will want evidence that proves intent beyond a doubt."

"You mean like actually planting the devices?"

"Acquiring them, at least. Failing that, we'll have to catch them in the act."

"Echo will be outside with the remote detonator. If he triggers it before we can stop him..." She didn't need to finish. Krister knew exactly what that meant.

"We will have officers stationed all around the building. Echo will need to be in range to use a radio detonator, so we'll find him."

"I hope you're right," she murmured.

Otherwise they were all history.

Avril was about to hang up when Krister said, "I have some other news you'll want to hear."

Something in his tone made her stomach tighten. "Yeah?"

"Rook's body washed up today in Lake Mälaren."

The blood drained from her face. A cold, hollow feeling opened up in her chest.

"Rook's dead?" she croaked.

Krister grunted. "Someone did a real number on him too. His body was covered in bruises, he had several broken bones, and he was missing two fingers on his left hand."

Her vision blurred at the edges. The room swayed. She sank into the nearest chair.

"Oh, God."

"Looks like he was tortured."

Bile burned her throat. She bent over, sucking in deep, measured breaths, willing the nausea away.

"Avril? Are you okay?"

She wasn't. Not even close.

They'd killed him.

Not just killed him—but made him suffer.

Because of her.

She pressed a trembling hand to her forehead, forcing herself to sit up straight. She couldn't break now.

"Avril, talk to me."

Her voice was barely a whisper. "I didn't think they'd actually kill him."

"Wait. You knew about this?"

"They thought he was a snitch," she whispered.

"A snitch? Why would they think that?" His voice dropped to a low whisper. "Avril, what did you do?"

"I got Karlsson to send him a bunch of emails. Fake instructions. Enough to make it look like he was feeding information to the police."

"What?" Krister exploded. "Jesus, Avril. What are you trying to do? Get yourself killed?"

"No." Her grip tightening around the phone. "I was trying to save the operation. Rook was onto me. He was going to expose me if I didn't get rid of him first. So I played him at his own game."

"You planted evidence," he hissed.

"I did what I had to do."

Silence stretched between them.

Avril tried to rationalize it. Rook wasn't a traitor. He hadn't deserved this. But it would have been him or her.

"Did he have proof you were undercover?"

"I saw it in his eyes," she said. "And there was the note."

A pause. "What note?"

She hesitated. "Someone slipped a note under the bookstore door. It said: 'He's onto you.'"

A loud thump on the other end told her he'd slammed his hand against the desk.

"Why didn't you tell me?"

"There wasn't time," she lied. "Besides, what does it matter now? Rook told me he didn't believe me. He said he was close to finding out who I was. If I hadn't acted, it'd be my body they'd be pulling out of that lake right now."

Krister was silent.

"I'll contact you when I know more," Avril said. With a heavy heart, she hung up the phone.

chapter
thirty-three

ENOUGH WAITING AROUND. TWO PEOPLE WERE DEAD, AN energy conglomerate was under threat, and Avril was done playing cat-and-mouse with Echo, Odin, and their band of misfits.

It was time to push back.

Digging through Runa's things had given her a lead. A utility bill made out to Jens Holst had an address on it. Runa had obviously handled the finances.

And so, that morning, Avril locked up the bookstore, pulled on her beanie and thick scarf, and set off.

Fang lived in a modern high-rise in central Stockholm, a far cry from the budget, rundown apartment she lived in. Through the tinted street-level windows, she spotted a state-of-the-art gym, a concierge and a vast lobby.

The gym made sense. Fang was former military, and now worked nightclub security, so he would prioritize keeping his body at peak condition. There wasn't much work for dishonorably discharged soldiers, though. Not unless you had the right connections. So how was he able to afford this? Was it thanks to Echo and the organization?

A coffee shop across the street provided the perfect vantage point. Avril ordered a coffee, claimed a booth with a clear line of sight to the lobby doors, and settled in to wait. Three quarters of an hour later, the glass doors opened, and Fang emerged. He wore a black puffer jacket, jeans and bright orange running shoes that clashed with the rest of his outfit. They made him stand out against the dull, gray backdrop of the street. Blending in clearly wasn't his priority today.

Or maybe he just never imagined he would be followed.

Fang wasted no time in setting off, taking giant strides. Leaping up from her table, Avril darted out of the café in pursuit. She kept well back, trying to blend into the remnants of the work crowd. At nine thirty, it was thinning out, but there were still enough people to give her cover.

Fang crossed an intersection, turned down a narrow street, and kept going. He didn't let up the pace, and Avril was panting to keep up. What was the hurry?

Then, she found out.

Echo.

Avril ducked into the shadowed alcove of a doorway. Echo stood outside a betting shop, hands in his pockets, watching Fang approach.

She frowned as she flattened herself against the door. A betting shop? Not exactly the kind of place she'd imagined Echo frequenting. The two men shook hands. Echo clasped Fang's arm, and said something to him that she couldn't hear before they stepped inside the shop.

Was this where Echo worked? Where he lived?

She surveyed the apartments above. Rundown brickwork, a faded red awning over the store, peeling window frames. What was the connection?

Making a note of the address, she set a mental reminder to ask Krister to check it out. He'd be able to find out who owned the apartments, or if they were rental accommodations.

She edged forward, careful to stay out of sight, and studied the building's façade. The sign on the awning read "Bet Mecca." No secondary branding, no promotional posters in the window.

Beside it, the door to the upstairs apartments was unmarked, except for a faded buzzer panel with peeling stickers where names should have been. It was a suitably nondescript building. The kind of place she'd imagine Echo might live.

Avril didn't loiter for long. Echo had sharp eyes, and he'd caught her following him once before. Backing away, she ducked into a nearby bookstore. It was warm and inviting, with low lighting and soft classical music playing through ceiling speakers. She pretended to browse while keeping an eye on the street.

What was Echo discussing with Fang?

Was he tightening security now that Rook had been exposed? Vetting a replacement?

Or arranging another hit?

Her.

The last possibility sat heavy in her gut.

One thing she didn't believe was that that Fang had killed Runa. He'd been too upset by her death to have any hand in it. No, she was pretty sure Echo had outsourced that task to someone else. Someone who wouldn't be identified by the CCTV cameras at the station.

Rook's body, however, bore all the earmarks of someone heavy-handed. Tortured, beaten, damaged. Someone paid to wield violence when necessary. Rook had been necessary.

Avril worked through the scenario in her head. Echo, acting as proxy for Odin, would have attempted to find out what Rook had told the law enforcement officers he'd been in contact with—and he'd have used Fang to do it.

Ironically, any national security agency would do exactly the same thing when trying to elicit information from a traitor or an enemy.

Avril left the bookstore and went to a nearby Lebanese restaurant to get something to eat. She wasn't hungry but needed somewhere to sit and wait. Whatever they were discussing, it warranted a good chunk of time.

She had just finished and was nursing a cup of peppermint tea when she saw the door to the betting shop open and Fang and Echo came out. They shook hands, turned, and walked in opposite directions.

Avril was ready.

Sneaking out, she watched both of them for a few seconds, then took off after Echo. She already knew where Fang lived. Echo was the one she wanted to find out about.

Extra cautious now, she tailed him for a block. For most of that time, he was on his phone talking to an unknown contact, oblivious to the fact he was being followed.

Then he stopped, turned, and looked up and down the street. Avril was ready. She sidestepped into an archway, immediately cast in shadow. A group of people hovered in front of her, providing a natural screen. There was no way he'd seen her.

She watched, waiting for something to happen. He glanced down at his phone, up again, and then narrowed his gaze as a black Mercedes swooped to a stop beside him. Squinting, Avril tried to make out the license plate.

Without a word, the door opened, and Echo slid inside. Avril groaned in frustration. She was going to lose him. Then, a taxi came to a halt right in front of the arch. A woman got out, thanked the driver and thrust some money through the window.

Avril glanced at the car containing Echo driving down the road and made a split-second decision. She darted out. "Are you free?"

The driver nodded.

She hopped in, pointing through the front windshield.

"Follow that Mercedes."

chapter
thirty-four

ECHO TURNED TO THE MAN SITTING IN THE BACK SEAT OF the car. "As-salaamu 'alaykum," he said respectfully. "How are the preparations coming along?"

The man, stocky, dark-eyed, and sharp-featured, didn't immediately reply. He glanced out the window and scanned the street. In the terror business, paranoia was second nature. His suit was impeccable, probably Savile Row, but it couldn't disguise the tension in his shoulders, or the loaded intensity in his gaze.

"On schedule," he said, his Arabic accent crisp but not heavy. He'd been educated in the West—Echo could tell by the English inflections on some words. "You?"

"Taken care of." Echo met his gaze evenly. "The groundwork is done. We'll be inside as planned with no issues."

The man nodded slowly. "Good. We need precise placement of the device."

"We've already mapped the interior," Echo said. "The structural weak points, the highest-density areas, and, of course, where the press will be stationed."

The man nodded. "We want maximum impact."

"And you'll get it. Do you have the package?"

The man shifted, pulling a slim, hard-shell case from beside him and placing it on his lap. He unlatched it and opened the lid, revealing a single laptop. It appeared ordinary at first glance, but beneath the false battery compartment and modified casing were carefully embedded components. Compact circuit boards, a lithium battery rigged as a power source, and a small plastic explosive charge, expertly molded to avoid detection.

Echo studied the device.

"It's configured with a dual triggering system," the man said. "Remote detonation via encrypted signal, and a timed failsafe in case anything goes wrong."

"It won't."

The man considered him for a moment, then nodded. "What about the distraction you mentioned?"

"In play," Echo assured him. "Our friends are fully committed."

There was a pause, then a satisfied nod. "Then all that remains is the execution."

Echo nodded. "And my payment."

Without a word, the man reached down, retrieved a compact black laptop from under the seat, and opened it on his knees. The screen glowed faintly as he navigated to a secure banking interface. With practiced ease, he keyed in a few commands, pausing only to glance at Echo.

"Now you have half, as per our agreement," he said, fingers still moving. "The rest will be in your account the day after the attack—assuming everything goes according to plan."

Echo tipped his head. "It will be a moment the world cannot ignore."

The dark eyes blazed. "Indeed."

They sat in silence for a moment, the weight of what they were planning hanging in the air. Outside, the city bustled, oblivious. People going about their lives, heading home from work, picking up groceries, laughing into their phones. A world that, in just over a week, would be irrevocably changed.

The Mercedes pulled into an underground garage beneath an unassuming commercial building. Echo got out, his shoes clicking against the concrete. "We won't speak again."

The man clasped his hand firmly. "Fi aman Allah," he said. May you be in God's protection.

Echo gave a slight nod.

Then he turned and walked toward an unmarked door that led to the stairwell. He didn't need to look back to know the man was watching him leave.

The plan was in motion. It couldn't be stopped now.

TWENTY MINUTES LATER, Echo stepped into his apartment, locking the door behind him. The sleek, minimalist space was a welcome relief to the grimy chaos of the city. He made himself a coffee and walked to the window, gazing at the skyline.

Rook's betrayal had hit him—and the organization—hard. Talk about bad timing. The cyber-security expert had denied any involvement with the police, but those emails were irrefutable. Although unsigned, they'd come from a legitimate police server.

Rook had claimed he was being set up, but the emails couldn't be faked, no matter how good someone was. He'd denied getting into that SUV, denied talking to the cops. And if it was just hearsay, Echo might have been tempted to believe him, but the emails were damming.

Before he'd died, Rook had told them he was being set up. Even insinuated Astrid may have had something to do with it.

"You're making a mistake trusting her," he'd warned, before Fang had delivered the final blows. Except he couldn't explain why. It was just a feeling. Totally unsubstantiated.

Rook had it out for Astrid from the start.

He thought about her innocence, her grief, her passion—all wrapped up in a petite package decorated with clear blue eyes and a platinum blond bow.

Was she keeping secrets?

Regardless, the new recruit was integral to his plan. He needed her to give the rest of the team access to the Nordic Energy corporate headquarters, then it wouldn't matter...

In a week and a half, he'd be sitting on a beach somewhere, sipping margaritas and thinking about the millions in his Swiss bank account.

Astrid, Odin and Terra Nova? He wouldn't give a fuck.

Not anymore.

chapter
thirty-five

KRISTER TAPPED HIS FINGERS IMPATIENTLY AGAINST THE desk as the system processed the license plate number Avril had sent him.

The seconds dragged on.

He leaned back in his chair, eyes drifting toward the cluttered whiteboard—their working case file for Terra Nova. It was a tangled mess of interconnecting lines, pinned photos, and scribbled notes. Names, locations, possible connections. With a big question mark in the middle.

Who was Odin?

The printer whirred. The results were in. He reached for the paper and scanned the entry.

"What?" he muttered out loud. They were diplomatic plates.

He sat back, confused. The vehicle was registered to the Kazakhstani embassy.

What the hell was Echo doing meeting with diplomats from Kazakhstan?

He searched for what he knew about the oil-rich nation. Kazakhstan had deep economic ties to Europe, and their state-owned energy companies had long been embroiled in corruption scandals, bribing politicians and strong-arming their way into oil and gas markets.

Was the Kazakh government backing Terra Nova?

But why? What was their aim?

To eliminate the competition? Corporate sabotage?

No doubt the collapse of Nordic Energy would open up opportunities for their competitors. Was that the game?

He sighed and rubbed his grainy eyes. With every new bit of evidence, this case got more and more complicated.

He added the information to an encrypted email and prepared to send it to Carl Lindholm. This was in their ballpark. Not his. They might be able to find out more. Before he could hit send, Freddie whispered, "Head's up."

He looked up.

His boss, Superintendent Leif Sundström, strode in, the hard set of his jaw making Krister's stomach sink. "Krister, a word in my office." Then he strode out again.

Shit. Now what?

He met Freddie's gaze and shrugged as he followed his boss out. Once in the neat, corner office on the same floor, Sundström turned to him. "I'm getting pressure from above to pull you off this investigation."

Krister's heart sank. "Which investigation? I'm working two homicides, as well as the undercover op with Säpo."

"That one," he grunted.

"Säpo want us off the case? It was them who asked for our help in the first place."

"I'm aware of that, but things have changed."

Krister tensed. "I can't pull Avril out now. She's close to getting us something on the attack."

Sundström sighed. He wasn't an unreasonable man, just at the mercy of those above him in the police hierarchy. "They don't want to pull her out, they want to take over. She's going to get a new handler. You're out."

Krister stared at him. "Sir, that's not going to work. You know what Avril is like. She needs… special handling."

She needed him.

"That's not our problem. She's an experienced FBI Special Agent, she will adapt. That's what she's been trained to do."

"She's not an undercover operative," he reminded him.

A shrug. "Regardless, it's out of my hands. You will no longer contact Avril Dahl while she is undercover. Do you hear me?"

Krister hesitated. To Säpo, Avril was just a pawn, useful for as long as she provided intelligence, disposable the moment she outlived her purpose. They weren't interested in keeping her safe. They weren't interested in her at all. They only cared about taking down Terra Nova.

"I'm serious, Krister. We don't have the time or the budget for this, and we sure as hell don't have the jurisdiction. This is not our fight."

His pulse pounded in his ears. "This isn't just about terrorism. There's something bigger happening here. Nordic Energy, the diplomatic link—"

"What diplomatic link?" Sundström interrupted.

Krister inhaled. "Avril saw Echo climb into a Mercedes Benz. She got the plates. It's registered to the Kazakhstani Embassy."

"Have you told Säpo?"

"I was just about to."

Sundström folded his arms across his chest. "Do it, and then you shut it down."

"What about Gustav Holmgren and Runa Wiklund's murders? They're connected to Terra Nova."

Sundström exhaled sharply, rubbing his temple like he was already tired of this conversation. "Säpo's taking over full control. We're done here."

Krister knew there was no point in arguing. Pulse pounding in his ears, he turned and left the Superintendent's office.

"ARE THEY SERIOUS?" Freddie blurted out once Krister had told them what had happened.

"Yeah, but Säpo isn't concerned about finding out who killed Runa, or Gustav Holmgren for that matter. Their focus is Terra Nova and the terrorist attack. Once they've brought them down, they'll let us move in and pick up the pieces."

"It'll be difficult to build a case against the perpetrators at that stage," Karlsson pointed out, and he wasn't wrong.

"I know." Krister hesitated. "I'm not backing off now. Avril is close, she said so herself. There's no way she'll work with anybody else, so we keep going. When we have a date, we'll share that intel with Säpo. Until then, we keep investigating the two homicides. We'll just have to keep it under wraps."

Both colleagues nodded.

Krister turned to Freddie. "Did you manage to talk to Gustav Holgren's kids?"

"Yeah, the son, Morten, is a big shot at Nordic Energy. He's being groomed to take over the company, and the board are talking about electing him to President."

Krister raised an eyebrow. "He got protection?"

"Yep, they all have, except the daughter. She works in Upsala. She refused when they asked her."

"What does she do?" Krister asked.

"School teacher. Isn't close with her father and only visits her mother occasionally. She did go after her father died, like Mrs. Holmgren said."

"Why wasn't she close to her father?" Krister's gaze slanted.

Freddie consulted his notes. "Because he's a selfish, misogynistic pig and she wants nothing to do with him—and I'm quoting."

Karlsson whistled. "No love lost there, then."

Indeed. That was very interesting.

"Can we get a warrant for the wife's cell data, as well as her bank accounts?" Krister asked.

"Not now we've been pulled off the case," Freddie said.

"Nobody knows we've been pulled off—yet." Krister reasoned. "Who's to say we didn't apply for it before I spoke with the Chief?"

Freddie broke into a grin. "I'll see what I can do."

chapter
thirty-six

AVRIL SAT IN HER LIVING ROOM, THE TELEVISION DRONING in the background. The news presenter was covering the upcoming World Summit, set to take place in Stockholm over the weekend—a meeting of world leaders to discuss economic policies, global security, and geopolitical alliances.

The stakes were high. Several major nations were on the brink of a new trade war, while others were pushing for sanctions over mounting international tensions. The world was watching, waiting to see if diplomacy would hold or if fractures between global powers would deepen.

Security was tight. No-fly zones had been established, and armed patrols were stationed at key locations. Social media was already buzzing with speculation. Would this be the summit where everything changed?

Her phone beeped, cutting through the noise. This was her real phone, not the burner. That could only mean one thing.

Echo.

Picking it up, she muted the television and read the message.

Kafé Tystnad, Slussgatan 7, Södertälje. 6PM Friday.

That was tomorrow.

There were no explanations, no instructions—just a place and a time. Avril blew out a slow breath. Maybe tomorrow they'd be given the date of the attack.

. . .

The address led Avril to a part of Södertälje she'd never been to before. A crumbling parade of stores—mostly pawn shops, a kebab take-out, and a liquor store with an epileptic neon sign. She walked past a massage parlor with blacked-out windows before spotting the café.

At six o'clock, it was still open. Geared toward people who drank coffee at all hours because they had nowhere else to go.

She pushed open the door and stepped inside.

The air smelled like burnt toast and old fryer grease. A couple of elderly men sat hunched over newspapers, coffee mugs in front of them. No one looked up as she entered.

Avril spotted Gaia sitting at the back. Next to her, Fang slouched, half-asleep, arms crossed over his chest. At another table, Thor sat with the participating members of his cell. She recognized some of them from the party.

Avril slid into the booth. "What's going on?"

Fang opened his eyes and grunted. He'd obviously had a late night bouncing at the club where he worked. Gaia shook her head. "Don't know. We're waiting for Echo."

As if on cue, the door creaked open and the man himself strode in, signature coat billowing behind him.

He scanned the café, his glasses catching the light. Then, his sharp, predatory gaze settled on them. He approached, halting between the two tables.

"Listen carefully," he said in a low voice. No preamble, no small talk. "We've been given the go-ahead. It's happening this weekend."

Electricity buzzed through the group. Fang, fully awake now, straightened up. Gaia gazed up at him, instantly alert. Thor was the only one who didn't appear surprised.

"We're going dark," Echo continued, meeting her gaze. "As of now, none of you are to go home. No outside contact. No phones." His eyes flicked to each of them in turn. "Until this is over, you do not exist."

Avril swallowed. She'd left her burner at home, but she had her legitimate phone with her. "Where are we staying?" she asked.

"There's a hotel next door. I've booked us all rooms."

It was a lockdown.

Avril had no doubt they'd be locked in, or at the very least supervised twenty-four seven. No one would be permitted to leave.

Echo glanced toward the door. "Finish your coffees and leave your devices on the table. We're leaving, now."

No one argued.

One by one, they drained their mugs, placed their phones on the table, and slid out of the booth. Avril followed them onto the street, her pulse racing.

This was not good. There was no time to warn Krister. No way of contacting him.

Thank goodness she'd told him about the meeting, hastily firing off a text with the address before she'd set out. That way, he'd know where she had gone when she didn't check in later.

They followed Echo a next door to an old hotel that looked like it was stuck in the seventies. Feeling desperate, Avril stuck her hand into her purse and felt around. Inside was her fake credit card, a loyalty card to a nearby grocery store, and a couple of bank notes. Grabbing the credit card, she dropped it against the wall, just before they were ushered inside.

Nobody noticed.

The walls were a shade of nicotine-stained beige. Above them, the overhead light hummed, casting a sickly glow over the cracked linoleum floor. A vending machine glowed in the corner, half-stocked with candy bars and bottled water that probably cost twice as much as anywhere else.

Without so much as a nod toward the grey-haired man at the reception desk, Echo led them upstairs. Fang remained in the lobby. It wasn't to guard them, it was to prevent them from leaving.

As Avril stepped inside the dingy room she was sharing with Gaia, a cold weight settled in her gut. There was no going back now.

"I'll be in to speak to each of you in turn," Echo said, ominously, his gaze lingering on all of them.

Avril shivered, but it wasn't from the cold. She didn't like surprises, and the evening had taken a sinister turn.

This weekend.

Somehow, she had to get a message to Krister. But how, with Gaia watching her every move?

They settled into their room, Gaia opting for the bed closest to the door, leaving Avril to take the one near the sealed window. Was that so she couldn't sneak out in the night?

The hotel had air conditioning, not that it was needed, but consequently, none of the windows opened. There was no way of escape.

Claustrophobic and jittery, Avril said she needed to use the bathroom, but in reality, she needed some alone time to pull herself together. Perching on the toilet seat, head in her hands, she tried to work out what to do next.

Would Krister figure out where they'd gone? Would he find her credit card and be able to trace her to the hotel? It was a stretch, and she couldn't count on that.

Maybe someone at the café had seen the direction they'd gone in? Would he check the CCTV in the street? When she didn't contact him, he would.

The thought gave her hope. Krister was resourceful. He'd find her.

AN HOUR TICKED BY. Avril wished she'd brought a book with her, or something to help kill the time. With no phones, they were left to talk amongst themselves or lie quietly alone with their thoughts. Still, it gave her time to think.

Eventually, when the sky had turned black outside the curtainless window, Echo made an appearance. Avril thought he looked tired, but then he'd probably spoken to several other members before he'd gotten to them. The responsibility of what lay ahead was weighing on him too.

Gaia, who'd been dozing, immediately sat up on the bed. Avril, who'd been sitting at the small table by the window, turned to face him.

"Sorry for the subterfuge," he said, but his expression was anything but apologetic. He was all business now, his posture tight and controlled. Avril noticed he held stapled sheets of paper in his hand. "It was necessary to prevent leaks. After what happened with Rook, we can't be too careful."

Gaia nodded sagely, while Avril just stared at him, saying nothing.

"Okay, let me get to your parts."

They both leaned forward, listening intently.

He placed a grubby plastic ID on the table in front of her. "Freyja, this is your employment card. It will give you access to the building. Fang will deliver your uniform later."

Before she could ask how, he continued, "You'll go in with the rest of the cleaning staff at seven tomorrow morning. The office should be relatively empty on a Saturday. The delivery entrance is at the back—that's where you'll let the rest of the team in." He placed the sheets of paper in front of her. "You can study the layout here."

She gave a nod and looked down at the schematics.

"Once they're inside, Gaia will take over." He turned to the older woman. "You'll show them where to plant the explosives. You've seen the schematics. We want to cause as much damage as possible."

"Gotcha."

"What if there are people inside?" Avril asked, then bit her tongue.

Shit, she was supposed to be a ruthless activist, not a nervous beginner concerned with other people's safety.

Echo gave her a sharp look.

"I just mean they might see something," she corrected, scrambling to correct her mistake. "We don't want anyone reporting us or alerting security."

He nodded. "I see your point. Gaia will handle that. It is not your concern." He hesitated, then said, "After you've let the team in, you need to leave."

He was giving her an out. Ensuring that she wasn't anywhere near the place when the devices detonated. Or maybe she was mistaking his altruism for paranoia. Perhaps he didn't want her around to compromise the op. Get cold feet or develop a conscience.

"How long do we have?" Gaia asked.

"A couple of hours, then it's show time."

He wasn't giving them the exact time of detonation. It could be while they were in there, it could be mid-morning or even during the afternoon. He wouldn't wait too long, though, for fear of the devices being discovered.

Then, everyone left in the building would be extinguished—unless Krister and the counterterrorism officers could get to Echo before he pushed the button.

Except they didn't know when.

Her heart sank.

It was going to be a massacre, and she had no way of stopping it.

chapter
thirty-seven

KRISTER WATCHED AVRIL WALK INSIDE THE DINGY HOTEL and frowned.

What the hell?

He sank lower in the driver's seat of the unmarked Volvo.

After his discussion with Sundström, he'd needed air. Needed time to think.

Taking one of the pool cars meant for surveillance ops, he'd found himself driving to the address Avril had sent him. It was both an act of defiance and a need to look out for her, now that they'd theoretically been pulled off the case. He still hadn't contacted Säpo with her details. Hadn't told them about the burner phone.

He should, but that could wait until tomorrow.

Right now, he was hoping to talk to her, tell her she had a new handler, but that he would still be there. Still have her back.

He'd arrived just in time to see her leave the café with a group of people, some of whom he recognized as members of Echo's cell and go into a nondescript hotel next door. He saw her dig into her purse, then her hand swung just a little too deliberately, and something small and dark fell onto the pavement.

Frowning, he waited until the little group had disappeared inside, and then cautiously got out of his car and crossed the street. He kept his pace casual, his coat pulled up against the cold. No one paid him any attention. At this time of the evening, they all had somewhere better to be.

As he passed the door to the hotel, he saw the hulking figure of Fang prowling around inside. It looked like he was guarding the entrance, providing protection for the group inside.

Keeping out of his line of sight, Krister bent to pick up the dropped item and saw it was a credit card. Avril's credit card—in her alias's name.

She'd been trying to send him a message.

He knew how her mind worked.

She'd already told him where the café was. When she didn't check in afterwards, he'd wonder where she was. He'd come looking, and hopefully, find the card.

It was a smart move, but a risky one. What if someone else had picked it up? A lot of people passed through this section of town. No guarantees it would be him.

Still, she'd had to try. He knew her burner would be back at the apartment, which left her with no other way of contacting him.

He stared inside the dimly lit hotel at the reception desk. A middle-aged man with greasy gray hair sat at the desk watching something on a computer or television screen beneath the counter. Chubby arms folded across his chest, he hadn't looked up once. Wasn't concerned there was a security guard in his lobby. That meant he was either being paid to turn a blind eye, or he was in on it. Krister was betting the former.

He strolled along to the café and took a look inside. A white-haired group of men played backgammon at a corner table, an old timer hunched over a cup of coffee, and two guys in dirty overalls tucked into greasy burgers and chips. The waiter, a gangly kid with long hair and bad skin, looked up as Krister entered.

"Hey." Krister flashed the kid his ID badge. "Got a minute?"

The kid shrugged. "Guess so."

Customer service obviously wasn't a top priority in this place.

Krister leaned in slightly. "I'm looking for some people. They met here earlier."

The kid frowned. "I don't know, man. I really—"

Krister pulled a photo up on his phone—one Avril had snapped a week ago of Echo. So far no facial recognition software had told them who he was. "Recognize this guy?"

The kid stared at it for a beat, then gave a nod. "He was in here earlier with a bunch of other people."

"You know him?" Krister asked.

"Nah. Never seen him before today."

"He's not a regular?"

A shake of the head.

"What about this guy?" Krister showed him a photograph of Fang.

The kid gave another nod. "Yeah, man. That guy was ripped. Looked like a bodybuilder or something."

"What about her?" He showed the kid a photo of Avril.

Another nod.

"Did you see where they went?"

"Out the door."

Krister sighed. No wonder the kid was working in this shitty place. "I was hoping you'd be more specific than that?"

"Nah, once they leave, that's it. I don't care where they go."

"You didn't overhear any of their conversation?" He gave the kid a hard look. "It's important."

The kid hesitated, then said, "I may have heard snippets, but only because I was clearing a nearby table."

Krister nodded. "Go on."

"I heard the first guy say something about it happening this weekend and that they were all checking into a hotel. Then they downed their drinks and walked out, leaving their cell phones on the table." He shook his head at the crazy behavior.

Krister tried to understand. "Whoa, go back to that first part. He definitely said it was happening this weekend?"

"Yeah."

"Did he say *what* was happening?"

"Not that I heard, but I wasn't there for very long. I cleaned up and went back to the kitchen. None of my business what the customers talk about, even if they walk out and leave their phones behind."

"What happened to them?" Krister asked. "The phones, I mean?"

"Some guy came in, put them in a bag, then left."

"What did he look like?"

"I don't know, man. Average height, brown hair, kinda stocky. Normal looking."

Great, that described half the men in Stockholm.

"They didn't say anything else?"

"That's all I heard." The kid looked over his shoulder. "Listen, man. I gotta get back to work."

Krister nodded and let him go.

He left the café deep in thought. Was the terrorist attack happening this weekend? Is that what Echo had meant? He turned right and walked back toward the hotel. Was that why they were all holed up here? Because Echo couldn't risk them divulging the details of the attack to anybody else. A slip of the tongue here, a drunken brag there. It was too risky.

He had to figure out if the attack was taking place on Saturday or Sunday, and what time.

Saturday would be his first guess, although the weekend was a strange time to do it, particularly if you were aiming for maximum damage. The building would be emptier than during the week.

Krister crossed the street back to his car, glancing up at the hotel. Four floors of windows overlooked the street. Was she in one of them?

Now it made sense why Fang was guarding the lobby. Not for protection, but to prevent anyone leaving. Until the attack, the activists were locked down—for the safety of the operation.

That meant Krister wasn't going anywhere either.

As long as Avril was inside that hotel, he would be out here, watching, waiting for them to make their move.

Settling down to wait, Krister reached for his phone and called Lindholm.

chapter
thirty-eight

THE EVENING WORE ON. AVRIL MADE POLITE CONVERSATION with Gaia, nodding along as the older woman talked about her university days, her disillusionment with the system, and how academia had become nothing more than a puppet for corporate interests.

Avril wasn't really listening.

Her mind was elsewhere. On the locked door, on the cell phones that had been confiscated in the café, on Echo who had seemed even more suspicious than usual. A slow, gnawing anxiety coiled in her gut.

Fang delivered takeout and a small suitcase of clothes. Gaia opened it on the bed and handed her a navy-blue coverall with the cleaning company's logo on the breast pocket. It looked worn, used. She placed it on the chair beside the bed, ready for the morning.

Avril watched as Gaia took out a smart business suit set and hung it up on a hanger in the empty closet. Avril could only assume she'd packed it ahead of time. The environmental scientist had known this day was coming, she just hadn't known when.

They ate, or rather Avril forced down a slice of cold pizza, knowing she'd need the sustenance for what lay ahead, even though she had no appetite. Afterwards, Gaia stretched and said, "I'm going to take a shower. It's been a long day."

Avril forced a smile. "Good idea."

As soon as Gaia disappeared into the small, yellow-lit bathroom and the shower sputtered to life, Avril moved.

She crossed the room swiftly and tried the door handle.

Locked.

She gritted her teeth. Of course.

She had expected as much, but the reality of it still sent a jolt of unease through her. She hadn't heard a key turn, hadn't seen Fang or anyone else secure it—so how the hell had they managed to lock them in?

She exhaled sharply through her nose, pressing her forehead against the cool wood of the door for a second, forcing herself to think.

Then she turned and looked at the only other entry or exit point—the window. Avril walked over to it and looked down. The streets outside were dimly lit, the glow of streetlamps casting long pools of amber light across the wet pavement. The drizzle from earlier had stopped, leaving everything slick and reflective.

She took a step closer. Then another.

A shadow moved below.

Avril's breath hitched.

At first, she thought she was imagining things, but then the figure stilled, positioned right under the glow of the nearest streetlamp.

Tall.

Broad.

Familiar.

Krister.

Her heart slammed against her ribs. She blinked, half-convinced her mind was playing tricks on her. How?

But it was him. She knew his stance, the way he held his weight slightly to one side, phone in hand, pretending to scroll. He wasn't looking at the hotel directly, but she knew he was aware of it. Aware of her.

The rush of elation snapped her out of her daze.

He found me.

The adrenaline sharpened her focus. Somehow, she needed to get a message to him. Spinning around, she scanning the room, searching for something—anything—she could write with. But of course, this wasn't the kind of place that offered complimentary notepads and pens. The drawers were empty, there was nothing in the closet, either. All she found under the bed was dust and an abandoned bottle cap.

Think!

She turned back to the window, pressing her palms against the glass. Was it tinted? From the inside, she could see clearly, but was that the same for someone looking up?

She hesitated, then hurried to the switch by the door and flicked the light on and off several times. Gaia, still in the bathroom, would never know.

After that, she left them on, even the nightstand lamps, blazing brightly. If it was dark outside and bright in here, then he had more chance of seeing her. She darted back to the window and peered down.

Please see me.

Please.

Krister turned, slow and deliberate, his head lifting just enough so that his face was fully illuminated by the streetlamp. He squinted, and for a terrifying moment, Avril thought maybe he'd missed it, or hadn't realized it was her.

But then their eyes locked.

Her stomach flipped.

Slowly, she lifted her hands.

One flat against the glass. The other raised—only her thumb extended. The number six.

Six days.

Saturday.

Tomorrow.

She held the gesture firm, forcing herself to stay still despite the pounding of her pulse.

Did he understand?

The seconds stretched, each one longer than the last. Her arms ached, her fingers pressed so hard against the glass that they tingled.

Krister didn't move.

Then, finally, he did.

His hand came up—casual, almost lazy—and he patted the hood of the car six times. Then he turned, ducked down, and climbed into it.

Avril exhaled shakily, stepping back from the window as her heart continued its frantic rhythm.

He knew.

Krister knew.

chapter
thirty-nine

KRISTER'S CAR DIDN'T MOVE. IT STAYED THERE ALL NIGHT. Every time Avril looked out of the window at the darkened street below, she saw the shadowy figure of her friend inside. One day, when this was over, she'd tell him how much that meant to her, just knowing he was there.

She found it impossible to sleep. It wasn't just the unfamiliar bed, the person breathing softly beside her, or the strange, distant noises of the rundown hotel. It was the weight of knowing that tomorrow she would walk into a building, open a door, and set in motion a chain of events that would lead to mass murder.

So much depended on Krister and the police finding Echo, and putting a stop to the detonation, that her gut was twisted into a painful knot, and she felt vaguely nauseous. What if they didn't find him? What if the bombs went off while the rest of the team were still inside?

It was a very real possibility.

Could they even trust Echo to wait until the team was out of the building and in the clear before he hit the trigger?

Absolutely not, the voice in her head screamed.

It would be far easier to blow them all up, eliminate everyone who had any knowledge of the crime. No loose ends.

After you've let the team in, you need to leave.

So why had he told her she could go?

She didn't flatter herself into thinking it was because he had a soft spot for her. The man wasn't capable of that. He had darkness inside of him, just like the Frost Killer had. She'd seen it in his eyes. Knew the type—a little too well.

He'd kill them all, given half a chance. Like lambs to the slaughter, the rest of the team would follow him blindly. They would give their lives for the cause. They just didn't know it yet.

But she did.

She scowled up at the ceiling in the dark hotel room. Gaia's breathing beside her was even and rhythmic.

How could she sleep? How could any of them?

Gaia was the one who would plant the bombs, the one who would set the timers, ensuring chaos and destruction. How could she live with that?

The hours crawled by, each minute stretching into an eternity.

Avril turned over and stared at the window. The weak glow from the rain-drenched streetlamps didn't extend this far up, and the blanket cloud cover meant she couldn't see any stars. Not a single one.

It was a black night.

AT SOME POINT, she must have drifted off because the next thing she knew, a loud pounding on the door yanked her violently from sleep.

Her pulse lurched. For a split second, she didn't know where she was. Then it slammed into her. The hotel. The attack.

It was today!

The door creaked open before she could even sit up, and Fang filled the frame. "Time to move," he growled. No attempt to lower his voice. No concern for the other guests still sleeping—if there were any. "We leave in thirty minutes."

The room was still cloaked in darkness, the sun refusing to rise on the atrocity they were about to commit.

Gaia yawned and stretched. She looked well-rested. Refreshed, even. Meanwhile, she had barely managed two hours.

"Mind if I take the bathroom first?" Avril croaked, her throat tight.

Gaia waved a hand. "Go ahead."

She padded across the cold floor, locking the door behind her before leaning over the sink.

Breathe.

The face staring back at her in the mirror was deathly pale, her blue eyes were smudged with exhaustion. She turned on the faucet, splashing icy water over her cheeks, gripping the porcelain as she forced herself to get a grip.

This was it.

Today, they would catch Terra Nova in the act.

Today, they would bring them down.

The knot in her stomach twisted tighter.

Breathing out slowly, she patted her face dry, then nodded to herself before exiting the bathroom.

She could do this.

Gaia barely glanced at her as she pulled the suitcase past, disappearing inside to get ready.

Avril moved mechanically, pulling on her jeans and a T-shirt under the navy-blue cleaner's overall that had been delivered last night. It still held the faint scent of its previous owner, which made her think they'd stolen it from an employee. It made sense. If security ran the ID, the name would check out.

She looped the ID around her neck.

Maria Baranowska.

That was who she was today. The real Maria had either been fired or was conveniently missing. She hoped it was the former.

Gaia emerged from the bathroom dressed in a crisp suit, her hair twisted into a sleek chignon. She looked every inch the successful businesswoman, perfectly at ease in a boardroom.

"Ready?" Gaia flashed a confident smile.

How could she be so relaxed?

Avril gave a tight nod. "Yes. Let's do this."

A CAR WAITED OUTSIDE, its engine idling in the predawn chill. Avril hesitated for half a second, scanning the street, but there was no sign of

Krister's vehicle. He must have pulled back, not wanting to arouse suspicion.

Right now, he was probably coordinating with Säpo, mobilizing the counterterrorism teams.

As their car pulled away from the curb, Avril ran through the police procedure in her head. There would be undercover officers disguised as commuters, street sweepers, delivery drivers. Even a coffee vendor or the homeless man on the corner. More in unmarked vehicles. They might even have snipers stationed on rooftops.

All waiting for the signal.

The car dropped them a block away from Nordic Energy's headquarters. Avril got out first, pulling her coat tighter around her like a security blanket. Her pulse ratcheted up as she approached the staff entrance, around the corner from the main entrance.

Something wasn't right. There were way too many people here for a weekend.

Pausing, she surveyed the crowd. People were pouring in. Some alone, some in groups, but they were all headed into the building that in a few hours' time would be blown sky high.

"What's going on?" she asked the security guard, as she flashed her stolen ID.

"There's a symposium on today. Something about new technology —" Avril barely heard the rest.

No, no, no.

Her stomach plummeted.

Echo had known. He had chosen this day for maximum impact. These people weren't employees. They were students, scientists, young professionals. People who had nothing to do with the oil industry.

Her hands balled into fists. She wanted to scream, to grab the attendees by the shoulders and tell them to leave. To run while they still had a chance.

But she couldn't.

A single misstep and she would blow her cover. Blow the entire op.

At least people wouldn't die, the voice on her shoulder said. But they'd never catch Echo—or Odin. They would live to plan another atrocity, one they might execute next time.

Avril clawed at the scratchy collar around her neck, feeling like she was suffocating. The guard let her through, and she proceeded into the building.

She walked across the large, spacious lobby, and made her way to a door that said, Staff Only. Following the layout in her head, she walked down a long corridor that led to the dining hall and kitchen.

She pushed open the door on the right and entered the empty kitchen. Her gaze fell on the loading door at the back. It could only be opened from the inside, like a fire door. There was no access from the outside. She knew from the schematics that it led to a loading dock where food deliveries were made.

Avril took a deep breath and closed her eyes.

Her next move would condemn her.

No choice. They needed this. They needed intent.

Exhaling, she pulled open the door, relishing the icy draft that swept in.

Standing back, she watched as one by one, Thor, Gaia, Fang, and the others slipped inside, backpacks slung over their shoulders.

Stuffed with explosives.

chapter
forty

KRISTER SAT IN HIS UNMARKED CAR, FINGERS DRUMMING against the steering wheel as he watched the entrance to Nordic Energy's corporate headquarters. People were still trickling in—dozens of youngsters, geeky types, all with their ID badges swinging from their lanyards, their faces bright with anticipation.

Most were in their twenties, fresh out of university, their whole lives ahead of them. They were walking into a ticking time bomb. Literally.

He called Lindholm on his private cellphone. "We need to shut it down. Stop the symposium."

Lindholm hesitated. "It's unfortunate there are so many people there today, but I still think we should wait a while longer. Give us a chance to catch the bastard. I've got every counterterrorism agent in Stockholm searching a two-mile radius. He has to be here somewhere."

Krister could hear the stress in his voice, and he got it. They were so close. But there were lives at stake. In his book, that trumped finding a psychotic eco-terrorist.

"Echo won't talk," Krister warned him. From what Avril had told him about the cell leader, he wasn't going to cave, no matter what Säpo did to him. "He won't lead you to Odin."

"We'll see about that," the Säpo agent murmured.

When they had talked last night, Krister had told him he thought it was happening today. Here. What they hadn't realized when they'd planned today's response was that the building would be packed with students.

"It's too risky," Krister persisted, gripping the phone.

Lindholm's voice was firm. "One hour. Give us one hour, and then we'll shut the whole thing down."

Krister sucked in a breath. For all they knew, the devices were already in place. If only he could speak to Avril. She might be able to reassure them, give them more time. But she was still inside. He'd seen her walk up the stairs to the staff entrance in her dark blue cleaner's shirt less than ten minutes ago.

"One hour," he repeated, feeling sick. He only hoped it wasn't too late.

HALF AN HOUR LATER, Krister tapped his earpiece. "Status?"

"No sign of Echo yet," came Lindholm's voice, even more gravelly than before. He sounded strained, as he should. He was playing with fire.

Krister exhaled through his nose, scanning the crowd. Where the hell was Echo? He was about to exit the car and join the search when his phone rang. It was Freddie calling on his private number,

Freddie, Karlsson and Ingrid were in the office, working on the two homicides. Luckily, the Superintendent didn't come in on weekends and so had no knowledge of the latest developments or Krister's involvement in the op. Since Lindholm didn't answer to him, he'd been left out of the loop.

That wouldn't go down well, but Krister figured in this case it was better to ask for forgiveness than permission, which he certainly wouldn't get.

He answered the call. "Krister."

"Boss, we've got an ID on that guy you asked us to look into weeks back," Freddie said. "The facial rec team finally flagged him."

Krister straightened in his seat.

It was the man Avril had mugged, although Krister had never told the rest of the team about that. Officially, the guy was just a person of interest connected to the investigation.

"And?"

"Name's Erik Haldorsson. Facilities manager at the Stockholm International Fairs and Congress Center. He's worked there for four years. Low-level guy, nothing flashy. No criminal record. No known ties to eco-terrorists or other extremist groups."

Krister frowned. That was odd. Avril had said there was a possibility it was a set-up, which meant the man was working with Terra Nova, or at least the Stockholm cell.

"You sure?"

"Yeah. He's clean."

Maybe Avril had been wrong. Maybe it wasn't a setup. He thought about the contents of the briefcase that he'd studied on the cloud. Diagrams, schematics, receipts, but nobody knew what for. Could it be the Convention Center?

There had also been a lanyard with an access card attached.

His blood ran cold. A facilities manager would have unrestricted access to every part of the Convention Center. Another thought hit him. Hadn't Runa met Echo somewhere near the convention center the morning she died?

A "special job," that's what Runa had told Avril.

"Shit," he muttered, gripping the phone.

"What?" Freddie asked.

Was it possible? Had they gotten the wrong location?

A chill descended as the pieces slowly slotted into place.

Krister cleared his throat. "Fred, you and Karlsson get over to the Convention Center. Speak to Security and ask them to pull the surveillance footage from the last week. I want to see if Runa Håkansson entered the building on the day she died."

There was a short silence.

Freddie's voice was taut. "You do realize what today is, right?"

Krister's stomach dropped.

The World Summit.

"The Summit starts in two hours. The entire place is locked down," Freddie continued. "They aren't going to let us near the place."

Fuck.

Heads of state, diplomats, high-ranking officials from NATO, the

EU, and the G7 would be there. The kind of people who made prime terrorist targets.

Krister's pulse pounded. There was no doubt in his mind now.

"We're at the wrong target," he whispered.

"What?" Freddie asked, hesitantly.

Krister swallowed over the bile rising in his throat. The police, Säpo, counterterrorism—all their resources were focused on Nordic Energy, but the real target was on the other side of the city.

The Summit.

He hissed out a breath. Terra Nova had played them perfectly.

Krister thought of the black Mercedes-Benz G-Class Avril had spotted outside the café, the one Echo had been meeting with. The diplomatic plates from Kazakhstan.

At first, he thought their involvement was tied to Nordic Energy. Maybe a competitor trying to eliminate their biggest rival. But that didn't add up. Kazakhstan wasn't interested in Nordic Energy. They had oil. They had power.

They also had growing tensions with the West.

The Summit. That's what this was all about. Western alliances. Sanctions. Trade deals. It was the perfect target.

Krister threw the car into gear and peeled away from the curb, tires screeching. "Meet me at the convention center. Now."

"But—"

"Now. We have to talk to Security. I think they're going to hit the World Summit. That's the real target. Nordic Energy is a decoy."

"What about the explosives?" Freddie asked.

"I suspect they're duds, they were never going to blow up a bunch of tech students."

Freddie exhaled. "But we don't know that for sure."

"I'll call Lindholm, get him to send in the bomb squad in. No reason to wait now."

"Holy shit." Freddie muttered. "We're on our way."

The moment Krister pulled up to the barrier checkpoint, he knew Fred was right. Getting inside was going to be a problem.

Cold Legacy

Armed security was stationed everywhere—both private and government. The U.S. Secret Service was most noticeable with their dark suits, earpieces, and sharp, assessing gazes. He noticed their hands never strayed far from the bulges beneath their jackets. They moved in tight formations, scanning the crowd with an air of controlled aggression, ready to neutralize any threat before it materialized.

He flashed his badge to the security officer at the gate. "Detective Krister Jansson, Regional Police, Serious Crimes Unit. I need to speak to your Head of Security. Now."

The guard blinked. "Not possible, sir. We're on heightened security measures. Only vetted personnel are allowed through."

"How soon are dignitaries arriving?"

"First motorcades start rolling in at eleven. The event begins at midday."

Krister checked his watch. It was just after nine o'clock. That gave them two hours to figure out if this place was wired to blow.

"I understand, but I really need to speak to whoever is in charge," Krister pushed.

The guard frowned. "That would be Anders Holm, the Chief of Security. But he's extremely busy—"

"This is a matter of national security." Krister barked. "I have intel that says you might be a target, and I don't have time for protocol. Now call him."

The guard hesitated, then nodded. "If you'll wait here." He took out his phone and turned his back on them.

Krister scanned the grounds. Not as vast a police presence as he would have expected but then again, he knew why. All counterterrorism units had been diverted to the Nordic Energy building. He spotted a couple of snipers on nearby buildings, but they would be from the Secret Service or other countries' Governmental Agencies, not Swedish.

He turned to survey the building, the sick feeling in his gut intensifying. Runa. The access card. Terra Nova had already been here.

A few moments later, a man in a crisp suit with heavily hooded eyes arrived. He introduced himself as Anders Holm, and despite his air of efficiency, he looked exhausted. There was a lot riding on him, and Krister was just about to ruin his day.

"Detective Jansson, I appreciate your concern, but we've prepared for all possible threats," he said wearily.

"Not for this one, you haven't," Krister told him coldly.

Holm's brow creased. "Excuse me?"

Krister pulled out his phone and held up a surveillance image of Runa from last week. "This woman was inside your building five days ago," he explained. "She didn't have security clearance, but she got in."

Holm's expression darkened. "How?"

"She had a stolen ID badge."

Holm's jaw clenched. "Whose?"

"Probably Erik Haldorsson's. He was mugged the week before and his briefcase stolen."

"Erik was mugged?"

"Didn't tell you about it, eh? Well, if you pull up his employee log, I think you'll find he clocked in at—"

He glanced at Fred who said, "08:23 AM."

"I need to check. Please wait here."

"Oh, no," Krister said. "We're coming with you." He wasn't going to give the Chief of Security any opportunity to cover this up to save his own skin, even though he didn't think he was the type.

Holm hurried across the lobby to an adjoining security room. "Check the entry logs for Monday morning," he barked at the operator, who glanced up in surprise.

As expected, Erik Haldsorsson had checked in at 08:23 AM.

"Now call up the lobby camera for the same time frame."

The operator obliged, and Krister leaned over his shoulder. "Do you see your facilities manager in that footage?"

Holm shook his head, but he'd gone white.

"Who was using his ID?" Holm massaged his temple. "What does it mean?"

Krister fixed his gaze on the man's face. "What it means, Mr. Holm, is that your security team let in a known terrorist—a week before the World Summit."

Holm stopped breathing.

chapter
forty-one

The team filed inside. Avril waited until Thor, the last man, stepped over the threshold before nodding at Gaia.

"Over to you," she said, her voice steady.

Gaia studied her, and for a brief moment, she saw her gaze soften. "Get out of here," she said, her hand on her arm. It was a weird gesture, surprisingly intimate for the hardened activist. "It'll be okay."

Avril looked up but Gaia appeared calm and composed—not at all fazed by the atrocity she was about to commit. Avril didn't understand it. How was inflicting mass murder on all these innocent people okay? She had spent years studying killers, analyzing their psychology, their justifications.

But this? This was something else.

"Why are you still here?" Thor barked, scowling at her. She noticed he was chewing gum. It smelled minty, vaguely familiar.

Annoyed, she said, "I'm going."

He stood there watching her as she stepped outside, and pulled the door closed behind her. For a moment, she didn't move.

How could she walk away from this?

How could she not do anything?

Thor had been adamant. He'd wanted her gone.

For a moment there, she'd been catapulted back to the museum where she'd met Odin. She recalled how he'd stepped closer and she'd felt his body heat. She'd also smelled a whiff of the same gum.

"Don't be ridiculous," she muttered, as she turned and walked away from the building. "A lot of people chew gum. It's a coincidence."

Except, like Krister, she didn't believe in them.

Could Thor have been the man standing behind her at the museum? She stopped moving and stared at the sidewalk, pulse racing. His voice was similar, but not the same. Still, he could have been putting that on.

Could Thor be Odin?

It sounded impossible, but actually, what did she really know about the mysterious leader of Terra Nova? He was smart. He was manipulative. It wouldn't surprise her if he'd been part of their little group all the time. Watching them from the inside, monitoring their every move, waiting for someone to slip up.

Back at the museum, she hadn't seen his face. Hadn't turned around. At the Zoom meeting he'd been blurred out, his voice disguised.

She caught her breath. Thor hadn't been at that meeting. They hadn't been introduced to the second cell yet. Could he have been the shady figure on the screen?

The hairs on her neck stood up. The more she thought about it, the more sense it made.

Odin could be one of them.

She set off again, deep in thought. Thor. Really?

Something was still off. Thor might be passionate and dedicated to the cause, but he came across as a big thug, not a manipulative mastermind.

She bit down on her lip. Of course, he could just be a very good actor. She shook her head and worked through the sequence of events. It was Echo who had told her she was meeting Odin, and she'd believed him. Why wouldn't she? She'd been so desperate to meet the enigmatic leader that she'd jumped at the chance.

As she walked, thoughts tumbled through her mind like Tetris blocks, slowly slotting into place. It would make more sense if Echo, or even Gaia, was Odin. They both had an air of authority about them. A fanaticism that was hard to ignore.

Except Echo had stood in front of her at the museum, covertly monitoring the situation, so it couldn't be him.

She stopped. Or could it?

Had that been an elaborate ploy to throw her off track?

Even as she considered the other possibilities, she realized she was right. Only Echo had the sheer magnetism that a leader of an eco-terrorist organization should have. Only he had the fanatical drive, the zeal, the passion to pull it off. He had the smoldering fire burning behind his eyes. Not Thor.

She was sure of it.

Somehow, Echo had used Thor to convince her Odin was someone else, when all the time, he'd been standing right in front of her.

Her hands fisted. God, how he'd played her for a fool.

Heat burned into her cheeks when she thought how readily she'd believed it. Because she'd wanted to.

Rounding the front of the building, Avril scanned the streets for Krister, or for any of the counterterrorism officers. They were well hidden, but she knew what to look for.

Making her way over to a hotdog vendor, she snapped, "I need to use your phone."

He glanced around nervously. "You want mustard or ketchup on that, lady?"

There was no time for this. "I'm an undercover agent with the Stockholm Police." Damn, she didn't have anything to show him. No ID or police credentials. "I've just been inside the building. I need to use your phone, now."

He hesitated. "Sorry, what do you—"

"Look, I'm telling the truth. My name is Avril Dahl. You can clear it with your superior. This is about the imminent terrorist threat. I need to use your phone right now."

He frowned. "Where's your badge?"

"I'm undercover," she hissed, praying he'd believe her. "Your phone. Now."

Unsure, he handed it over.

Grabbing it, she called Krister's number. Thankfully, he picked up on the second ring. "Detective Jansson."

"Krister, it's me."

"Jesus, Avril. You okay? Whose number is this?"

"One of the undercover officers. I need to talk to you. Something about this setup doesn't feel right. I can't put my finger on it, but everyone is acting weird. They're too calm." She hesitated, closing her eyes against her personal humiliation. "Also, I'm pretty sure Echo is Odin. I think he's been playing us this whole time."

Playing me.

A heavy pause.

"Krister?"

"You could be right," came the muted response. "I think the Nordic Energy attack is a diversion."

"What?" Her mind raced, connecting the dots. A diversion? The thought had never even occurred to her.

"Think about it, Avril. Where was Runa killed? What had she done that day?"

"The Säpo surveillance team put her in the vicinity of the Convention Center."

"Yeah, and earlier today we found out that the man you mugged, a guy called Haldorsson, is the Facilities Manager at the center."

Avril took a moment to process this. "His briefcase—" She thought about the plans, the documents, receipts. The access card. "Oh, God."

"It gets worse," Krister continued. "The morning she died, Runa accessed the center using Haldorsson's keycard."

Her mind was spinning. "Why would she do that?" Then it fell into place and she gasped. "Oh, my God. The World Summit. I saw it on the news."

Was she doomed to blindness? Echo had tricked them. All this time they'd been led to believe Nordic Energy was the target, when in fact, it was somewhere else entirely.

Krister let out a loud breath. "Exactly. What if Runa came here to scout it out? The Convention Center could be the real target."

Avril clutched the top of the hotdog stand, earning her a strange look from the undercover vendor. "Those men in the café, the Mercedes—"

"Yeah, we traced the number plate to the Kazakhstan Embassy.

Could be a rogue terror cell or a faction of an existing one. Anyway, my guess is they are the real drivers behind this. I think they used Terra Nova to provide a distraction."

"Oh, God," she whispered. "Do you think Echo knows?"

"I'm sure of it." Krister's voice hardened. "He met with them. They must have offered him a deal."

"He sold out?" she couldn't believe it.

"Everyone has their limits."

All this time she'd thought he was truly passionate about the cause, and he'd been using their agenda for his own personal gain.

"Why else would he get you to mug Haldorsson?" Krister added.

She'd thought that was just a test, but in reality, Haldorsson had been the real target. They'd needed his keycard to gain access to the Convention Center.

"What about the break-in at Henrik Ahlström's house? Why did he make us steal the Nordic Energy schematics?"

"An elaborate smoke screen," Krister replied grimly. "To make us believe that was the legitimate target."

Avil bent over like she'd been sucker punched. "You're saying he knew?" Her voice was a hoarse whisper.

Krister grunted. "If you want my honest opinion, I think Echo was playing us all along. My guess is he knew who you were right from the start, and he was using you to feed false information back to us."

A flush of shame spread throughout her body.

Echo had played her at her own game. He'd out manipulated her, and she hadn't seen it coming. All the while, she thought she'd been playing him.

Then she remembered Rook, and how devastated Echo had been at his betrayal. How unraveled he'd been that evening in her apartment.

"Not from the start," she decided. "He eliminated Rook because of me."

"Well, after that, then."

Avril let out a humiliated groan. "I can't believe I didn't see it. I feel so stupid."

"Don't. Echo—or, rather, Odin—is smart. He used you to plant information. He used everyone. I doubt the rest of the team knows the full story either."

Avril gritted her teeth, trying but failing to keep the rage at bay. "Where are you?"

"At the Convention Center. The dignitaries are arriving soon, and we don't know where the device or devices are. We've got less than an hour to find them."

"I'll let you go then," she said brusquely. "What about here? I've just let the team in with backpacks that I thought were filled with explosives."

"Those were probably just for show. I called Lindholm. He's already moving in, arresting people."

"Are you sure?" She glanced around, hit by a pang of doubt. "There are hundreds of kids here. How do you know Echo isn't planning to blow up this place too? A two-pronged attack."

"I don't know for sure," he admitted. "But murdering innocent kids isn't part of their MO. Besides, they've already killed Gustav Holmgren. Nordic Energy's share price has tanked. What good is blowing up their HQ too? You said yourself the members were acting strangely."

"Yeah, too relaxed for what they were about to do." Then she knew Krister was right. "Because they weren't actually going to blow the place. Everybody knew but me."

She felt like such a fool.

It's going to be okay.

Gaia had been trying to tell her not to worry, that they weren't going to hurt anyone, but she hadn't understood. Hadn't understood any of it.

Avril swept a hand over her hair, ripping out the elastic band that kept her ponytail in place. It must have been Gaia who'd sent her that note at the bookstore, warning her about Rook. Underneath the tough, activist façade, Gaia cared.

"What about Echo?" she whispered. "Where is he?"

"Not there," Krister said, grimly. "He's going to be here at the Convention Center, his finger poised on that trigger, about to cause the biggest global catastrophe of our time."

chapter
forty-two

ODIN MOVED QUICKLY, WEAVING THROUGH THE controlled chaos of the Stockholm Convention Center. The summit was less than an hour from opening, and the air was thick with tension. Security teams patrolled the hallways, gazes vigilant. Aides and diplomats hurried between rooms carrying folders and portable microphones. Last-minute adjustments were being made to the auditorium seating and the lectern.

It was all going according to plan.

He adjusted his lanyard, keeping his head down as he strode toward the stairwell. Elevators were too risky—too many eyes, too many potential witnesses. He needed to retrieve the device and plant it in position as the dignitaries arrived and filed into the auditorium for the welcome speech.

And what a fiery speech it would be.

He was about to disappear into the stairwell when he spotted a vaguely familiar figure entering the lobby.

Krister Jansson. Stockholm's Serious Crimes lead detective and the man he suspected was Astrid's—or Avril, as he now knew her name was —handler. She thought she was so clever, infiltrating his organization, playing him for a fool.

For a while, he had been taken in, he couldn't deny it. That stung. It wasn't often someone managed to pull the wool over his eyes. But after

Rook's betrayal, when he'd analyzed her phone data, he'd realized Rook had been right all along. It was the lack of activity on both her phone and social media accounts that had condemned her. Nobody was that inactive. Not even an introverted, grief-stricken activist.

He studied Jansson and his blood ran cold. What was he doing here?

The law enforcement officer was scanning the vast entrance area with a sharp, assessing gaze. He was looking for something. Or someone.

He was looking for him.

A flicker of unease settled in Odin's gut as he disappeared into the stairwell, pulling the door closed behind him. He moved fast, taking the stairs two at a time until he reached the sixth floor. Did the detective know? Had he figured it out?

Säpo should still be chasing ghosts at Nordic Energy. The decoy was designed to buy him time, to keep every available counterterrorism unit focused on the wrong target while he slipped under the radar.

If they'd figured it out, that meant they'd be apprehending Thor and the team. It wouldn't be long before they searched the backpacks and realized the explosives were duds. Fakes. No triggers, no real explosive payload—just enough components to look real to the untrained eye but they wouldn't pass muster when inspected by an expert.

Odin took a slow breath. It didn't matter.

It was too late for them to stop *this*.

The sixth floor was empty, just as he knew it would be. The entire administrative wing had been closed for the duration of the summit. Access was restricted to essential personnel—security teams, event organizers, and last but not least, the facilities manager.

Odin glanced down at the lanyard around his neck.

It had been a perfect plan.

Freyja had performed well when she'd mugged Haldorsson and stolen his briefcase. He gave a soft snort. She was tough, that one. She'd gone through with the assault even though she was an officer of the law. Had she even considered not doing it? He wondered whether she'd told Jansson about it. Not that it mattered, anyway. Neither of them had known what it was really for.

Earlier this week, Runa had used the access card to gain entry to the conference center. When the Human Resources Manager had gone to the restroom, she'd breezed into his office and stolen his laptop bag right out from under his desk. He thought he'd left it in the staff canteen, according to the report he'd filed with Security.

Fool.

It had taken only a few days to make the necessary modifications. A hidden compartment built into the lining housing 600 grams of C-4, molded and packed tight to avoid detection. The detonator was concealed within, set to be triggered by a remote signal.

It was beautiful in its simplicity. No wires, no bulky components. The weight difference was negligible. The best part was, it was already inside the building, waiting for him.

Odin stepped up to the office door, reached into his pocket, and retrieved a slim tool. He picked the lock in seconds, slipping inside and shutting the door behind him. Without wasting any time, he headed for the desk.

Reaching underneath, he grabbed the laptop bag. It hadn't been hard to secret it back into the building. Not Runa this time. He'd returned it himself, since the HR Manager was off sick. Poor thing had come down with a vicious bout of food poisoning. It was so bad he'd had to be hospitalized. There was no danger of death now that he wasn't ingesting the toxin anymore. He'd make a full recovery. They weren't monsters.

Except by then it would be too late. His role in the attack would be cemented.

Odin smirked as he pulled the laptop bag out and set it on the desk. Opening it, he lifted the flap just enough to see the compartment was still closed. Everything was intact. Perfect.

Now for the final step.

He reached into his pocket and removed the second lanyard. It read: *Political Advisor – Republic of Tajikistan.*

The real advisor had been conveniently detained at Almaty International Airport, caught up in a bureaucratic nightmare orchestrated by their Kazakhstani friends. A misplaced visa stamp, a sudden "security concern," an unfortunate clerical error—just enough to keep him grounded indefinitely. The poor bastard wouldn't be making it to the summit.

Odin's fake credentials wouldn't get him through the primary security checkpoints, but since he was already inside the building, nobody would question his presence in the auditorium.

Which was all he needed.

Slipping the new lanyard over his head, he closed the briefcase and straightened his tie. He wore a smart but non-descript suit in a dull gray. The kind that made people look right past you. Adjusting his glasses, Odin picked up the case and left the office.

As he emerged from the stairwell into the lobby, he wondered whether Detective Jansson and his sidekick were still inside.

Had they seen the surveillance footage of Runa? Did they know she had entered the facility days before?

Staff members moved quickly, event coordinators whispered into headsets, security teams checked IDs at every turn. The dignitaries were filing in now, all patted down and scanned as they came through the front entrance.

He smiled like he belonged there, even accepted a glass of champagne from a hovering waiter. Jansson was nowhere in sight.

Good.

There was a brief window before the welcome presentation began. Downing his champagne, he made his way into the auditorium.

chapter
forty-three

KRISTER STOOD IN THE DIM SURVEILLANCE OFFICE, HIS GAZE on the monitors as the delegates filed into the Convention Center. The welcoming ceremony was being held in the main auditorium, a grand space lined with rows of seats facing an elevated stage. It was here that the opening remarks would be delivered.

After that, the delegates would transition into the designated negotiation chamber. This was an expansive, high-security hall shaped like an amphitheater and fitted with individual desks and interpreter booths.

He wondered which would be the target.

"We've swept both venues three times," Holm stated, rubbing his perspiring forehead. "We've also had the dogs through there. They're clean."

Krister watched the endless procession of politicians, advisors, and security detail on the monitors. "Could someone bring a bomb in with them?"

Holm shook his head. "Not through security. Everyone is screened at multiple checkpoints. We're using state-of-the-art luggage scanners, magnetometers, handheld wands, and explosive trace detectors. Nothing is getting past that, I don't care how good they are."

Krister thought for a long moment. "What if the bomb is already here?" he said quietly.

Holm narrowed his gaze. "How do you mean? I told you, we—"

"Not in the auditorium or the negotiation chamber, but somewhere else. What if it was smuggled in beforehand and left in a storage closet or a maintenance closet? If it's already in the building, all Echo has to do is retrieve it and plant it in either of the two rooms."

Holm stiffened. "That would mean—"

"He could be doing it right now."

Holm swore under his breath. "How would they have gotten it in?"

"I don't know, but if we could trace the woman's movements earlier this week, we might be able to find out."

Krister turned to the security officer seated at the console. "Pull up the surveillance footage from Monday morning again. See if you can track her movements through the building."

The operator's fingers flew across the keyboard, scrolling through hours of footage. "There are blind spots," he murmured. "We lose her in the stairwell and in some of the back offices."

"What about the elevator landings? Any movement there?"

"Maybe." The officer tapped at the keyboard, speeding through timestamps.

Krister's pulse pounded. This was going to take too long.

"I'm going to check it out," he told Holm. "Call me the second you figure out where she went."

Holm hesitated, eyes flicking between Krister and the monitors. "I've got to return to my post," he said. "I'll have Nilsson update you."

Krister gave the man his number, then went back out into the lobby. Echo wasn't the type to risk exposure. He'd have the device hidden inside the building, ready to be retrieved when the time came, Krister was sure of it.

Delegates were still arriving, greeting each other, and talking in small clusters. Their security details were never far away, standing silently watching. Krister wove through the crowd, looking for anything out of place.

Many of the delegates carried briefcases and phones, but they'd all been herded in through the man entrance and would have been searched, scanned and admitted.

Krister entered the auditorium. It was filling up fast, but there was also a line of uniformed security personnel along the perimeter, all focused on the incoming VIPs.

If there was a bomb here, where the hell was it?

He left and made his way down a short corridor, toward the negotiation chamber. Two uniformed officers stood at the entrance, guarding the room. He flashed his credentials, and they stepped aside.

The round chamber was mostly empty, aside from a handful of aides who were arranging documents, adjusting microphones and testing earpieces. Krister circled the perimeter, scanning the desks, but apart from the aides, all of whom had already been searched, everything appeared normal. He couldn't see anything suspicious.

His phone vibrated in his pocket. "Tell me you found something," he barked, answering it.

Nilsson's voice was subdued. "I've managed to find out where the woman went. To the sixth floor. She must have taken the stairs."

Krister frowned. "Sixth floor? What's up there?"

"The administrative offices, sir. They're all empty today, though."

"You see anyone up there earlier?" If that's where Runa had planted the bomb, then someone would have gone up to retrieve it.

"I'll check."

Krister swore under his breath. "Keep me posted."

He turned sharply, retracing his steps. If Runa had gone to the sixth floor, it wasn't for sightseeing. And if Echo was in the building, he was either on his way there—or coming from there now.

chapter
forty-four

THE HOTDOG VENDOR TOOK HER TO SEE CARL LINDHOLM, who was pacing up and down beside an unmarked police van, his finger pressed tightly to his earpiece. She could tell by his clenched jaw and red face that Krister's theory had been correct.

Thank God.

"So they really are duds?" he asked, his gaze flicking up as he caught sight of her.

Avril raised a hand in a silent greeting. He scowled at her, then cursed, and hung up.

"They weren't wired to detonate," he groaned. "The whole thing was a fucking setup."

"I heard. Did you catch them?"

He nodded. "Yeah, we did. All except Echo. He wasn't there."

Avril doubted he ever had been.

A sense of relief swept through her. The subterfuge was over. She was out. No more pretending to be Astrid, no more clandestine meetings, no more worrying about whether they'd discover who she really was.

He'd always known, anyway.

"What happens to them now?" she asked.

His gaze hardened. "They'll be interrogated, charged, and sent to jail to await trial. We'll push them to give up Odin."

Cold Legacy

Avril didn't tell him her theory. Not yet. There wasn't enough to go on, even if she was convinced.

Lindholm glanced around at the various teams he had employed, and his face crumpled. "What a farce."

"Gaia was in on it," she told him, remembering her calm demeanor. "She's an engineer—she'd know the difference between real explosives and duds."

He nodded grimly. "We'll keep that in mind during interrogations."

"The others probably had no clue," Avril continued. "They're fanatical enough to believe they were blowing up innocent people for the greater good."

Lindholm exhaled sharply. "What a fucking disaster. We've just burned countless hours and resources on a ghost attack, leaving the real target virtually unprotected."

Avril sucked in a breath. "You know about the Convention Center?"

"Yeah, I spoke to Detective Janssen earlier. He told me to start arresting people. I was about to head over there now." He gestured sharply at two officers. "You're with me. Move."

Avril ran to keep up. "Can I catch a ride?"

She got a grunt in response.

They piled into a dark blue Säpo-issue Volvo XC90 and peeled away from the Nordic Energy perimeter, emergency lights flashing. Lindholm's hands were tight on the wheel as he navigated the streets, weaving aggressively through the thinning morning traffic.

The radio crackled. "Säpo Command to Unit Five. What's your status?"

Lindholm pressed his earpiece. "Unit Five en route to Convention Center. ETA four minutes."

"Copy that. We're sending additional units. Keep this channel open."

The Volvo skidded to a halt outside a police barricade. They were still two blocks from the Convention Center. Avril looked out of the window in dismay. Already, armored vehicles were rolling up to the front entrance and delegates were filing in.

Uniformed officers were checking credentials.

"This could take a while," Lindholm murmured.

"I'm going to need a weapon," Avril said.

Lindholm hesitated, then leaned over and took a spare out of the glove compartment. He checked it, then handed it to her.

Wordlessly, Avril climbed out of the vehicle. If Echo was planning to detonate, he'd have to be inside by now.

"I'll take a walk around the perimeter," she told him, tucking the gun into the back of her jeans then pulling her shirt over it. "Echo will have found another way in. He can't go through the front."

Lindholm turned to the other officer. "Bergström, go with her."

Bergström, solidly built with a military buzz cut, fell into step beside her as they cut away from the main security perimeter.

The back of the building was significantly quieter. It was still cordoned off, but there were fewer police officers and no media. Just a loading dock, where caterers and maintenance staff were making last-minute deliveries.

That's when Avril saw him.

A figure in a dark suit, moving quickly away from the service exit.

Her breath hitched.

Echo.

"Bergström, over there!" she hissed. "That's him."

Echo had just slipped through a side gate, barely noticeable in the weak morning light. He wasn't heading for an entrance. He was leaving.

Avril's stomach flipped.

"He's already placed the bomb," she hissed. If he was getting out, that meant it was in situ and set to detonate soon. "We need to stop him," she said urgently.

Bergström was already keying his radio. "Unit Five, we've got eyes on the suspect, heading west on foot through the service exit."

Lindholm's voice came through immediately. "Keep him in sight, but do not engage. Backup is on the way."

Bergström nodded. "Copy that."

The Säpo agent started to move forward, but Avril was faster. Echo was slipping into the alleyway behind the loading docks. If she lost him now, she might never catch him again.

"He's getting away," she hissed, and took off running.

chapter
forty-five

KRISTER PUSHED THROUGH THE SECURITY DOORS INTO THE auditorium, heart hammering. The delegates were all seated, their voices a low murmur of diplomatic small talk. The stage was set for the opening speeches, and the air crackled with anticipation.

Krister took a moment and stood still, taking everything in. The rows of seats, closely packed; the aisle down the middle; the stage with its impressive podium, ready for the opening remarks—and he felt the sheer weight of political importance in the room.

It was in here, he was sure of it. Somewhere in this chamber, death was waiting.

He spotted Holm and some of his team across the room, earpieces in, hands hovering near their holsters. Their expressions were grim, but alert. A silent shake from the Chief's head confirmed it—they hadn't found anything either.

Yet.

Krister's mind raced. The device had been here all along—on floor six. That's why Runa had used the Facilities Manager's card and come in. Somehow, Terra Nova had returned the laptop bag to the office, and today, Echo had retrieved it. He'd been here, of that he was sure. They just had to find it.

His earpiece crackled. "Krister, we've found something."

He spun around. "Fred, where are you?"

"In the seating area," Freddie murmured, his voice low so as not to cause alarm. "Row E, seat 14. We've got a laptop bag positioned under a chair, hidden beneath a gray jacket."

Krister scanned the midsection of the auditorium. A hand went up. Freddie and Karlsson both stood in the middle of the jostling bodies, white-faced and serious.

Krister hurried over, dodging suited legs and briefcases and attaché bags. When he saw the laptop bag, he knew this was it. The chair was vacant, but the jacket draped casually over the back suggested someone was sitting there. Security wouldn't—and hadn't—questioned it.

He was both relieved and petrified. All around Row E, Seat 14, diplomats were sitting, directly in the blast zone, oblivious to the danger they were in.

Krister got on the radio. "Holm, it's Jansson. It's in the auditorium. We have to evacuate. Now."

Holm looked across. "Are you sure?"

"One hundred percent." He didn't have to open it to know what was inside. He recognized the strap from the CCTV video at the station. This was the bag Runa had been carrying when she'd died.

"Sniffer dogs missed it," Freddie muttered, shaking his head. "It must be a device that doesn't emit detectable vapors."

Krister swore under his breath. That meant it was military-grade plastic explosives—C4 or Semtex—designed to evade detection. The detonator was likely electronic, remote-activated. If Echo was still in range, he could trigger it at any second.

Holm cursed, but began issuing orders into his radio, then he went to speak to the Mayor, who would have to make an announcement.

"Get hold of Lindholm," Krister told Fred, "and call the bomb squad."

"Excuse me, ladies and gentlemen. Our security teams have detected an imminent threat and I'm afraid we have to evacuate the building. Could you please clear the auditorium. There is no need to panic, but if you could leave in an orderly fashion as quickly as possible. Thank you."

Krister watched as security teams moved methodically but urgently, approaching heads of state, their aides, their bodyguards—whispering in their ears, guiding them out with steady hands.

It started as a slow ripple—delegates rising, confused but compliant. Then it picked up momentum. Chairs scraped. Murmurs turned into urgent voices.

Still, not fast enough.

Krister's eyes locked onto the gray jacket in Row E. Beneath it, just visible, the laptop bag containing the bomb.

His entire body felt cold. This was it.

If it detonated now, the entire summit would be obliterated. The front row, the stage, the surrounding areas. Shrapnel would rip through flesh, bone, and steel like butter. The blast would collapse the ceiling, turn bodies into torn fragments, and send a message that would echo across the world.

He couldn't let that happen.

"Get out of here," he muttered to Freddie and Karlsson, before taking a step toward the chair with the device underneath it.

They glanced at each other.

"Boss, let's wait for the bomb squad," Karlsson urged. But Krister barely heard him. His world had narrowed. Nothing else mattered but the laptop bag and the reality of what he had to do.

Get it out of here.

"Krister, wait!" Freddie called as he moved toward it.

But he couldn't wait. He wouldn't.

"There's no time," he rasped. Even now, the auditorium was still half-full. Echo could detonate the device at any moment. He couldn't let that happen.

Each step felt like wading through molasses. His breath was steady, but inside, his pulse pounded so hard he thought his ribs would crack.

As he reached the chair, his hands trembled. He wiped his palms on his trousers, then reached out for the laptop bag. His fingertips brushed the handle.

No beep, no click. Not yet.

He carefully slid it out from underneath the chair.

Freddie's voice, wavering from the middle aisle. "Krister, for the love of God, don't move it. Wait for the bomb squad."

But if they waited, Echo might trigger it remotely.

Krister lifted it.

Was the weight off? Or was he imagining it?

He straightened up, holding the laptop bag steady, heart hammering like it was about to jump out of his chest. His thoughts flashed to Avril. Would he ever see her again?

He thought about her stubbornness, her fire, the way she'd held her own inside Terra Nova. She was still out there, completely unaware he was standing here, one second away from turning into nothing but red mist.

If he died, at least he'd die saving the summit, saving peace.

He gave a soft snort. That was as noble a death as he could hope for.

"This way." He heard Holm's voice. Urgent, yet precise. Why was he still here? "There's a fire exit behind the stage."

Grateful for the direction, he forced himself not to run. Any sudden movement could trigger a pressure switch.

Instead, he walked, slow and steady, each step bringing him closer to the exit, further from the chaos of the auditorium.

One foot after the other.

The stage was empty, and up ahead, he saw Holm beckoning. "This way. Follow me."

A cold draft, and he rounded the stage and saw the open doors. He didn't look up, didn't know where Fred and Karlsson were. All he knew was he had to keep going.

Outside, security was setting up a perimeter, keeping everyone back. He walked into the center of a plaza and paused. Was this clear enough?

Armed security swarmed the area, but from beyond the cordon. Only Holm was crazy enough to stand with him in the square. He appreciated the support more than Holm would ever know.

The bomb squad had arrived, dressed head to toe in protective gear.

"Put it down slowly!" one of them called.

Krister glanced up, sweat soaking through his shirt.

"Krister, you're clear," Holm said, making up and down movements with his hand. "Just—just put it down."

Gently, he lowered it onto the pavement. His hands shook as he took a step back. Then another. His knees buckled, and he sank down onto the cold concrete.

Cold Legacy

The bomb squad descended, their team moving in surgically, shields raised, a technician opening his tool kit to examine the briefcase.

Firm arms grabbed his and lifted him to his feet. It was Holm. "Come on, let's get out of here. It's out of your hands now."

Krister allowed Holm to lead him to the cordon, where Freddie and Karlsson were waiting. "Jesus, boss. That's the craziest thing I've ever seen anyone do," Karlsson muttered.

Freddie elbowed him in the ribs. "Shut up."

"Will they disarm it here?" Krister croaked, looking up as Lindholm came over.

Holm shrugged, but Lindholm had heard the question. "No. They'll take it to a controlled detonation site. It's too risky to dismantle it here."

Krister finally exhaled—a breath he hadn't realized he was holding.

They all watched as a robotic arm extended, gently cradling the briefcase, moving it into a blast-proof containment unit. The doors sealed shut with a final, heavy clunk.

It was over.

Krister leaned against a low wall, weak with relief. Around them, the security teams barked orders, directing snipers, coordinating evacuation logistics, but he barely heard them.

His job was done.

"Where's Avril?" he muttered, just as a Säpo agent with a buzz cut came running around the side of the building and into the plaza.

"Sir, Avril Dahl has gone in pursuit of the suspect," he panted, stopping in front of Lindholm.

Krister's head shot up. "What?"

"She took off before I could stop her. He's on foot, heading west. I lost them near the canal."

"Has she got backup?" Krister demanded.

The man shook his head. "No, sir. She's on her own."

chapter
forty-six

THE MOMENT AVRIL SAW ECHO SLIP THROUGH THE BACK exit, she bolted. The cold Stockholm air bit at her exposed skin, but she ignored it. This was it. This was her moment.

He was fast, weaving through the narrow alleys behind the Convention Center, but she was faster. She had prepared for this. Her FBI training kicked in as she calculated angles, anticipated his movements, read his body language.

Ahead, Echo vaulted over a metal railing, landing smoothly on the pavement below, then darted left, disappearing behind a row of stacked shipping containers in what looked like a construction site.

Avril pushed harder, her breath burning in her throat as she followed. Pulling the gun from her waistband, she ducked under the railing, rounded the corner and raced along beside the looming containers. In the distance, she heard the wail of multiple sirens. Had they found something? Was there still time to get everyone out?

She'd have heard the explosion if the device had been triggered. Unless it was on a remote timer. Maybe those sirens would have to pick up the pieces. The thought made her shiver with dread.

Echo was leading her away from the Convention Center, away from where the security presence was strongest.

Bergström had given up. He'd lost them half a mile back and now it was just her and Echo, their footsteps the only two on the path.

Cold Legacy

She wasn't stupid. He wanted this confrontation as much as she did.

Her legs burned, but she didn't slow down. She chased him past a row of abandoned industrial buildings, the scent of oil and damp asphalt filling her nostrils. A chain-link fence loomed ahead, topped with barbed wire.

He was trapped.

Without breaking stride, Echo launched himself at the fence, scaled it like it was nothing, and landed on the other side. He barely even looked winded.

Shit.

Avril muttered the curse but didn't hesitate. She stuffed the gun back into her jeans and jumped, gripping the freezing metal, and heaving herself up. The barbed wire at the top cut through the denim, but she ignored the sting, swinging one leg over and dropping down hard on the other side.

She grunted, then looked up, but Echo was nowhere to be seen.

What? How did that happen? She'd been right behind him.

Breath ragged, she surveyed the immediate area. On her left was a construction site, partially dug up, concrete blocks waiting to be laid, an abandoned crane like a hulking metallic monster lurking in the corner.

On her left, a small verge and a dip to a path that ran alongside a canal. The water was dark and deep, and she didn't think he'd gone down there. Ahead was a parked truck, stacks of wooden pallets and piles of building materials.

Avril stood still and listened, but it was silent, other than the muted sirens far away.

She threw her hands down in frustration.

She'd lost him.

Or maybe he was hiding.

She moved forward, slowly, listening for any whisper of movement. Her instincts screamed at her that he was still here.

Waiting.

She was the prey now.

Avril rounded a pile of bricks and froze. She felt a presence behind her, but too late. Before she could react, a hand clamped over her wrist, twisting it with expert precision. Her gun was yanked from her grip, and she was spun around, slammed up against the cold brick wall.

Echo.

His breath ghosted against her cheek, his grip like iron.

Avril struggled, but he pinned her easily, the weight of his body holding her in place. She felt the sharp edges of the bricks cut into her hands. He was strong, stronger than he looked. His glasses were gone, and in their place were the burning, intense eyes of a man who had nothing left to lose.

"Hello, Avril." Hearing him say her real name sent shivers down her spine. It confirmed everything.

"How long have you known?" she hissed, breathing hard.

"Since Rook." His voice faltered, and she saw the flash of anger. "I had him killed because of you."

Her stomach twisted.

"He would have exposed me." She forced herself to hold his gaze. "He was getting too close."

A smirk played at his lips, but there was no humor behind it. Just a cold realization. "I believed you over him. You fooled me. That doesn't happen often."

"You're Odin, aren't you?" she demanded.

His eyes darkened, the smirk fading.

"You're too smart for your own good, Special Agent."

Her breath caught in her throat.

"I don't work for the FBI anymore."

"I know."

She swallowed, staring into those dark pits. He was still curious about her, she could tell. There were questions there. Questions he wanted answered. Echo was all about control. He had to connect the dots.

"All that stuff about your mother dying. Was it real?"

She hesitated.

"Tell me," he hissed.

A nod. "Yes. She was murdered."

Why she was telling him the truth, she had no idea. But there was something about the way he looked at her, like he was peeling away the layers of her soul, and she couldn't help herself.

He nodded, as if he'd suspected it all along.

"I knew it. Your grief was too real. That's what fooled me." Then, with a low chuckle, he added, "Well played."

"What about you?" she whispered.

"Oh, I have my darkness too," he replied. "But then, you already know that."

She didn't answer, just stared at his eyes, hollow embers, cracks of fire filled with secrets. "Maybe I'll tell you about it one day."

Avril's jaw clenched. "You won't get a chance. Your plan won't succeed."

Echo turned his gaze toward the Convention Center. "How do you know I haven't already?"

"We'd have heard the explosion. You haven't had time to detonate it. They'll find the bomb before it's too late."

To her surprise, he shrugged.

"Don't you care?" she pressed.

"That wasn't my fight." He leaned in, his voice almost a whisper. "The Freedom Front was using me. Using Terra Nova to further their own ends."

Avril frowned. "The distraction?"

He nodded. "Nordic Energy, all of it. A smokescreen."

"What about the Summit?" She tried to move her hands, but he kept them pinned against the bricks.

"It was always their beef with the West. Not mine."

His tone was almost indifferent, like he wasn't about to become the most wanted man in the world.

"But you're a terrorist."

"No, Avril. I'm a businessman. They already paid me half the money upfront."

His eyes flickered. A micro expression. He was lying. Odin wasn't indifferent.

"Did you ever care?" she whispered. "Or was this always just about the money?"

"You see a lot, don't you?"

"So do you," she countered.

He tilted his head. "I saw through you."

She knew he wasn't talking about her alias. "We were talking about you."

"I cared. Very deeply. But I soon learned that nothing was ever going to change. Idealistic bullshit. I cared, but the world doesn't."

"So you sold out."

A shrug. "If you like. It seemed like the smart thing to do."

"What about the others? Gaia, Fang, Thor? Don't they matter?"

A sniff. "They'll be okay. I made sure they didn't know anything. Not really."

Avril studied him. "You didn't blow up Gustav Holmgren, did you?"

He gave a low chuckle. "You just work that out?" He shook his head. "Of course not. But the timing was too convenient not to take advantage of it."

He was all about playing games.

"As fun as this has been, Avril, it's time for me to go."

She shifted her head, trying to see if help was on the way.

He leaned in, his lips so close to her cheek she could feel his breath. "Now I'm going to disappear. And nobody—not you, not Säpo, not Interpol—will ever be able to find me."

Avril believed him.

Unless she could stop him.

She moved before he could react, twisting out of his grip, but he was faster.

His arm snapped around her throat, yanking her back against him.

And then she felt it. The cold steel of a gun pressed to her temple.

"Don't," he murmured against her ear, calm, almost gentle. "I don't want to hurt you."

Shouts rang out behind them and Avril exhaled in relief. They were here.

They had him.

But he also had her.

A red laser dot danced over her chest then rose higher, until it stilled on Echo. A sniper locking onto his target.

"Put the weapon down!" someone ordered through a megaphone.

Echo laughed softly, pressing the barrel tighter against her skull.

"Let's not be hasty," he called out, dragging her toward the verge. Avril's pulse thundered in her ears. She could feel the tension in his body, the calculating stillness as he assessed his options.

And she knew the moment he made his decision.

His lips barely moved as he whispered against her ear. Words only for her.

"I'll be seeing you, Avril."

Then, without warning, he shoved her forward, releasing her at the exact same second he turned and sprinted toward the water.

Avril hit the ground hard, gasping for breath—just in time to see Echo dive off the verge into the dark, freezing river below.

Gunfire erupted, pockmarking the surface of the water.

But he was already gone.

chapter
forty-seven

"HE MIGHT COME AFTER YOU," KRISTER SAID, THE NEXT morning.

They were seated in the Stockholm Serious Crime Unit's boardroom, undergoing a formal debriefing. The room smelled of burnt coffee and stress, and the table was cluttered with case files, half-empty water bottles, and a pile of evidence reports.

Through the large windows, the city outside looked normal, like nothing had happened. Just another day in the Swedish capital.

Last night, after Echo had dived into the river and vanished, Säpo had launched a full-scale manhunt. They had divers in the water, helicopters sweeping the airspace, tactical teams scouring the riverbanks, and checkpoints set up at major transit hubs.

None of it mattered.

He was gone.

She didn't meet Krister's gaze. "I doubt he will. That would be suicide, and he doesn't want to be caught. He's got the money, now he'll vanish to some tropical island where he can enjoy it. I don't see him returning."

I'll be seeing you, Avril.

Even as she said it, she knew that wasn't how Echo operated. He was patient, like a predator stalking its prey, and maybe not now, maybe not tomorrow, but one day, their paths would cross again.

Cold Legacy

He'd make sure of it.

She shoved the thought aside and focused on what Fred was saying.

"The bomb squad successfully disposed of the device," he reported, flipping through his notes. "It was packed with eight kilos of C-4. That's enough to level the entire auditorium."

"Do we know who was behind it? I mean, who the terrorists were who paid Echo to create the diversion and plant the real bomb at the Convention Center?"

Joanna Johansson, a senior officer from the National Operations Department shook her head. They handled serious organized crime, terrorism, and national security threats.

"Not yet, but we're working on it. With those diplomatic plates you gave us, and the Kazakhstan connection, we have several leads."

Avril gave a tight nod. She hoped they found the organization responsible. If that device had gone off during the summit, they'd be looking at a mass casualty event. Diplomatic leaders, security personnel, civilians.

"Thank God you got there in time." Johansson looked at Krister with something between admiration and disbelief, as if she couldn't quite believe the man had carried an active explosive out of the building with his bare hands.

Krister just shrugged. "It wasn't a choice," he muttered. "It was either that or risk being blown to hell anyway."

Fred chuckled, shaking his head. "That's going down in history as one of the craziest things ever done in this department."

Avril smiled. She had always known Krister was brave.

Even as a kid, he had looked out for her, put her safety before his own, carried her home when she'd fallen skiing and sprained her ankle. That was who Krister was.

A hero.

And now, thanks to him, the Summit was still going ahead. The world had come dangerously close to a diplomatic catastrophe, but instead of pushing the nations apart, the attack had done the opposite. It had unified them.

The summit's postponement had been brief. Now that the bomb

had been removed and the threat neutralized, the meeting was set to continue later today.

Poetic justice.

Avril took a slow breath. "How did you know Runa had been to the Convention Center?"

Krister turned to her. "It was an educated guess. She told you that Echo had given her a task, right? A secret one."

Avril nodded, her chest constricting as she recalled that morning in her apartment. Runa had been so eager to please, with absolutely no idea what Echo had in store for her.

"Then she ended up dead," he said grimly. "That told me one thing—she knew something Echo couldn't afford for anyone else to know."

Fred pulled up an image on his tablet. "We still don't know who actually pushed Runa," he said. "But we have a lead."

The screen displayed a grainy image from a security camera outside what looked like Älvsjö Station. A man in a dark jacket with the hood up walked purposefully through the crowd. They could just about make out his features. In his hand, was the laptop bag that had been used to plant the bomb.

"Who is he?" Avril squinted at the image. She didn't recognize him. He wasn't from the eco-cell, either Echo's or Thor's.

"We think he's a contract killer," Krister said grimly. "He's popped up on Säpo's radar before."

"That's the laptop bag that Runa stole on the day she died," Krister pointed to the screen.

"She must've brought it to him," Avril whispered. "She had no idea it was going to be used to plant a bomb."

Krister nodded. "That's why Echo had her killed. She was a loose end."

Avril clenched her jaw.

Runa had thought she was doing something good for the cause, but like everyone else, she had been a tool to be used and discarded.

Echo had outplayed them all.

"He likes to keep his hands clean," Krister muttered.

Avril gave a tight nod. To her knowledge, Echo had never personally killed anyone. He always outsourced. He had ordered Fang to kill Rook and a hitman to push Runa onto the train tracks.

That didn't make him less guilty.

If anything, it made him even more dangerous, because he didn't see people as people. They were pawns, used when necessary. Eliminated when they became a liability.

She recalled the way he had looked at her when he'd had her pinned against the pile of bricks. With familiarity, something more than just recognition. She couldn't deny they had a connection, twisted and strange as it was.

Not love, not attraction, but something else.

An obsession?

He saw himself in me, she realized.

She had spent ten years hunting her mother's murderer, a serial killer who had butchered fifty women. That obsession had consumed her, had driven her to sacrifice her personal life, relationships, stability.

Echo had been the same way.

She didn't know about his past, but it had to be traumatic for him to have become the man he was today.

She had spent a decade chasing a monster.

He had spent a decade becoming one.

She recognized the fire behind his eyes. His passion was real.

That's why he let me live.

Krister's voice pulled her back to the present. "You okay?"

She turned to face him. He was looking at her the same way he always did, with a warm glow in his eyes. Krister, so steady, unwavering, and protective. He had stayed outside her hotel window all night, making sure she was safe. He had risked his life to carry a bomb out of a crowded building.

He was the one constant in her life.

And now, she realized, he always would be.

She offered him a small, genuine smile.

"Yes," she said. "I am now."

epilogue

ONE WEEK LATER...

AVRIL WATCHED as Krister set two mugs of coffee down on the kitchen table and slid into the chair opposite her. The scent of the dark-roast blend filled the small space, making it feel warmer than it was. The sky outside was still a bruised shade of gray, but there were early signs of spring. Melting snowbanks, the drip of water from the eaves, tufts of grass poking through the soggy ground.

Avril wrapped her hands around the mug, absorbing its heat. She was still processing everything that had happened. Terra Nova, Nordic Energy, the bomb, the way Echo had looked at her before he disappeared into the river, whispering those final words in her ear.

I'll be seeing you, Avril.

They'd haunted her dreams, but now, here with Krister, they didn't seem quite so potent.

"I heard you solved Gustav Holmgren's murder."

He smiled, his light brown hair still damp from his morning shower. "Yeah, once we got hold of the wife's phone records, we saw she'd made some calls to a known criminal."

"He made the bomb?"

"No, but he put her in touch with the man who did. We arrested him yesterday."

"I can't believe it was her this whole time. She must have really hated her husband to have done that to him."

Krister gave a sage nod. "She watched him burn."

Avril shuddered. "Did she confess?"

"Eventually. She had no choice. We had footage of her planting it in his car the night before the explosion. The neighbors picked it up on their home surveillance camera."

"That was lucky," Avril said.

"Yeah, we may not have had enough to prosecute, otherwise." He hesitated. "Turns out he'd been having an affair, as well as ignoring her for the latter half of their marriage."

Avril shook her head. "He sure underestimated her."

Krister's eyebrow quirked. He took a sip of coffee, then said, "I talked to Sundström this morning."

She smiled. "Has he forgiven you for getting involved?" Freddie had told her how the Chief had warned Krister off the case, but he'd ignored him. That's why he'd been outside her window, and that's how he'd known when they'd moved on the corporate headquarters.

Krister's lips curved. "He's getting there. Although, that wasn't what we spoke about."

"It wasn't?"

"No, we were talking about you."

Before she could press him further, he set a printed document on the table between them. Her name was at the top.

She exhaled sharply. "A job offer?"

"It's official." Krister placed a pen down next to it. "We had to fight Säpo for you—Lindholm is your biggest fan—but I'm happy to say we won that one. All you have to do is sign, and you can start Monday."

She stared at the bold black lettering at the top of the page. She was no longer an outsider. No longer a temporary consultant, a borrowed agent, an interloper that nobody wanted around. She was one of them now.

Her fingers brushed over the papers. "How do you know I'll accept?"

Krister smiled. "I know you, Avril. You want to work, you need to work. You'll be bored doing anything else but catching bad guys."

She let out a breathless laugh.

Stockholm was always meant to be temporary. A quick trip to sort out her father's things, sell the house and move on. But somewhere along the way, it had changed into so much more.

It was home.

She glanced at Krister, who was leaning back with his arms crossed, watching her. There was a sparkle in his eye. A challenge.

She smirked. He was right. This was what she needed to fill the emptiness she'd been carrying around with her these last few weeks. It would give her a sense of purpose again. That's what had been missing from her life.

"All right," she said, picking up the pen and signing.

She was here to stay.

Avril Dahl's story continues in *Cold Mercy*... click the link below: https://www.amazon.com/dp/B0F7RHF86L

Join the L.T. Ryan reader family & receive a free copy of the Rachel Hatch story, *Fractured*. Click the link below to get started: https://ltryan.com/rachel-hatch-newsletter-signup-1

about the author

L.T. Ryan is a *USA Today* and international bestselling author. The new age of publishing offered L.T. the opportunity to blend his passions for creating, marketing, and technology to reach audiences with his popular Jack Noble series.

Living in central Virginia with his wife, the youngest of his three daughters, and their three dogs, L.T. enjoys staring out his window at the trees and mountains while he should be writing, as well as reading, hiking, running, and playing with gadgets. See what he's up to at http://ltryan.com.

Social Medial Links:
- Facebook (L.T. Ryan): https://www.facebook.com/LTRyanAuthor
- Facebook (Jack Noble Page): https://www.facebook.com/JackNobleBooks/
- Twitter: https://twitter.com/LTRyanWrites
- Goodreads: http://www.goodreads.com/author/show/6151659.L_T_Ryan

---

Biba Pearce is a crime writer and author of the Kenzie Gilmore, Dalton Savage and DCI Rob Miller series. Her books have been shortlisted for the Feathered Quill and the CWA Debut Dagger awards, and The Marlow Murders was voted best crime fiction book in the Indie Excellence Book Awards.

Biba lives in leafy Surrey with her family and when she isn't writing, can be found walking along the Thames River path - near to where many of her books are set - or rambling through the countryside.

Download a FREE Kenzie Gilmore prequel novella at her website bibapearce.com.

also by l.t. ryan

Find All of L.T. Ryan's Books on Amazon Today!

The Jack Noble Series
The Recruit (free)
The First Deception (Prequel 1)
Noble Beginnings
A Deadly Distance
Ripple Effect (Bear Logan)
Thin Line
Noble Intentions
When Dead in Greece
Noble Retribution
Noble Betrayal
Never Go Home
Beyond Betrayal (Clarissa Abbot)
Noble Judgment
Never Cry Mercy

Deadline

End Game

Noble Ultimatum

Noble Legend

Noble Revenge

Never Look Back

Bear Logan Series

Ripple Effect

Blowback

Take Down

Deep State

Bear & Mandy Logan Series

Close to Home

Under the Surface

The Last Stop

Over the Edge

Between the Lies

Caught in the Web

Rachel Hatch Series

Drift

Downburst

Fever Burn

Smoke Signal

Firewalk

Whitewater

Aftershock

Whirlwind

Tsunami

Fastrope

Sidewinder

Redaction

Mirage (Coming Soon)

Mitch Tanner Series

The Depth of Darkness

Into The Darkness

Deliver Us From Darkness

Cassie Quinn Series

Path of Bones

Whisper of Bones

Symphony of Bones

Etched in Shadow

Concealed in Shadow

Betrayed in Shadow

Born from Ashes

Return to Ashes

Risen from Ashes (Coming Soon)

Blake Brier Series

Unmasked

Unleashed

Uncharted

Drawpoint

Contrail

Detachment

Clear

Quarry

Dalton Savage Series

Savage Grounds

Scorched Earth

Cold Sky

The Frost Killer

Crimson Moon

Dust Devil (Coming Soon)

Maddie Castle Series

The Handler

Tracking Justice

Hunting Grounds

Vanished Trails

Smoldering Lies

Field of Bones

Beneath the Grove (Coming Soon)

Affliction Z Series

Affliction Z: Patient Zero

Affliction Z: Abandoned Hope

Affliction Z: Descended in Blood

Affliction Z : Fractured Part 1

Affliction Z: Fractured Part 2 (Fall 2021)

Alex Hayes Series

Fractured Verdict

11th Hour Witness

Buried Testimony

Stella LaRosa Series

Black Rose

Red Ink
Black Gold
White Lies

Avril Dahl Series
Cold Reckoning
Cold Legacy
Cold Mercy (Pre-Order)

Savannah Shadows Series
Echos of Guilt
The Silence Before
Dead Air (Pre-Order)

Receive a free copy of The Recruit. Visit:

https://ltryan.com/jack-noble-newsletter-signup-1

Made in United States
North Haven, CT
05 July 2025